Chapter 1

In the country of Runway Four, in the n[illegible] of Bludgeon City, jus[illegible] over the Regal Canal, the Lie District is found. If you drill [illegible] it via Google Maps, your eyes fall on a vast warren of bleak houses, the layout broken in key parts by a grim prison, a mental institution, and a large Gothic cathedral, rebadged as Secular Hall. Nestled deep in this maze of misery is Rodent Street where lives a man of little renown and even less significance. He dwells in a pokey little room—his very own rathole—in a house of spartan flats. He is tall, fair-haired and twenty-five years old. His name is Grudge Galmount.

***

Grudge was alone in the rathole with only his thoughts for company. His Spanish girlfriend, one Beatrice Marcos, was back in Madrid. The pair had enjoyed, if that's the word, a six-month relationship while she lived in Bludgeon to improve her English. Her mother—a well-off widow—had encouraged her daughter to travel. Now, from her mother's apartment in Sol, Beatrice had written Galmount a long, lecturing letter—her second in a week—in which she urged him to change his ways and reverse the downward spiral of his life. The letter's tone jarred with Grudge. Propped up by pillows on his rickety bed, he mulled over his reply. He considered this for a trial run:

My sweetest Bea,

I am sick of you and your fucking letters...

But he trailed off right there. He didn't have the heart to go on in such a bitter vein towards the woman he loved most in the world. At least he told himself he loved her. The emotionally erratic Galmount was prone to falling hopelessly in love. Since reaching adulthood, he had given several people his all. Bea was just the latest in a longish line.

Nonetheless, he was hostile towards her letters, and fed up with her pleas for him to change. The word itself—*change*—filled him with dread. He thought how easy things could be if he were left alone to find his artistic destiny. He saw himself, drink in hand—a phantasmal composite of many a hero—busily working at a desk writing something of great import; and churning out such wonderful stuff on a daily basis, like it was going out of fashion. Hell, he'd set the fashion!

However, he quickly killed this daydream. The rathole was cold and he crashed back to earth from his skysailing. His hopes of being a writer were just that: hopes. His current station in life prevented him from fulfilling any sort of ambition. The heroes of whom he'd read—in contraband books—lived in free lands where it was possible to realise your dreams. No such luck for Grudge Galmount in the land of Runway Four. He knew in the depths of his soul that in essence he was a drudge. Drudge Galmount, he said to himself, and laughed. His laughter, though, was hollow.

A promo calendar from the local prison, Downland, stared at him. He noted with displeasure the date: Friday the 13th. It explains the foulness of my mood, he mused, an unlucky low. He felt his heart was being eaten away by fang-toothed maggots in their legion. As for his mind, there was a beast in there whose horns were beginning to push out of Grudge's skull. The initial prodding had become a violent pain moving ever outwards as the demon sought supremacy. Grudge sought desperately to assess his life's situation. The summation was succinct. In his professional life (he knew it was a joke to use such a term) he amounted to nothing. And in his private affairs, things weren't much better. Worst of all were the people who hurt him and forgot it quickly, as just part of their makeup to inflict wounds.

He looked at the calendar again. *Locking Them Up*, it read, *Looking After You.* Who's looking after me? he wondered, as the weight of his worries bore down on him like a squadron of shrieking dive bombers. Closing his eyes, he whispered to God, asking the Creator to bring him succour— and some much needed luck.

His faith—he still didn't know where it came from—had held firm in spite of everything that had happened to him. As far as he knew, the government had not yet devised a way to read people's thoughts. He was sure they were working on it. In the meantime, while he could, Grudge talked to God—a lot.

Around this time, early in ____, Grudge acquired a set of dumbbells and through constant repetitions began to muscle up in his arms and chest.

The crew with whom he worked, surprised by this change in Galmount's physique, began to call him Big Grudge. The nickname was apt for, by the age of twenty-five, he burned with resentments. Also, in the same period, Beatrice asked Galmount what brought him the most happiness. "Writing," he replied instantly. "When I can," he'd added, realising that up to then he had written nothing of note.

***

Runway Four operated under a strange blend of communist authoritarianism and free-market capitalism. Essentially, it was a socialist market economy run by a dictatorship. In a nod to history it had named its currency the goldmark. R4 was governed by a cabal of twenty-five key politicians—not unlike China—who from their privileged Politburo positions controlled the population with great power. There was a Standing Committee, too, comprised of a vile bunch of seven fiends all of whom deserved to die. The queen of these ants was a man named Chairman Young. Grudge Galmount was but a drone in his colony.

Mornings he woke around five. The other tenants in the house were usually up, washing, eating and preparing to leave for their menial jobs. These were the first sounds of Grudge's day as heard through paper-thin walls: ants stirring.

His daily shift at the coffin factory began at seven. He would shave, shower, all that stuff, as best he could in his rathole's tiny bathroom. He considered it a stroke of luck to have his own toilet. Many of the houses let in the Lie District came with communal bathrooms. The idea of sharing in the smells and soapsuds of others was a ghastly prospect. It was a small luxury: his own crapper.

He generally had little for breakfast. Youth was on his side, not to mention money, or the lack of it, as a reason for his fasting. A cup of tea and a rolled-up cigarette was often the height of his sustenance. Sometimes, if feeling flush, he'd buy a banana in the corner shop on the way to the tram. More often than not, though, he walked the three kilometres to Revenue Road because he had no money to take public transport. In recent weeks his money situation had improved to a degree, due to the fact he had foresworn alcohol and drugs in his latest attempt to better himself and perhaps even turn his life around.

For as long as he lives, Grudge will not forget the feeling of emptiness that assailed him crossing the River Plur at Tubb Bridge to start his shift. The factory—drab as Russia under the Communists—was located halfway down the cheerless Revenue Road. It was the most prominent building thereon having recently undergone an extension that had increased its size but done nothing for its zero architectural merit. The death industry thrived in the city, and in the world. The government preached a mantra of export-led boom. Freshly made coffins were being sent to all corners of the globe. The local market, too—Bludgeon and its surrounds—was tightly boxed off.

Wormwood Coffin Manufacturers—Caskets of Craft Since 1877 read the sign above the main entrance. Grudge thought *Work Will Imprison You* would have been a far better blurb.

This particular morning was just like any other. He entered the building and punched the time clock at reception before walking along the corridor that led to the factory floor, a.k.a. the Fabrication Hall. Several other drones filed along with him facing their day forlornly. Beneath a banner that proclaimed *Unleash the Transformative Phase of Economic Growth* the shift began as always: wordlessly, like an unloved medical procedure one must carry out each day.

In the main, Grudge's spot was at the end of the line—the final nails and finishing touches—before the casket was taken to a garage area to be loaded onto a truck and delivered locally or internationally. The thriving firm of *Wormwood* had dozens of undertakers on their books.

Grudge generally put in a twelve-hour day, six days a week, extended at times when orders were out the door. On the seventh day he tried to emulate God and rest as best he could.

Chairman Young was fond of saying that he wanted Runway Four to be the best country in the world to do business with; and his wish was coming to pass. Notwithstanding their many stark suburbs, the cities, in particular Bludgeon, gleamed with the sheen of new money at their cores. The countryside, on the other hand, was a desolate, agrarian place of subsistence and concentration camps. Camp Thirteen being the most notorious. Woe to any citizen who transgressed. It was to the camps—referred to as corrective thinking centres—that they were sent.

Each day, Grudge got a fifteen-minute morning and afternoon break plus a maximum of forty minutes to take his lunch. These rest times were generous compared to what had gone before when employees worked the entire twelve hours with just a meagre ten-minute stop for food. The break times had improved as the economy had soared ahead. *Wormwood's* current boss, Noel Bowe—no slouch in the tyrannical department—introduced these better working conditions purely in the belief that they would bolster his bottom line; which was exactly what had happened.

Nationally, Chairman Young liked to espouse a philosophy he referred to as the *Happy Worker*—in reality a complete sham but promoted constantly as it allowed the Chairman to tell himself he was being progressive.

Grudge's immediate supervisor—whom he loathed—was a woman called Mary Dawn. Because of her place in the pecking order, she got to sit at a desk all day in a corner of the Fabrication Hall. She had telephone and computer privileges that were the envy of Grudge and his fellow workers. She knew it, too, and seemed to take a perverse pleasure in rubbing their noses in it, often talking inanely for long stretches to friends, or her elderly mother. Mary was a thirty-five-year-old spinster who lived with her parents. She was married to the job. On more than one occasion she had told Grudge: "Rank has its privileges." In his view, her arrogance, frequently conveyed in such haughty statements, evinced a personality type that was quite possibly psychotic. Still, he grinned as best he could and bore this contumely from his superior day upon day. The plan was to plot his way out of his current life through guile. So, he hammered away. There was always a new body in need of a coffin.

He nodded a curt hello to his two co-workers on the line this morning, Mordechai Levy and Joe O'Keeffe. Then, without further ado, he buried himself in work, trying to shut out all thoughts of his troubled life, Beatrice, his awful living quarters, and the hateful eye of Mary Dawn. Casket after casket rolled up in front of his hands. But his plan to shut out the world was made impossible by the incessant banter between Mordechai and Joe. Within reason, banter was permitted on the factory floor as long as the workers, in Noel Bowe's phrase, "still got the work done." Today's badinage was quite funny Grudge was forced to admit and it helped somewhat to ease his mental pain. They were discussing a girl in another section whom they both liked—a delectable creature named Amy Reville—each man staking his claim to Amy's affection and telling the other in no uncertain terms to butt out. This argument was conducted in a mock serious fashion, as Joe and Mordechai knew full well that Amy had a boyfriend in the police. Any pursuit of her was bound to get nowhere. Grudge knew Amy, too, and had bumped into her round the factory from time to time. He had once walked to the tram with her and talked about music. There was no doubt she was good-looking and seemed to have a pleasant personality. Though, he wasn't going there. He was content with Beatrice and his stop-and-go relationship with that Spanish handful.

As the morning wore on, Joe and Mordechai continued their banter to the extent that the humour of the exchange faded. One or two workers from other lines joined in and it all became tiresome. Grudge wished he was a tortoise and could withdraw into his shell. He tried to focus on the morning break due soon. The chat switched from Amy to broader themes. A recent spate of horrific murders in the nation—including two in Bludgeon the night before—came up. The killings—they'd been going on for a year now—had gripped people's imagination, and Grudge's co-workers were no exception. True crime is more exciting than the fictive. The consensus on the floor was the perpetrator, though a particularly fiendish and evasive killer, would be caught soon; very little, if anything, escaped the authorities in Runway Four.

The talk careened wildly in terms of theme when a particular fucker two lines down, with whom Grudge did not see eye to eye, Séamus Cronin, grew vocal on the subject of nationalism. Grudge and Cronin had argued in the past about politics and Cronin seemed to be spoiling for a fight. This was no surprise as he was an argumentative bastard at the best of times. Grudge didn't rise to the bait, preferring to keep his head down and coast as best he could towards tea.

After what seemed like an eternity, break time came. At the sound of a horn, Grudge and the other drones dropped tools and filed towards one of the factory's basement canteens. There were two of same at this lower level used—appropriately enough—for the low-level workers. Up on the third floor there was a bigger, plusher affair reserved strictly for senior management.

The basement canteens were spartan sorry places more to be endured than enjoyed. Each contained a boiler for tea, rudimentary tables and chairs and—in a sop to luxuriousness—a microwave oven. Staff huddled together, supping and masticating their humble fare like it was work in itself. Some conversed, while others read from library books, government newspapers, or scanned severely censored smartphones.

There was more talk than usual today. The banter out on the floor had got people in chatty mode. The previous night's murders were at the forefront of every conversation. The news had reported that the mutilated bodies of two care-in-the-community outpatients, Martha Murtagh and Celia Sellers, had been discovered in their sheltered housing in Goat Park, a street in the Lie District close to the Grange Asylum. The asylum, situated several hundred metres from the boundary line with Truth, was an overcrowded place of banally evil enterprise. It had something of Hell's lack of imagination.

The police seemed convinced that the deaths were the work of the same person responsible for the string of killings in the past few months. Citizens were afraid and at the same time enthralled by the horrifying murders.

The entire care-in-the-community idea was a perestroika-like initiative from the Chairman—a sop to liberalism so to speak—wherein he could paint himself as a benign and caring leader. It also took the pressure off the country's overflowing mental asylums. Broken people were given small houses outside the walls of the institutions in nothing more than a cosmetic exercise.

On those occasions when he bestrode the world stage, Chairman Young liked to boast to other world leaders about his benevolent regime and he often cited his beloved care-in-the-community initiative as an example thereof. Of course, perestroika R4-style was merely an opening up of society to make more money and nothing else. There was no benevolent side to it at all. Every one of those outpatients was monitored and accounted for to the extent of having no freedom whatsoever. If they infringed the government's strictures in any way they were instantly returned to the horrors of the asylum. It seemed, though, from the reports, that the horrors of the asylum would have been preferable to the flaying incurred by Martha and Celia.

In the canteen Grudge sat as far from Séamus Cronin as he could. Cronin lived with his mother, a widow, and did not have a girlfriend. Grudge imagined that Séamus spent a lot of his nights accessing whatever pornographic websites he could find behind the great firewall of Runway Four. The world's porn merchants were most inventive not to say ingenious and there was quite a proliferation of smut available online even in such a heavily censored land like R4. Cronin always came across as angry and confrontational. Luckily for Grudge, his nemesis seemed more interested in some biscuits this morning than having a pop at Galmount.

Grudge sat with Mordechai and Joe. As always, they talked in fits and starts about everything and anything. Football came up—a subject on which Grudge was clueless. Joe and Mordechai were the exact opposite. They followed national and international leagues with a passion that most people in the country kept for self-preservation. They ribbed Galmount frequently over his lack of sporting knowledge. He answered their jibes with a vacant stare.

The rumour doing the rounds of an imminent pay cut was also chewed over for a bit. One of capitalism's golden tenets had gained a lot of ground in R4 of late: the imperative to *"keep costs down"*, and in the eyes of the captains of industry that meant, principally, cutting wages. Noel Bowe was all for it.

—"I'm fucked if they cut my pay," Joe said. "I mean I've borrowed so much these past few years. I'm up to my tits in debt."

—"It's moobs for a man, not tits," Mordechai pointed out, in his own uniquely mordant manner. Levy's wit often fell flat but in this case it stuttered along with some degree of mobility. A little smile appeared at the corner of Grudge's mouth.

—"I think he means you're up to your *moobs* in debt, Joe," Grudge said.

O'Keeffe was the one wearing a vacant stare now. Generally, when things got quick-witted or quick-fire, he quickly got lost.

The government newspapers—a daily tabloid and a broadsheet, *The Orb* and *The Inquisitor*—were open under their noses. Pictures of the exterior of the latest murder house, along with photographs of the victims extracted from their Asylum patient files, took prominence on the front pages. The headlines screamed: *Butchery in Lie*, *Death in the Community*, *Fresh Murders*, with the promise of more details and further pictures—shots of the butchered corpses—on the inside pages. As ever, the press had their sources, and a scurrilous police photographer had provided the goods.

The fifteen minutes of morning break was almost up and by now an audible buzz was about the room on the subject of these murders most foul. People were animated by the heinous crimes. Joe and Mordechai began to vent on the topic, too.
—"I hope they get the fucker soon," was Grudge's contribution to the discussion. "He must be one sick bastard! Look at the details, he chopped them to bits."
—"I wouldn't count on the police to find him that quickly, Big Grudge," Mordechai said. "Of course, it would be a different story if it was you blogging against the government. They'd be around to your gaff in a second."
—"Easy, Mord," Joe said, throwing his eyes towards the listening device attached to the canteen wall. "Watch what you're saying, you never know when they're monitoring you."
Mordechai put his finger to his lips and smiled. Grudge nodded. It was an unusually perceptive remark from Joe.
The horn blasted again. The drones returned to the factory floor and resumed their chores.

***

After work that evening Grudge decided to visit a place that was in many ways a throwback to a bygone era: the local library. In this age of digitalisation and internet access it might seem unusual that the place remained open at all. The explanation lay in the fact that Chairman Young was said to be a lover of books—mind you, nothing too strenuous for the Great Helmsman. He contented himself with minimally taxing reads. His near fetishisation of the book had its roots in his early sexualisation at the hands of a nursemaid who had fondled him whilst reading him tales of Bo Peep, bears and a boy who cried wolf. Young loved the smell of a book, open in his hands, with its paper pages smooth to the touch and its black ink flowing forward in marvellous momentum. Reading thus was a sensation that could not be beaten, according to the Chairman, and, most unusually for a dictator, he encouraged citizens to make use of the many libraries in Runway Four. There were dozens of them lending books approved by government censors. Riskier reads reached R4 via smuggling.

Grudge himself was a keen reader, though not quite voracious. His mind was prone to drift. Nevertheless, books had survived the crisis of late postmodernism, as well as the strictures of the R4 state, and Grudge Galmount was a beneficiary of that happy fact.
He hopped on a tram on Revenue Road and paid the fare to the Lie District. He was in no mood for walking. He had the fare as he'd been taking things easy in recent weeks; going home early and working out with his weights before reading himself to sleep. He had fallen off the wagon just once. He could only recall snippets and prayed it was nothing too wild.
Twenty minutes later, the tram pulled to a stop outside the library. The building dated from a distant age: *'Erected in 1934'* read the stone above the door. Once inside, Grudge hoped to get his hands on some Sherlock Holmes. The current killer abroad, causing such a frisson of fear, had whetted his appetite for some meat-and-potatoes nineteenth-century crime fiction. Conan Doyle was not on the government's banned list.
He entered the library, passed a forty-something bespectacled spinster at the front desk, and turned left in the direction of Crime. An evening crowd was in, with most noses buried. The odd reader stared round the room in what Grudge took as far less than momentary wonder. Arriving at the crime shelves, he began to browse, casting a cold eye on Black, Burke and Connolly—all unbanned—before doubling back to a chunk of Conan Doyle titles. His hand was on the spine of the Hound of the Baskervilles when an attractive young lady, early twenties, glided past grabbing his attention.
He felt that familiar twinge in his loins and quickly abandoned his search for Sherlock Holmes. He walked through the library pursuing the vision. He found her at a computer screen in the online area where she had just sat down and taken off her coat, intent on engaging the search engine. Grudge, captivated by now, walked over and, as casually as he could, asked.
—"Good evening, Ms.?"
She looked up, surprised to be addressed out of the blue, but answered warmly.
—"Eh, hello, do I know you?"
—"Grudge Galmount," Grudge said, with a smile on his face.
The girl laughed.

—“That’s a nice alliterative name. I’m Sally Popplewell,” she replied.
This was good, Grudge thought, eminently positive in fact. She wanted to converse. My name even registered in her head. He scrambled for something to say.
—“You seem familiar, Sally. I thought for a moment I knew you. You look like the sister of a friend,” he lied. “Pardon me if I’m interrupting. Are you researching?”
—“As a matter of fact I am,” Sally said, sounding for all the world like she was glad to have been asked the question. “I mostly work at home but I came down to the library to get a break from the four walls. I’m looking to find out how many similar murders have been committed over the years; similar to this fiend that’s on the loose. I’m a freelance journalist. Trying to make a name for myself I guess you could say.”
—“Fascinating line of work,” Grudge said. “I’m in coffins myself.”
Sally looked startled and then laughed thinking this fellow was merely cracking a joke.
—“No, seriously,” Grudge said. “I work at *Wormwood Coffin Manufacturers* on Revenue Road. I’m on the assembly line. I was on my way home and decided to pop into the library for some crime fiction. These murders are on my mind, too.”
Then, Grudge knew that he had to be brave and seize the day.
—“Would you fancy going for a coffee, Sally? There’s a little café around the corner. We seem to have a mutual interest in murder. It could be fun.”
She hesitated, sizing him up, before acceding to his request.
—“Why not? I’ve been working on this story all day. I could use a break.”
She logged off her computer and picked up her things.
The café was a comfortable place in its own way. They ordered coffees and continued chatting.
—“I’m an only child. I live with my parents in the Truth District,” Sally explained. “My father didn’t want me to go into journalism in case I offended the government with something I wrote. But I got around him. I’ve always been daddy’s girl and able to get my own way. So far I’ve managed to stay on the right side of the powers that be. They’re as anxious as everybody else is to catch this killer. Any

work I do on this story can only meet with their favour. And what about you, Grudge, what are your living arrangements?"
—"A real loner me," Grudge laughed. "I'm stuck in my flat up in Rodent Street. It's just around the corner from here, actually. I like it that way, though. I'm an only child, too. My parents were killed in Camp Thirteen when I was an infant. I was raised in the Arenta state orphanage. You probably know it. It's in the Truth District."
—"Arenta," Sally said. "Too right I've heard of it. An awful place by all accounts. You seem very together for someone who's been through that hellhole."
—"Well, I am what I am," Grudge said, rather obliquely. "I simply go to work each day and keep my head down. I've been at *Wormwood* since I was eighteen. No sense in getting on the wrong side of this government. You're just dispatched if you do. I'll end up like my parents, killed in a camp. I don't want any trouble. I take a drink now and again but it's nothing serious. I don't do drugs."
He was lying to a degree here. Still, he wasn't going to confess to this girl on their first evening together the true extent of his destructive relationship with alcohol and other substances. Besides, wasn't it under control these days, his destructiveness?
Sally nodded and looked at him intensely.
—"Why were your parents sent to the camp?" she asked.
—"For expressing religious beliefs. A nurse in Arenta told me all this. My mam and dad, Gerard and Sarah, were people of strong faith. I was conceived when my mother was forty-five, and when that happened they let everybody in the neighbourhood know that it was down to God, that I was their little miracle. Some shitbag neighbour ratted them out and they were hauled off to Camp Thirteen. *"Worship of a Deity other than Chairman Young"* was the official charge. At Camp Thirteen I presume they were worked to the bone, though I've no definite knowledge of what actually happened to them. I guess they eventually died of starvation and overwork."
—"I'm sorry. That's awful," Sally said, with kindness in her eyes. Looking into those warm eyes, her face framed by ringlets of soft black hair, Grudge was seized by an urge to have her in his life from this day forth. It struck him that Beatrice was simply too far away in Madrid, and that his relationship with her was impossible to conduct. Come to think of it, was he really in love with Beatrice at all, or was he just childishly attached to the notion of their bond? These deep

questions presented themselves to his smitten head with an urgency for which he was in no way prepared.
It was getting on for nine. The café was about to close. The owner scrunched up his apron and told Grudge and Sally he would be shutting the doors in five minutes.
The gallant Grudge walked Sally to her tram stop and saw her onto a car emblazoned with pro-government graffiti that was heading to Truth. Small parties of fervent citizens regularly painted pro-regime slogans in various places around Bludgeon. The authorities in the main approved these displays of fanaticism such was the creativity of the graffiti whorls on walls, pavements and trams. It all gave a nice aesthetic bent to Bludgeon's otherwise bleak streetscape.
To Galmount's surprise, Sally agreed to meet with him the following week for another coffee. She gave him her number and he secured a time and date.
—"Good luck with your research into the psycho!" he shouted, and skipped away from the stop elated at how his evening with Ms. Sally Popplewell had gone.
When he reached Rodent Street, however, his upbeat mood nosedived on seeing his landlord's car parked outside his domicile. She, for it was a she—Lydia Morten—always travelled in style on the back of her earnings from the slum dwellings she controlled, as well as a music career that had longed since reached its zenith but was nonetheless ticking along in a fair to middling manner just the same. She had parked her menacing 4x4 Audi at the front door of the rathole building. Luckily for Grudge, she was just leaving when he arrived. As ever, her younger, muscular, lapdog boyfriend, Conan, accompanied her. Seeing Grudge coming hesitantly up the garden path, Lydia exclaimed in her usual shrill tone.
—"You owe me some money, Grudge. You're two weeks in arrears now. Have you got it?"
Grudge could only look at his shoes and pray for the moment to pass. This harridan never failed to reduce him to straw. He'd been a bloody fool, he told himself, to squander those two rent payments on a spree. Finally he mumbled.
—"I'm getting paid next Saturday and will have it then. If Conan calls at seven I'll make sure to be here."
—"You mean *when* I call," Conan snarled. "Saturday at seven. We're not a bloody charity."

The pair of them climbed into the Audi and sped away. Grudge despised them.

Chapter 2

In the rathole as he lay on the rickety bed he couldn't get the thought of Sally Popplewell out of his head. All notion of writing a fresh letter to Beatrice—an idea that had struck him during his work shift—was put to one side. Good old-fashioned lust was very firmly on his mind. Unable to contain it, he stripped from the waist down and brought himself off swiftly, all the while keeping the image of Sally's mouth—her words coming forth through perfect white teeth—uppermost in his mind. When she had talked about journalism it was clear that she had a calling. Her earnestness on the subject was obvious, and the image of her talking with such raptness provided Grudge with a most stimulating memory.
After cleaning up, he lay back on his pillow, breathed deeply, and reconsidered writing to Bea—this time ending their relationship:

My sweetest Bea,

It pains me to have to tell you that we have no future together...

But he allowed the words to peter out at that point. He couldn't finish things with Beatrice. He still had feelings for her. The days they'd spent together surely meant something. Was he that fickle that he would discard her like an old coat as soon as someone newer, nearer (and nicer looking!) came along? Sadly, the answer was yes. At base, his deepest loyalty was to himself and the sating of his own desires. If Beatrice were to return to Bludgeon—something well within the bounds of possibility—he knew that he would choose Sally over Bea in a heartbeat. And yet, compounding his caddishness, he didn't have the balls to write the words that needed to be written. He tossed his pen and paper aside and lay there, sleepy now, like an orangutan on zoo grass catching some rays.
Sally Popplewell swam through his head, an alluring mermaid laden with promise and mystery. Again, the image of her mouth stimulated him and he was almost going to have a second run at it—there being

no hand like your own hand—except that Ann-Marie from the flat down the hall called out his name as she knocked on his door. Grudge got up, opened it slightly, and looked out at his worried-looking
neighbour. Fifty, single and poor, Ann-Marie had an awful lot of time on her hands. She worked mornings only—the result of a mysterious disability—and spent most of her life indoors twitching at her curtains and rubbing against her walls. She was a watcher and a listener, and (usefully) a good source of information. She seemed to know everything about everybody.
—"Yes, Ann-Marie, what is it?" Grudge asked, flustered from his masturbatory exertions.
—"I just wanted to warn you, Grudge. Lydia and Conan were here."
—"I know they were," he said, impatiently. "I met them on my way in. What do you want to warn me about?"
—"They want you out. I overheard them talking in the hall. Conan said he'd evict you if you didn't pay your arrears."
She was clearly a lonely woman and Grudge felt sorry for her.
—"Thanks for the heads up, Ann-Marie. I know they'd like to see the back of me, but don't you fret: I'm paying my arrears next Saturday. Now, if you don't mind, goodnight."
—"Yeah, goodnight," Ann-Marie said. "I'm just trying to help."
She turned her spindly frame and headed back to her lonely flat.
Grudge closed his door and lay on the bed once more. It had started to rain and the drops, like the tears of a spurned lover, pelted off the grimy windowpane that looked onto the backyard. Within minutes he nodded off. Before reaching deep sleep, he roamed the glades of REM for a spell: as though propelled from a launch pad he took to the air over a field of lush green grass. He felt exhilarated to be flying so and strangely familiar with the feeling—it wasn't something new to him at all. Hurtling towards him at great speed he saw Sally flying, too. She hovered in midair smiling and spoke indecipherably to him before their lips locked in a kiss so intense it sent him to the slumberous depths like a knockout drug.
His time in the depths was short-lived however. The rain persisted and indeed got heavier and its rattling on the window stirred him after half an hour. He sat up and reached for a book from a small pile on his locker, feeling a tinge of regret that he hadn't managed to get a Sherlock Holmes from the library. Of course, meeting Sally had

more than compensated for that failure. The book—a postmodern affair—entertained in its own way, even though the constant intrusion of the authorial voice irritated Grudge. He yearned for simpler formats and easier ways to tell stories. Nonetheless, despite these misgivings, the novel held him and he read on.

He was alert and insomniac and his eyes darted through the paragraphs not unlike somebody on cocaine. Another half hour passed when a set piece on ethnic cleansing emerged from the pages. Unable to stomach disturbing scenes of bound men and boys being shot in a forest clearing, he put the book down and stared blankly at the walls. If he listened hard enough—not that he cared to—he could hear the truck driver in the flat above snoring like a hog; the intrusion of the neighbourly snuffle so to speak.

Grudge's gaze was blank as the sun but his mind was full of topics. It raced down a myriad of paths. Despite the pleasure of meeting Sally earlier, his pliable mood was easily turned into one of anxiety and gloom. He knew that at this rate he would have great difficulty getting back to sleep. The thought of facing the next day at the factory feeling exhausted was a nightmare. He wished that he could move on from his current circumstances, find a better, more intellectually stimulating, position, but it was impossible—people of his class were destined to work menially, in his case producing coffins, the ultimate in stultifying labour.

Now awake in the middle of the night in his bleak room, he almost wept to think that the apogee of his career progression was to wind up in *Wormwood.*

The rain kept coming down, and his mind raced on, until Grudge decided that enough was enough. He *had* to get some sleep. He'd been trying to avoid substances since his recent spree and was succeeding more or less. He was the kind of guy who could easily do temperance, but once a drug got in his system, one was too many and a million not enough. He was loath to dabble in sleeping medication. Nevertheless, he had kept a couple of *Stilnoct* tablets offside in case of emergency, and getting some shuteye was just that. He reached into his bedside locker for the pills bought from a street dealer near Secular Hall. He filled a small cup with water, popped three in his mouth, felt their effects in minutes, hopped back to bed, grew wonderfully languorous, and went out cold.

***

The next day in the Fabrication Hall the talk, in the main, was still of murder. Specifically, the two women mutilated and killed in their sheltered housing two nights earlier. Their house in Goat Park opposite the Grange Asylum was now a cordoned off crime scene. The press was in overdrive reporting the killings and everyone in *Wormwood* and beyond was agog at the gruesome events. From all accounts, the two middle-aged victims—only recently released from the Grange—had had the torments of Hell visited upon them prior to their deaths.
In the canteen, Séamus Cronin thought it great fun to rib Grudge on the subject.
—"What were you up to two nights ago, Galmount?" he sneered, in a voice fully audible to the room. Several people sniggered at his witless gibe.
—"What do you mean?" Grudge asked sheepishly. He was still tired and woozy from last night's pills.
—"Well, there have been two more murders," Cronin said. "Any criminologist would tell you that the typical profile of these perpetrators is a loner with no friends who lives on his own. That about sums you up, Grudgie!"
Cronin fell about the place guffawing at his remark, and its Sherlock Holmes-like level of deduction. The canteen erupted, too, as the grinning nitwits that passed for his colleagues all looked to Grudge who was deep in discomfort. It was at moments like this he wished the ground would open and swallow him whole. He thought how wonderful it would be if he could become a fallen leaf and disappear down a fast-flowing river. He scrambled in his head for a witty retort but nothing came. When he did speak it was all rather weak.
—"C'mon, Séamus. I'm just trying to have a quiet break. Besides, it's not really funny making jokes about those murders. From what I've read the two women met a terrible death."
—"From what you've read?" Cronin asked, laying his incredulity on thick. "Sure weren't you fucking there?"
And once more the fools brayed. The poor fellow just couldn't win.
Later that afternoon as Grudge grappled with a particularly tricky brass handle, Mary Dawn approached and asked him to come upstairs to the senior management's suite of offices. He grew

alarmed, for this could only mean one thing: he was in some kind of trouble.
—"I'll be right with you, Mary," he said, putting his tool down and running his hand through his hair trying to imagine what it was all about. Creeping anxiety threatened to suffocate him. There was the shift during his mini-bender about two weeks back when he had come to work under the influence of vodka and synthetic cocaine. He believed he'd masked his inebriation well; maybe not. He had to admit those few days were a blur. Details remained sketchy and were still only coming to light a fortnight on. Walking down a street, travelling on the tram, or in the rathole, he would suddenly catch a glimpse of his strung out self, clasp his head and think: Oh my God! So, it was quite conceivable that he had made a holy show of himself in the workplace and blanked the whole thing out. Or, if not a holy show, at least, possibly, that he had been stoned enough for people to know it. The funny thing was, though, nobody had said anything to him afterwards. Cronin and his ilk would surely have brought it up if they'd known that he was high on the job. Not to mention Mary Dawn!
Then again, Grudge being his own worst critic and an inveterate worrier, perhaps he simply floated along during his spree benumbed and whistling past the graveyard of the world. Maybe the worst thing he had done was to not eat enough, and ignore Ann-Marie in the hallway as he came and went and she sought to pass the time of day with him.
Whatever had happened, *mea maxima culpa* now, he thought.
Mary signalled she was growing impatient. She paced back and forth at her desk looking at her watch and wearing a stern expression that told him to get a move on. In his anxiety he kicked over a container of nails to the annoyance of Mordechai and another chap working with him that day called Pole Wallace. Pole leaned down sighing and began putting the nails back in their box as Grudge joined Mary at her desk and the two of them headed towards the elevators.
Grudge could feel the beady eyes of co-workers upon him and felt all he was missing in terms of appearance was a noose round his neck.
Wordlessly, he entered the lift with Mary. As the contraption headed skyward, the thunderous silence between them was close to

unbearable. He had to speak if only to alleviate his growing sense of panic. He piped up.
—"What's this about, Mary, am I in trouble?"
Her nose crinkled the way a person's might upon entering a stinking toilet. Grudge wondered if his voice was really that bad.
—"Noel will speak to you in a minute," she answered, clearly not wishing to give anything away.
The Noel she referred to was Noel Bowe, the managing director of *Wormwood.* Christ, Grudge thought, this must be fucking serious if we're going to meet the big cheese himself. He rubbed his brow where beads of cold sweat formed, racking his brain to remember the day he'd arrived to work high. He could've sworn he had kept it all well hidden; he would soon find out.
The elevator came to a halt on the plush third floor. Grudge and Mary emerged still not speaking. They proceeded down a quiet corridor with offices on either side containing Bowe's closest lieutenants, sundry minions, and a smattering of the firm's most obsequious flunkies. There was also a room with a clerical support staff—what used to be called a typing pool in the old days. Swimming in this pool was a shoal of attractive girls selected for the job on the basis of their looks alone. The lieutenants—all male—were the most senior members of the firm and each was as cold and calculating a shark as one could meet. Grudge's own nose crinkled as he walked along the deep-pile carpet detecting in the air the unmistakable spoor of rutting males.
Wormwood's business was lucrative and recession-proof; the happiest of happy mixtures. As wags round Bludgeon were wont to say: people were dying today who never died before. Bowe was a Party man through and through. The kind of chap Chairman Young liked to be seen with on social occasions; a gala dinner here, or a trip to the racetrack there. Noel Bowe, noble captain of industry, was the embodiment of Runway Four's economic miracle—as the Chairman liked to call the recent surge in export figures. How the Supreme Commander relished hyperbole and spin!
In Young's view, Bowe was an example to the plebs of what could be achieved by a strong work ethic and a good nose for making money. There was no problem in the Chairman's mind with Bowe's utter ruthlessness and his willingness to have anybody who stood in

his way eradicated. That philosophy—a sort of smile-as-you-kill, can-do spirit—had taken him to the top of *Wormwood's* greasy pole. Of course, the only people Noel smiled at whilst doing the killing were Party bosses and bigwigs; the lower orders meant nothing to him other than acting as a source of backbreaking labour to help increase *Wormwood's* wealth. His manner was openly contemptuous towards the dogsbodies of the factory floor. Bowe's loyalty to the Party was paramount. It went to the very core of his being. It was not unheard of him to betray dissenters. He had done so—and would do so again—in his professional and private life. Quite a few folk had gone to early graves on account of Noel Bowe. He was known to be a lover of surveillance—a malign gadget-freak—and such things as listening devices and cameras were commonplace in his factory. To Noel, Grudge Galmount was a tadpole. Dealing with him would be a picnic.

Reaching Bowe's rosewood office door, Mary rapped on the polished wood and in they went. An anteroom with an attractive secretary was their first port of call. She was expecting them.

—"Mr. Bowe will see you now," she chirped, waving her hand towards a further door—again of polished rosewood—that led to the sanctum sanctorum.

Grudge and Mary took their signal and walked inside to meet the boss.

The room—opulent and vast—told its own tale of money, power and a life of preferment. Grudge tried to guess how much native forest had been felled to create the place.

The great man was at his desk eating segments of satsuma. The ball bearings of an office toy knocked back and forth before him.

His stare was that of a raptor, his focus fixed on Galmount.

It seemed that Noel Bowe wanted to get straight down to business.

—"Take a seat both of you," he said, indicating two plush chairs. "This won't take long."

They positioned themselves on the rich lining of the seats and waited for Bowe to speak.

—"Grudge Galmount," Noel said. "I have asked Mary to bring you up here today as I am extremely concerned and indeed angry regarding some recent behaviour on your part. As a matter of fact, I've been annoyed about your misdeed for a fortnight now, going over and over it in my head. I've waited till now to speak to you as I

wanted to see whether or not it was a one-off occurrence. Luckily for you, it seems to have been an isolated incident. That's not to excuse it, however, and I have to say: I am stunned by your effrontery."
Grudge felt his Adam's apple jerk. He didn't want to think about it, but he knew his heart was beating faster than a suicide bomber about to pull the cord. Was Bowe really saying this stuff? He was afraid to even contemplate an answer.
—"You may have thought at the time that you were being clever and getting away with your outrageousness. Mary knew what was going on, as did I, once it was brought to my attention. Here at *Wormwood* we have the finest high-definition surveillance cameras, and excellent microphones. They picked up your every facial tic, as well as the mumbled dirge you spoke. When she showed me, I told Mary we'd not act straightaway, although she was keen to do so. I felt a period of further monitoring was necessary. I wanted to see if the situation was grave enough to warrant calling in the police."
Jesus Christ, Grudge thought, the police! He was sure now that it was all to do with the day he'd turned up stoned. The sin of being intoxicated on the job was one of the biggest no-nos in Runway Four. In the eyes of the authorities it displayed complete contempt for Chairman Young's *Happy Worker* philosophy.
In *Wormwood*, Noel Bowe saw himself very much as the eyes and ears of the Party; and, boy, had Grudge Galmount transgressed.
Mary's face was an ugly mix of sanctimony and rapt attentiveness, while Grudge for his part simply wished that Bowe would get to the point. The man's wearisome volubility only prolonged the agony.
—Whilst I don't blame Mary for your misdeeds—she's an exemplary employee—from now on she'll manage you much more tightly. You're under a level of scrutiny, Galmount, that will teach you to respect your job, respect this proud firm, and respect your country. For the past fortnight, Mary's been monitoring the video grabs of you on the line with a closeness not seen heretofore. She will continue to do so going forward. I've been receiving daily reports on your behaviour, a practice we will maintain indefinitely. I've asked Mary to put anything she deems out of the ordinary in a mail and send it straight to this office. Your toilet visits and your breaks are scrutinized more than your colleagues, the majority of whom give no trouble at all. You brought this on yourself, Galmount. You can wear that hangdog expression all you like.

You'll get no sympathy from me. Just be thankful I haven't notified the law—not yet anyway. Of course, if you step out of line again you will be shown no mercy."
A short silence ensued. Grudge was delighted that Noel had shut up for a moment. He was disappointed by his reference to a hangdog expression, convinced he'd been showing a mature responsible face; evidently not.
Noel popped another segment of satsuma into his mouth and reached for a TV remote on the desk.
—"We are going to watch some footage," he announced. "Turn around, look over there."
He zapped a flatscreen mounted on the wall. Their heads turned and all three stared. The picture flickered and lit up: showtime. Grudge didn't even want to be in this taxing theatre. Sweaty-palmed and dry-lipped, he sat in the incongruously comfortable chair, his head full of dread, fearing the worst. He had forgotten just how watched his workplace was.
The "movie" opened with a wide pan of the Fabrication Hall. Ten a.m. and the date—the seventh of ____ in the year ____—flashed in bright green at the bottom of the screen. A morning shift was proceeding in its typically tedious manner. At the various points along the assembly line the workers' heads were down. For whatever reason, there wasn't much raillery to be heard on this particular day; just the noise of tools and machinery and the ringing of telephones on supervisors' desks. These supervisors—strategically placed for maximum watchfulness—did their thing: watched intently.
Mary and Noel, too, watched intently the emerging picture. As did Grudge, who was burning inside at the unfairness of it all, this tormenting trap he had fallen into. On top of everything else, his nerves were shot.
Presently, the camera began to zoom in. He saw himself—that anaesthetised man from a fortnight back—with his hammer in his hand banging at a casket. He worked robotically, his head down like everyone else's. Why is Bowe showing me this, Grudge wondered, there's nothing out of the ordinary? The reason soon became clear. The angle switched. Another camera, positioned on the floor, zoomed up towards Grudge's face.
The film jogged his memory. He really had—to use the vernacular—been "off his box" that morning. His features, every contour in high-

definition, filled the screen. The eyes bloodshot, the skin a pallid hue of junkie white, and the lips dry and thin. Moreover, they moved continuously for Grudge was reciting a snippet of Romantic verse—in a loop, and softly—which the hi-tech microphone had picked up as loud and clear as—well—a bell:

My heart aches, and a drowsy numbness pains
My sense, as though of hemlock I had drunk...

Over and over he said it while pounding his tool in a sloppy syncopated rhythm. He was smiling, too, with the dreamy-eyed expression of the inebriated. He looked shambolic. If he thought at the time that the noise and activity of the Fabrication Hall would conceal his sottishness, he was wrong. The evidence was before his eyes in Noel Bowe's office and his neck was on the line. They had him bang to rights.
—"I think we can say without doubt that you are intoxicated in that footage, Galmount," Bowe said, his face pinched with anger.
Mary the toady looked on delighting in Grudge's exposure. She was ruthless, heartless, but unfortunately for Grudge she was far from voiceless, proclaiming.
—"I am so sorry, sir, that this happened on my watch. It disgusts me to see Grudge in that condition on the film, and to think that he was in such a state on my assembly line. I feel *I've* let *Wormwood* down, never mind him."
—"Ridiculous, Mary," the boss answered. "You did nothing wrong. As I said, you're an exemplary employee. In point of fact, you did all the initial monitoring on this and you brought it to my attention. You are only to be praised for your behaviour in the matter."
Grudge's sense of trepidation began to subside a little. He realised that while he was definitely receiving a dressing down, he was to some degree being given a chance. It appeared that Noel would not be calling in the police just yet. If he was reading the gist of this conversation correctly, it seemed the Government's corrective thinking facilities would have to wait another day to welcome Grudge Galmount into their unloving embrace. He could just about tolerate the sanctimonious crap spouting from Noel and Mary, if it meant he was not to be arrested. He was well aware that Noel had the power to have him jailed and the key thrown away. He decided

there and then, though, to buck up and not give either of them the chance again to catch him stoned on the job. He would stick to lifting his weights and working on his sobriety.
He felt the need to say something to ease things, and to defend himself in some way.
—"This won't happen again, Mr. Bowe. I know it looks bad and I'm not going to deny that I am under the influence in those scenes but…"
—"Shut up right there, Galmount!" Noel snapped. "I don't want your excuses. You're a disgrace. If there's any repeat of this behaviour, I'll have Government rehabilitation officers all over you like pigeons around vomit. You think you're clever with your centuries-old verse—yes, I looked up the lines—but you're not. You're just a stupid, drunken serf and don't ever forget it. Take him out of here, Mary. He's to be watched non-stop!"
Mary nodded in her typically obsequious way.
—"Absolutely, Mr. Bowe, I will do just that," she said.
With nary another word, she shoved Grudge's elbow and shunted him out of the room. The pair made the dreary descent to the factory floor. In the lift, Grudge was acutely aware how much he despised Mary.
Back on the assembly line Levy and Wallace said nothing to him. He felt swamped by travails and worked on his caskets in an effort to forget all else. He could sense the whispering of colleagues who knew he was in deep doo-doo. Well, he thought, it gives them something to talk about.
Mary returned to the commanding position of her desk where, between filing her nails, browsing the internet, and phoning a friend, she managed to keep a vigilant eye on her most disgraceful employee: the messed up young man from Rodent Street.
If she were to be honest with herself—an unlikely scenario—she'd have to admit that he was also her most desirable member of staff. She had always found him attractive in a vulnerable sort of way. Invariably, though, and perhaps inevitably, her inner sadist always got the upper hand when it came to Grudge and she never followed her heart.
She noticed his diligent approach to the work since coming back from Noel's office; his newfound zeal with his tool. In fact, he was going at it hammer and tongs. Good, she thought, it meant the talk

with Bowe had frightened him and perhaps now he would pull up his socks and become the model employee she always knew he could be; a model employee she looked forward to bullying all the more as soon as he emerged.
After a while, as he hammered, quite unknown to Mary, Grudge's mind began to fixate on the best ways he could think to murder the bitch. Eventually, towards the end of his shift, he grew tired of these killing fantasies and roamed into the divine mental terrain where Sally Popplewell dwelt.
He couldn't wait to see her next week.

Chapter 3

As it turned out, he didn't have to wait a week to see Sally. That evening just after seven, hitting Revenue Road following his shift, with depression and fear swirling in his gut, Grudge's cellphone rang. Wonderful, he thought, seeing Sally's name flash on the screen.
He was hungry and nervy and heading to a cheap falafel place on Domina. He preferred that to returning straight to Rodent Street. A call from Sally was just the fillip he needed. He felt his mood lift instantly.
—"Hi, Grudge. It's Sally Popplewell. Remember me?" she asked, in her sweetest voice.
—"Sally! Of course I remember you. How could I forget such a pretty girl?" Grudge—a charmer to his fingertips—shouted above the din of the rush hour traffic. "What can I do for you?"
—"Well," Sally went on. "You can do me a favour, that's what. I know we said we'd meet up next week, but something's come up in the meantime. I'm going to need some assistance and I think you'll find this rather interesting. Plus, I really enjoyed the other night so why wait a week?"
Grudge felt lucky. What great compensation for the agonies earlier with Mary Dawn and Noel Bowe, Sally, a beautiful woman, talking sweetly down the phone to him. Thank you, God. He was intrigued, too, about what she meant by "something's come up".
—"Sure," he said, trying to sound calm. "The other night was fun."

He wanted to play it cool, feeling he was in with a chance of a genuine relationship with this girl—something he yearned for more than the half-hearted long-distance kind he had with Beatrice.
—"But what do you mean by something's come up? And where do you want to meet?"
He wanted hard information from Sally. There had been enough beating about the bush.
—"Well," Sally explained. "The editor of *The Inquisitor*, Jeff Kern—a highly influential man as I'm sure you know—really liked some freelance stuff I sent him recently and asked me to go to Goat Park where the care-in-the-community women were killed and report back from the house. Luckily, I've been researching Bludgeon and R4 murders for a while now, so I ought to be able to produce something special. He's got me police clearance to enter the house through his contacts in the force. I'm *so* flattered. I mean this is the editor of *The Inquisitor* I'm talking about. He said he liked the pieces I sent in. Several were published in the last few months but they were just piddling articles really—the city's litter problem, trams running late, that kind of thing. I could hardly believe it when he phoned me last night. I've to show up tomorrow evening at the house, flash some ID and the police will let me in to have a look round. I mean, how lucky's that for a wannabe journalist?" she laughed.
Grudge noticed with a delightful twinge that her laugh was the sexiest he had ever heard.
—"Wow," he said. "You've certainly impressed the right person there in terms of furthering your career. Jeff Kern is just about R4's top man in newspapers."
He had to hand it to her, talk about attracting good attention.
—"And let me guess, you want me to come with you?" he added.
Grudge, on University Green at this stage, crossed the street at a pedestrian light while a snake of thick traffic idled. He was relishing this phone call, the rat's nest of cares in his head untangled for now. His confidence lifted purely from talking to this veritable angel.
He beat a path through the evening crowds, with all the poise and command of a grand old duke leading a platoon up a hill. It was amazing the effect speaking to Sally had on him. Butterflies danced in his stomach and he felt like a man in the grip of a powerfully euphoric drug. What a contrast to the cowed figure he had cut in

Bowe's office that afternoon where he'd felt all of an inch tall. Undoubtedly, she was a magical girl to change him so. Anyone looking at Grudge sashaying down Domina—and quite a few passersby did take notice—would have thought they saw a man at the top of his game: proud, happy, and without a care in the world. If they had looked closer, though,—and, again, some did—they would have noticed the shabby condition of his raiment and realised he wasn't such a hotshot after all.

Nonetheless, the illusion held quite well and Galmount galloped along the street, his juices flowing in anticipation of his falafel meal and his tail up at the prospect of meeting Sally so soon again.

—"Exactly, Grudge. I respectfully request the pleasure of your company when I step inside such a scene of utter barbarity."

Grudge found the formality in her tone wonderfully flirtatious and played along eagerly.

—"Well, Ms. Popplewell, it sounds as though you will need a strong masculine presence tomorrow evening. It gives me enormous pleasure to provide you with somebody who fits the bill perfectly: me!" he laughed down the phone.

—"That's great. I've absolutely no doubt you'll be the perfect companion. But, joking aside, Jeff Kern has warned me it's far from pretty inside that house. It's extremely harrowing. Everything's preserved for forensics. It won't be cleaned up for a couple of days. Kern has swung it that we can traipse through despite the investigation. He's got some power. Apparently, you can still see clumps of hair matted in blood and stuck to the walls."

—"Oh my God, how gross! I know some pictures have been in the press already but I haven't bothered to look. Seems I'll be seeing things for real now. I presume the bodies have been removed to the morgue?"

—"Yes. The autopsies are today as far as I know. Kern sent a photographer and another reporter around this morning to shoot the site and do a basic facts-of-the-story piece. He wants something a little more in-depth from me. I'm hoping inspiration strikes hard. There's no need for us to take photographs. We'll just go room to room and I'll record my impressions into the phone. It might be a bit traumatising to do it on my own, that's why I'd like you there."

—"Ready, willing and able," Grudge said. "Just tell me where and when to meet?"

—“Okay, let’s say seven-thirty tomorrow evening? You’ll be finished work by then, right?”
—“I sure will.”
—“In that case, there’s a filthy butcher’s shop on the East Circular Road, with flies in the window. Do you know it?”
—“Unfortunately, yes. I’m embarrassed to say I’ve bought meat there from time to time.”
—“Right, well, we’ll rendezvous outside it. The horror house is just a couple of minutes away.”
—“You got it, Sally. I’ll be there,” Grudge said. “Seven-thirty tomorrow evening.”
Pleased, naturally, by this conversation with Sally, Grudge was also a tad apprehensive to think he’d be visiting a murder scene, with near untrammelled access, the following evening. What a challenge to take on.
—“See you then. Byeee!” she rang off, to go wherever it was that a young freelance journalist, single and living with her parents, vanished to of an evening.
Grudge continued along the street, with the traffic booming and the crowds teeming, hoping Sally, when she got home, would think of him fondly, at regular bursts, throughout the night.
With a grin on his face—in sharp contrast to his demeanour when clocking off—he entered the falafel joint. He was famished. Cooking smells sent saliva sluicing round his mouth. One of the great advantages of his abstemious periods was having a lot more money to spend on food. One of the great disadvantages was his tendency to binge eat and gain weight. This time round, however, on his latest stab at temperate living, he was trying to ditch the binging, and was making a good fist of it, too. Between eating the correct amount of calories per day, not giving in to cravings for sweets and cakes, and his weightlifting exercises in the evening, the result was a healthier and happier Grudge all round.
Nonetheless, he loved to eat and had no qualms about scoffing a meal of less than nutritious fast food, reasoning that he still wouldn’t exceed his daily calorie count.
Here at the falafel joint—*Taste of Persia*—he was a familiar face who always ordered the same thing: a tub of mushy peas, a cola (diet), French fries in garlic sauce and one of their speciality kebabs. Seeing Grudge, the serf behind the counter smiled.

—"Your usual, sir?"
—"Yes, please," Grudge said, licking his lips.
He slid out of the place half an hour later—his belly full—and headed for Rodent Street.

***

The following evening—Thursday—at seven-thirty Grudge stood on the East Circular Road, at the shop with the flies, waiting for Sally Popplewell. A poster beside him read: *'Hail the Great Ideology of Chairman Young'*. As usual at that hour the footpath was crammed with citizens returning from labour to the relative comfort of their hovels and the contentment that a square meal and several hours of television bring. Cars and trams, too, stuffed with souls poured down the thoroughfare.
Selecting various faces from this scene, Grudge was struck by the fact that nobody seemed to be smiling. Such is life, he thought, under an oppressive regime. Although, it had to be said, the regime made strenuous efforts to propagandise a benign caring image. People could more or less live where they wanted to—that is to say, where they could afford to live. There was still a healthy market in private property in the country; albeit skewed in favour of landlords, of whom there were many. Poorer folk rented; Grudge's rathole being a case in point. A form of capitalism—one which principally enriched the Party members at the top, and their families—was allowed to flourish.
The authorities bestowed these landlords with generous reliefs in buying and owning property, leaving the less well off to sink or swim in a sea of inequality. It was a controlled dictatorial capitalism—production and commerce thriving under the government's steely eye. Business orders were on the rise. If one was to believe the propaganda—and in this instance it was true—exports were booming. The country earned billions by sending abroad the many goods manufactured in harsh conditions at home. As one example, hundreds of people in democracies were being buried in *Wormwood* coffins on a daily basis.
The retail sector, too, was enjoying a prosperous period. There was no doubt that people had more money in their pockets. In reality, though, it was a pittance that trickled down to the lower orders, enough to keep food in their bellies and roofs over their heads, and

leave them with the price of a few gimcracks or some cheap and nasty garments.
The stewardship of Chairman Young saw all the country's power and wealth invested in venal Party honchos. To compound the injustice, those on society's bottom tiers were told that they mattered—that they were more than mere factory fodder—and that Runway Four had their best interests at heart.
The massed ranks of the poor saw through these lies. They craved the freedom to express themselves openly and to go wherever they so desired. They were not to be bought off by three hot meals a day and a place to sleep at night. Nor did it matter to them one iota that on paper the economic statistics of the country were so impressive, or that shops and factories were thriving. The shop owners, the factory owners, the landlords were all Party men who bragged that they were wealth creators. In truth, they were misers who paid minimal wages and hoarded their money out of pure greed.
The threat of a potential uprising in R4—a Prole Spring—was an ever clear and present danger for the government. Hence, the incessantly oppressive surveillance tactics of the powers that be.
It occurred to Grudge that under such a dispensation, it was no surprise that the little people were not smiling.
Curiously, internet access was quite liberally available in Runway Four. But it wasn't as though people's online habits went unobserved. The state utilised a form of software—created by an Irish startup—that allowed it to eavesdrop on all web activity within its borders. A massive bureaucracy had built up around the collating of citizens' electronic data. Everybody knew about the surveillance. It was part of everyday life. People also knew that many a person had been carted off for corrective thinking over something they had written online. Therefore, there was a constant cautiousness to internet posts and searches.
The regime drew the line at Runway Fourians leaving the state of their own free will. Though this had been changing in recent times as Chairman Young wanted to see "our best and our brightest" go abroad to gain skills and return in due course as better citizens. Permission had to be sought—and was seldom granted—for foreign travel. This desire to keep everybody within the country's borders was a sign of the regime's control-freakery. Grudge himself had never set foot outside the land. It was unheard of for someone of his

social standing to do so. To begin with, he wouldn't have had the money to buy a ticket, the prices of which were set at exorbitant rates.

Although the benign and caring image was forever being sold, the system in its day to day form was something entirely different. Still, Grudge thought, in the grand scheme of things, how bad is it? He had heard of other places—North Korea for example—that were effectively open concentration camps. At least here in R4 the constraints, though tight, allowed for some individuality to peep through, and the operation of a semblance of a free market. Sure, there was Camp Thirteen, and others of its ilk, for those who contravened the law (and, oftentimes, for those who didn't!). There was, too, the hellhole of Downland Prison in the Lie District close to Grudge's home. But, at the same time, a gloss of civilised prosperity lay across the land that Galmount knew was lacking on other shores. Of course the gloss soon faded in certain grottier parts of the cities, and in rural areas it wasn't there at all. He consoled himself that he could have been born somewhere worse; nurturing an attitude of gratitude that he knew would help him in the long run.

The vehicles and pedestrians kept coming—a rushing river in which the minnow Grudge felt infinitesimal. He didn't let the feeling swamp him, though. Instead, he focused in on Sally believing that her recent entry into his life was a sign of hope. After all, didn't angels sometimes appear out of nowhere? He zeroed in on the occasional moments of peace his current spell of sober living were bringing to his soul. He lifted his eyes beyond the bustle of rush hour and felt the pull of the skies. Hell, the way he was feeling, even the air in his lungs he understood to be a gift.

By the force of his will, he shepherded his thoughts into positive terrain and was psychologically empowered. The surge of certainty soon passed, however, and he felt small again, a speck in the crowd. He saw himself back in *Wormwood* on the line, a beaten and bent bondservant. Nonetheless, these little epiphanies were building towards something—he knew not what—only that everything would be revealed, if he could just learn to wait.

Mustn't grumble, as the Britishers say, Sally is on her way. He was struck by how powerful was the thought of her, sweeping all his sorrows aside.

He expected she would appear at any minute and, sure enough, from out of the crowd he spotted her, as lovely as he remembered her from two nights before: tall and slim, with a lithe and flawless stride; a fine bounce indeed. Her dark hair jounced gently upon her shoulders. Her face, with its pretty porcelain complexion, reminded him of an actress—Keira somebody—who had been famous once. As she neared, Grudge was struck by her sensuality. The swish of her hips thrilled him.

She came alongside with a prepossessing look on her face. His eyes lit up in pleasure. Before he could say anything, she planted a small but meaningful kiss on his cheek. He was taken aback but wonderfully flattered. He pulled her lightly at the waist, kissing her similarly. He was quite good at flirtatiousness, once he got going.

—"Well hi!" she gushed, as pleased by Grudge's kiss as he was with hers. "Thanks for coming. Sorry I'm a bit late. I got so wrapped up researching murders online that I didn't notice the time. Then my father came home from work and mum insisted I eat some dinner with them. I was actually starving after all those hours on the computer. Dinner was a treat. So, here I am. That's my excuse. Hope you'll accept it."

—"Of course," Grudge laughed. "I'm just worried about the effect of all that murderous research. It can't be good for a girl's psychological health."

—"Oh, don't worry about me. I'm made of steely stuff. I've got the ability to compartmentalise all the death and gore. It's work. It's what I have to do. It's my calling. Last night in bed I unwound by listening to classical music. There are ways and means, Grudge."

—"If you say so. Anyway, thanks for having me on this field trip. It looks like we're heading for another compartment. This one's called *Satanic Slayings* and it's to be found in a house down the road."

—"That's right. Goat Park. Let's go."

They made a beeline off the East Circular to the quieter Downrath Place. Goat Park was five minutes away and Grudge felt a twinge of fear at the prospect of what they might see at their destination. Sally seemed calm and he found her presence reassuring. She had chosen him to come along, and required him to be strong and composed, and that was what he intended to be. He put aside his fear and instead relished the fact of her company.

—“I’ve a lot of examining to do,” she said. “I want to drill down into it. I really believe that if I just stand there and look at the scene, the words will come. I’ll give Jeff Kern something special for his paper.”
Grudge knew it was entirely inappropriate at that point, particularly in light of what she was saying, but nevertheless he felt a lust rise inside him at the sight of her moving lips. Luckily, he still managed to take in her words.
—“Well,” he said. “This will certainly make a difference from my run-of-the-mill evenings of late. That’s an almost mystical notion, by the way, the idea you’ll just stand there acting as a conduit for the words to travel down.”
—“Hmm. Now you’re getting all deep on me, Grudge. I like it. Make me a channel of your words, God!”
At this, she threw her head back laughing, exposing neat white teeth. Oh, that mouth! It was all he could do not to grab her on the spot and kiss it.
Presently, they reached Goat Park: Victorian, down-at-heel, with the entrance to the Grange Asylum looming large on one side of the street. There was no problem finding the murder house. There was yellow police tape around its garden gate and a policeman, barely out of short trousers, standing on duty.
The house was one of several red-bricks with small gardens on a nondescript row—the sheltered housing so beloved of Chairman Young. This is going to be intense, Grudge thought.
He looked over at the asylum. A security van pulled up to the barrier with a fresh batch of citizens to incarcerate. The scene, part and parcel of the quotidian intercourse of R4 life, was rendered poignant by the thought that had the women stayed in the Grange—with all its ghastliness—their fate would have been far better than what had befallen them in their halfway house. That he was about to enter and survey the blood-spattered site, in the company of such a bright, charismatic woman as Sally, gave Grudge pause for thought. In his mind’s eye, he saw himself squirming in Bowe’s office the day before: cornered, weak and powerless. Then he looked at Sally, who was looking to him at this hour for protection and stability. It was a strange turn of events.
The policeman looked bored out of his mind, like he’d rather be at home playing computer games and chomping pizza, or watching

rubbish TV. His superiors knew all about the importance of optics and had placed him at the house to let folk know that this case was being taken seriously and worked on an ongoing basis. His sergeant had radioed him earlier to inform him that Sally and another man would be coming to take a look around with a view to writing a story for *The Inquisitor*. He greeted their arrival with the impassive stare of the deeply uninterested.
—"Hi," Sally said, and introduced herself, furnishing her national ID card to the officer. Grudge showed his, too.
The officer looked at their papers and took a sidelong glance at Grudge, who let a small smile form on his lips. The officer responded not one jot. Grudge wasn't surprised. This rank of policeman did donkey work for low pay. He wouldn't smile either, if it was him in the young fellow's shoes.
—"That's fine," he said. "I was told to expect you. The front door's open. Try not to touch too much, but take as long as you like. I don't go off duty till midnight so it doesn't bother me. Be warned, though, it's not a pretty sight."
—"Thanks," Sally said. "I think we're big enough and bold enough to handle it."
He lowered the yellow tape to allow them step over. Sally went first up the garden path. Grudge followed.
—"There's just one more thing," the gossoon shouted after them. "You might need some nose pegs!"
Excited now, they paid him no heed.
The front door creaked as the intrepid pair pushed it open and stepped inside the house. The hallway was creepily quiet, a silence more pronounced perhaps in light of the fact that they both knew what had taken place within these walls only days beforehand. A stenchy smell hung in the air stronger than the kind that often wafts from pavement vents onto city streets.
—"Pew!" Grudge said. "That's pretty rancid."
—"It's stinky alright," Sally said. "But it can't be the bodies. They went to the morgue on Tuesday."
—"Must be a sewer blowing in from somewhere."
Still, the smell unnerved him and he saw how his pat explanation did not quite fit.
It struck him, in fact, that there was something otherworldly about this odour. It seemed to permeate every cubic centimetre of the air.

This was no passing wind. It lingered, on close terms with death, and the bringers of death. It was the smell of an airborne plague that has descended on a town and killed the inhabitants.
—"Bad and all as the whiff is," Sally said. "We're going have to hold our noses and get through this. Let's work."
She had become semi-transfixed. A look of utmost concentration flooded her face, like a method actor getting into character. This was how seriously she considered the craft of journalism: her vocation.
Grudge pinched his nostrils and waited as she took the lead.
She moved ahead of him slowly, scouring the walls and floor, her eyes, beady as a bird of prey's, glistening in their sockets. What was it that she sought: clues, inspiration, communion with the dead, communion with the Devil?
Harking back to an old ambition, Grudge thought he might get some fiction out of the situation: *Ghosts of Goat Park* had a nice ring to it. But he checked himself and stopped his mind wandering. Unlike his writing, which he'd yet to practise in earnest, this was serious and he needed to focus. If ever there was a time to keep his wits about him, it was now.
Sally tapped the *voice memos* facility on her phone. The high priestess was about to deliver a sermon that, one day, would stir the souls of a large congregation. Grudge—her ardent helpmeet—stood in thrall.
He unpinched his nostrils and was relieved that the foulness had left the air. In its place a somewhat neutral scent had taken hold, neither pleasant nor unpleasant. If anything, it was redolent of old suburbia—musty, with a hint of perfume—sometime in the nineteen-seventies. Doggerel entered his skull: *"strange drains indeed, most peculiar, mama."*
—"Funny, the smell's gone," Sally said, momentarily emerging from her trance.
—"Not before time!"
They entered the kitchen. Sally—devoted and in the zone—listened to her calling, as the dying listen. Her keen eyes trained on all before her. No detail, however small, went unnoticed.
She began to record the scene into her phone, factual descriptions along with her impressions. "They liked Scandinavian," she noted. She outlined the type of cupboards—IKEAesque and ivory—and the tables and the chairs. She opened the presses and recorded their

contents: crockery, food, pots and pans. The victims—Martha and Celia—had liked to cook and took full advantage of the fact that they could prepare their own meals away from the regimented dining patterns they'd been subjected to in the asylum. Canny shoppers, they'd used the little money they earned from cleaning jobs to buy the best food possible within their budget. Grudge espied a shelf of cookery books on one wall—as did Sally who, continuing her "sermon", noted it into her phone.

Grudge was impressed with her eye for detail. Nonetheless, he was curious and couldn't resist asking.

—"Why don't you just take some photographs, it would save you all that dictation?"

—"Kern has enough photographs," she said. "The photographer he sent yesterday saw to that. A police snapper leaked some corpse shots, too."

—"But for your own convenience," Grudge persisted. "Why not just photograph the scene and write the article from the comfort of home by looking back at the pictures?"

—"This is what I do, Grudge. I don't mean to sound pretentious but, it's like you said earlier, I'm the pipe down which the words come. I've got to voice my impressions as soon as I see them. Working off a photograph later would be too sterile. The alchemy is here. I'm in the middle of the magic now."

—"That's fair enough. Your faith is strong, girl. I defer to your expertise. In fact at this point I'm sensing I should shut up."

—"Don't be silly. I value what you say. As it happens, I need you here. I couldn't do this without you."

Her words warmed him. No one had spoken to him as nicely in years. He was honoured.

—"If you wouldn't mind, though, just keep quiet for the next few minutes," she laughed.

He complied. They continued round the kitchen. Sally scrutinized hither and yon, recording it all into her phone. Grudge's heart went out to the poor women who had made their meals here and washed their delph in the Belfast sink. A sense of unease came over him—a feeling that he was treading in the Devil's footsteps. He didn't relish the thought of going upstairs to where Martha and Celia had been slain in their beds. Still, for the second time that evening, he steeled himself for Sally's sake.

Next, they went into a small laundry nook just off the kitchen where the washing machine was. Even here Sally took a thorough inventory of the mundane details: the type of washing powder, the basket, the bowl of pegs. Grudge began to think that she was going too far with her exact itemisation of every single thing. What she was doing was really the job of the forensic police, he felt. As a journalist she should skim through these parts of the house and get straight to the crux of the matter, namely, the bedrooms where the sensational killings had taken place. She must have read his mind for she turned and addressed him.
—"I know you think I'm being finickity mentioning the minutest things, but it all helps, believe me. When I listen back to this stuff the real prose flows. This method has worked for me before with lesser articles."
—"Like I said, your faith is strong. I don't doubt you'll get the best article you can."
—"I want to give Jeff Kern—and his readers—a piece of writing on a grand scale. Something he'd give his life to publish. So please, Grudge, just bear with me."
—"I'm right beside you, girl. Keep doing what you're doing."
And that was exactly what she did. Scoping around, composing her long prose poem of the damned—its first draft—and retaining a rapt expression on her face.
With the kitchen and nook examined, they returned to the hall. She looked in a small storage area under the stairs. There was nothing there of real interest, unless you considered umbrellas, a vacuum cleaner and the poor victims' coats to be earth-shattering discoveries. As the object of his desire took her inventory, Grudge was seized by the feeling that what they were doing was borderline sacrilegious. He grew upset on behalf of the murdered women to be traipsing round the sacred site of their deaths so intrusively. It just seemed wrong to him and, for an instant, he regretted coming—despite the chance it gave him to spend time with Sally.
The foul odour returned as quickly as it had vanished and once again Grudge pinched his nose to impede the fetid scent.
Sally for her part now seemed impervious to the smell—never mentioning it—and went about her business still, to all intents and purposes, transfixed.

Grudge started to think that the police would have been all over everything already, and that that was enough. Was it really necessary for Galmount and Popplewell to trample over things, too?
But, then, as changeable as the air were Grudge's feelings and once more he took, with relish, to his role as helper to this strong-willed, beautiful woman. He no longer regretted coming. Rather, he felt meant to be there.
He removed his hand from his face and sniffed the air. Strangely, the mephitic bouquet was gone again and things were back to that seventies suburban savour; he had the feeling tricks were being played.
Something impelled him to break Sally's spell.
—"Is there anything else I can do at the moment, besides just sticking to your side?"
Her eyes widened and it took her a second to focus on what he'd said.
—"Not now. Just come round with me and take in everything you see. I'll ask for your impression later. It'll be good to get an ordinary Joe's perspective, if I may call you that?"
—"By all means, go right ahead," Grudge said. "Ordinary Joe kind of suits me."
They headed into the small living room off the hallway. Grudge glanced outside through the front window. The gossoon policeman was still standing guard, chatting away on his cellphone; placing bets at the bookies, Grudge imagined, or trying to entice some poor girl out on a date. The street was so bland, dully quiet—the most striking feature of Goat Park was the asylum entrance. The rest of the place was as humdrum as a thousand other streets in Bludgeon City. Again, he thought of the victims, living here quietly, watching TV, glancing out that same window from time to time, their days rooted in tiresome ordinariness and state control. The thought that at some point they would be virtually crucified under this roof would have been unimaginable to them.
Sally continued with the voice memo. She remained in her semi-trancelike state, flowing in and out of attentiveness to Grudge, devoting most of her energies to tabulation. Everything in these downstairs rooms was undisturbed. The scene was as it had been throughout Martha and Celia's lives; the gruesomeness—that grotesque upheaval—had gone on upstairs.

Police forensics had been all over the house in search of clues: DNA, fingerprints and the like. No clues had been found. The investigators were baffled. It was as though the perpetrator was a ghost.
—"Okay, are you ready?" Sally asked, suddenly. "It's time to go upstairs and see where the real action took place."
—"I'm as ready as I'll ever be," Grudge said, keeping his tone light. "Let's do it."
Upstairs, Sally took in the bathroom first. Again, all was ordinary here, sparsely furnished with no signs of struggle or violence. The landing itself was bare with little of note to catch the eye. A picture framed on the wall of two spring lambs—their fleece, yes, as white as snow—struck a poignant chord with Grudge. How apt, he thought, in light of the slaughter.
They entered the first of the two bedrooms, Celia's. Here, the picture changed completely. Grudge and Sally stood staring at a scene of suggested horror. The key thing missing of course was the body itself—Celia was on ice in the morgue awaiting her imminent burial. The post mortems were complete and two lonely spots had been set aside in the potter's field for her and Martha.
The sheets on the bed, the walls with their cheap and nasty wallpaper, the carpet, even the lightshade on the ceiling bulb, were all smeared with the stains of the blood that was a by-product of the violent death that had taken place here. In one spot on the carpet Grudge noticed with a wince a clump of bloody hair that he guessed had been discarded during the mutilation process.
Although an amateur, Sally went about her business with a good deal of professionalism. As before, she took stock of the detail of the room and recorded her observations.
—"Can I make a point?" Grudge interrupted.
—"What is it?
—"Why the hell haven't the police cleaned up this room yet? And I presume the one next door is just as bad."
—"It could be laziness on their part, or more likely a lack of resources. From what I hear, they're ploughing all their energy into checking CCTV at the moment. According to Jeff Kern, it's thrown up zilch so far."
—"That man certainly has the inside track," Grudge said.
—"He sure does. But look, no doubt the police will get around to cleaning up eventually. In the meantime, it gives me a great chance

to get a feel for what went down here. My story will be all the better for it."
She was putting her work ahead of any empathy for the victims. Later, perhaps weeks down the road, when the ink was dry on her piece, she might spare them a sympathetic thought.
They finished up in the first bedroom and moved on to the second, Martha's, where they met an equally devilish scene; more blood smears everywhere and the still palpable air of a horrific death. Sally worked while Grudge looked on, nausea and sadness swirling in his brain. He was tearful in fact and tried to hide his welling tears from Sally, not for any macho reasons but simply to stay strong for her when she needed him.
Minutes later, she concluded her analysis of the room.
—"Right, I'm done," she said, attending to Grudge again. "That's enough horror for one day. I think we both need to get out of this house, and fast!"
—"I couldn't agree with you more."
—"All the same, I reckon I've got the makings of a brilliant story here. Now the real work begins. I've got to go home and write it all up."
—"That won't be a problem. You strike me as quite the professional."
—"Thanks," she said, and to his great delight reached over and kissed him on the cheek again.
They headed down the stairs and back outside. Oddly enough, as they were leaving, the vile smell re-emerged. What the hell is it? Grudge wondered. It can't be just a drain problem. He was glad to be going. If it was a plague, he didn't want to catch it.
They thanked the unseasoned sentinel at the garden gate for his cooperation. His smart aleck surliness seemed to have left him. He must have bagged that date over the phone.
—"Good luck with your story," he shouted after them, as the two sleuths headed back towards Downrath Place and the East Circular Road.
It was getting late so they decided against coffee. As before, Grudge walked her to her tram stop. As they waited, she asked for his impression of the house they had just visited—his ordinary Joe perspective. He gave it to her short and sweet: the place reeked of evil. Sally promised to incorporate his view into her article.

They shared their first full-on kiss—a thirty-second smooch—as the tram trundled into sight. They vowed to meet for a longer date in the near future.
—"There's always the possibility," Grudge said. "That the killer is not of this world."
Sally shook her head and climbed on board the tram.
A drained but happy Grudge returned to Rodent Street. He slept beautifully that night.

Chapter 4

The next morning at the coffin factory Grudge began to feel oppressed again. The full extent of his ensnarement hit home. At the best of times the factory was an oppressive place, but now Mary Dawn had devised an even more elaborate way to control him. Calling him over to her desk when he arrived at work, she explained that from now on, when he wished to use the toilet, he would have to notify her first. All his good feelings from the previous night's work with Sally vanished within those first three minutes of his morning shift.
He viewed Mary's new stricture as an outrageous breach of his privacy. What next? Would he have to specify defecation or urination when popping out to the loo? But, then again, what could he do? He had shot himself in the foot so to speak by turning up stoned to work that accursed day.
Noel Bowe had had his stern chat and this was the upshot: more petty rules and a stifling sense of surveillance. He wished he'd had more cop on than to turn up high. He was paying for it now. The sheer indignity of it all: having to tell Mary Dawn whenever he wanted to take a piss!
Such rules were typical of *Wormwood* and its ethos. Stay in your staff's faces at all times, let them know they are being watched and make life doubly difficult for anyone who doesn't tow the line.
Hammering away on a fresh casket, Grudge's depression was grave. What a change from last night when working with Sally anything had seemed possible. In order to lift his mood, he tried to think thoughts of her. It was his version of cognitive behavioural therapy.
Mordechai Levy standing nearby must have sensed Grudge's downbeat mood for he chimed in with an attempt at a joke.

—"Hey, Grudge, did you know that when Jesus was a boy, he was a wayward child? His parents couldn't handle the messiah"
Actually, punning on the composer's name as Mordechai did was not such a bad effort and despite his gloominess Grudge allowed himself a chuckle.
On an optimistic note, he continued working at his CBT and told himself, from past experience, the low feeling swamping him would eventually flee. Such optimism spurred him on towards lunch break.
In the canteen eating a sandwich of rubbery ham and washing it down with some fruity coffee, he started to feel human again. He was looking forward to his next encounter with Sally.
Unfortunately, his lifting mood sank on the arrival of Séamus Cronin to eat his lunch. As ever, Cronin found that chink in Grudge's armour—his sensitivity—and ploughed straight in to exploit it.
—"Hey, there's Galmount!" he sneered.
Other workers pricked up their ears accustomed to these bouts of slagging between the pair, knowing it could get sparky.
Grudge reddened and looked up from a copy of *The Inquisitor*. He was on edge straightaway. For some reason this Cronin prick always reduced him to jelly. Invariably, following an encounter with Cronin, in which Galmount came off worst, Grudge would think of the best things he could have said *afterwards* when it was too late. He tensed up now expecting fresh mockery from Séamus, and sure enough, as suicidal depression follows a bipolar high, Cronin's snide remarks rang out.
—"Well, aren't you the dark horse, Galmount?" he boomed, throwing his big thick head around the room in an effort to pull in an audience. This he did with ease as the sheep-like workers paused to listen to what the bully had to say.
Grudge, weakened and snared, could only look questioningly at his attacker and await the next sentence. Where, he wondered, is the fucker heading with this?
—"You were seen last night in the Lie District, ya sneaky prick, walking along the street with an absolute beaut of a wan. Where'd you get her, Galmount? Off the net? Was she a prozzy, cos you certainly couldn't pull a bird like that under your own steam?"
Cronin laughed at what he thought was his deep wit.
Grudge felt anger rise. He was becoming protective of Sally even though they'd only been acquainted a short time. Something told

him he was in for the long haul with this woman. To hear this loutish oaf make a mockery of her, and for the great ape to insinuate that Sally was some class of a prostitute, was too much for Grudge's ears. He had to take several deep breaths to stop himself from exploding. In response the best he could muster was.
—"She's a friend of mine."
He said it apologetically.
—"A friend?" his tormenter asked, sounding amazed. "A girl like that wouldn't hang around with the likes of you. I'm telling you: you must have been paying her."
One or two of the canteen pond life began to laugh, incensing Grudge all the more. He felt himself tremble, and prayed hard that he might keep a lid on his emotions. He knew that the last thing he could withstand was an explosion of anger from inside. It could send him back drinking, or into the realm of mental illness. Cronin, sensing he had an audience, continued with his cruel gibes, lathering it on thick.
—"Galmount, the day you pull a girl like that would be a miracle. Look at the state of you. You're in bits. I can see you shaking. Some whore, was she? Are you on drugs with all that shaking? I think it's rehab for you, lad, or worse: corrective thinking."
Grudge tried with all his might to stay calm. Keeping himself in check, he spoke in as measured a tone as he could manage.
—"Hey, Cronin," he said. "I'd appreciate if you wouldn't refer to my friend like that." Grudge was sticking to his line—true as it happened—that Sally was his friend. Cronin looked taken aback.
—"Sally, that's her name, is a really smashing person, and it's totally unfair of you to describe her in that way."
Cronin was offended. He couldn't let this upstart show him up in front of the crowd. He would have to fight back with something extra cruel.
—"Fuckoff, Galmount," he said. "I'll say what I want, and I certainly won't be watching my words for a little prick like you. She must be hard up this Sally to be seen with you of an evening. I mean, is she mentally defective?"
Grudge was boiling inside and would have willingly murdered Cronin on the spot. But he managed to control himself. He said nothing. All eyes were upon him now. Instead, he gave Cronin the

filthiest and bravest look he could summon, gathered himself, and fled the canteen like a bullet.
Cronin addressed the room, a stupid sneer on his face.
—"It must be the pussy's time of the month!"
The pond life guffawed.
Grudge spent the rest of the day working quietly at his station ignoring Mordechai and Pole Wallace who both jabbered on regarding sport and so forth. Inside, he was still seething over Cronin. His brain burned with a resentment that was almost a physical pain. He tried not to dwell on the many ways possible to murder his nemesis. He was sufficiently intelligent to know that dwelling thus would only serve to eat him up. Cronin, none the wiser, not privy to Grudge's thoughts, was no doubt going about his business oblivious to the torment he had inflicted.
Grudge, therefore, kept his head down and trudged on with his coffin-making tasks. Mary Dawn scrutinized him. He tried ever so hard to stay positive, reflecting on things such as art, literature and Sally Popplewell—all the while maintaining a stony silence towards colleagues.
At clocking off time—sacred seven p.m.—he was suddenly swamped with an enormous wave of craving that crashed against his delicate mindscape. Thoughts of weed as opposed to drink assailed him violently. The craving kept growing and intensified as he walked the streets to the rathole for his evening meal. It simply wouldn't do! He was going to have to scratch the itch.
Dreck LeBlanc was a hash dealer whom Grudge had often used in the past. He lived with his woman and their small child in an upstairs flat over a chemist shop several miles beyond the Lie District in a place called The Numb. LeBlanc had been dealing hash since Adam was a boy, rarely peddling anything harder than the weed. He had once got his hands on a consignment of Class A powder and had had no difficulty shifting it, but found that the kind of customer the drug brought to his door was far too unstable and dangerous. In The Numb, Dreck dealt with impunity because he dealt a good deal to the local police, in particular several mid-ranking officers with lots of sway who for years had ensured that the heat stayed off LeBlanc. Dreck liked a quiet life, just the little lady and the childer, living comfortably on the profits of his weed sales. He stuck to the plant

and thrived off it, attracting, week upon week, a far more relaxed and infinitely less threatening clientele than those crazy cokeheads. Dreck insisted that his customers call between six and ten in the evening, absolutely no later as it disturbed his sleeping child and his long-time girlfriend hated it, too. She was known to throw ferocious fits of temper when stoners showed up beyond the ten o'clock mark.

Grudge scampered out of town battling himself in a mental war, oblivious to the crowds and traffic being so wrapped up in his own pain and craving. People on the pavement steered clear lest he was a nutcase hoping for a fight. His war concerned the rights and wrongs of going back on drugs. He knew deep down that he should avoid them entirely, especially in light of his recent visit to Noel Bowe's office and all that was revealed to him there.

Finally, after about half an hour's walking, he prevailed in the battle with himself. He would head to The Numb, see LeBlanc and purchase a week's supply of hashish. The way he reasoned it: it was only a soft drug, it wasn't going to break his budget, its effects on him were far milder and less harmful than alcohol, and he was under so much pressure at work that he needed something to keep him from going mad. He would moderate his usage, confining his intake to a few smokes at night when his imaginative mind could loosen up and wander at its leisure. It would keep him relaxed around Sally on the many future dates that he hoped would arise. If his mind was chilled from smoking the night before, the work pressure would not show when he met her face to face. Such were the cunning rationalisations that his addictive brain engaged in to justify his slip, when abstinence would have been a far better course for him to take. At Parn Square he hopped on a tram, paid the fare to The Numb, and sat back in happy anticipation.

Through the streets the tram trundled. Grudge drank in the scene with a painterly eye. How drab the city was; Soviet-style in its aspect; occasionally enlivened by the graffiti whorls of pro-regime slogans. Bludgeon seemed like something from that book, a smuggled copy of which he'd read as a teenager, with a year—Nineteen something or other—for its title. The authorities hated that one for sure, how eerily prescient its author had been to come up with a society so totalitarian, oppressive, dystopian (all the right words filled Grudge's head) and he, Grudge Galmount, a prole on a tram, had fetched up in just such a world, with its trod-upon citizenry

scurrying homeward to their hovels. In the mix, too, was the political signage looming large on every street corner; the scarifying symbols of the omnipotent Party.
Grudge counted his blessings, though, in one regard: the approach of the Party to controlling its citizens. In Runway Four, people had some degree of leeway to live ostensibly free lives. It was only if one repeatedly broke strictures and was wantonly disobedient, that one found the secret police knocking at one's door. The Party—*We Are Troops of the Party*, went the song—pinned its hopes on the god of market forces to feed the bellies, warm the bodies, and pacify the minds of the populace. It was a strategy that was actually working. In global terms R4 was a high achiever on lists of positive economic indicators. The money was rolling in, manufacturing was burgeoning, and the country exported to the four corners of the globe.
Grudge pondered the fact that in a roundabout way this wealth flowing into the national coffers was responsible for the degree of personal autonomy he had in being able to catch a tram and head to The Numb to buy some drugs.
Presently, he reached his stop, alighted and made for LeBlanc's place above the chemist shop. It was just gone eight so he knew that he was well within the permitted hours to call; no chance of LeBlanc's woman throwing a fit.
He came to the row of shops, and saw the chemist's green neon cross and the light on in LeBlanc's flat above. By now he was a quivering globule of flesh at the thought of getting high. Small stabs of excited joy darted from his heart and tingled his stomach. The obliteration of pain through weed was the cause of his incipient bliss.
He reached for the bell and pressed it hard. After a moment he heard footsteps hurrying down the stairs and into the hallway. The door opened and Dreck LeBlanc stood there in a white vest and jog pants looking for all the world like he hadn't a care in it.
—"Grudge Galmount," he said. "Haven't seen you in a while. Where've you been? Did the secret police finally get their mitts on ya?"
—"Hi, Dreck," Grudge said. "No, it's nothing as serious as the secret police. I've been nowhere really, just giving the old weed a miss for a spell. It was affecting my breathing."

This was a lie on Grudge's part. So far so good when it came to smoking. He had suffered no respiratory complaints from the habit. He just didn't want to get up on his high abstinence horse with a drug dealer and start banging on to LeBlanc about his wish to live a sober life and foreswear all drugs. The door would have been slammed in his face. So he continued for a moment with his "bad for my health" ruse.
—"I was waking up after a night's smoking coughing and spluttering my guts out. I saw blood in my spit one morning," he embellished the facts further. "So I said to myself, enough is enough. I'll knock this smoking lark on the head for a bit."
Dreck LeBlanc seemed wholly uninterested in Grudge's talk of smoking and ill-health. He stood in his doorway fidgeting, with a half grin on his face. He did like Galmount but the guy was awfully fond of rabbiting on about things to such an extent that you just wished he'd shut the fuck up.
—"Fair enough, Grudge," LeBlanc said. "Tell me something I don't know. Smoking is bad for your health. No shit, Sherlock!"
At this witticism, the drug dealer laughed and coughed, his own wheezy chest testament to his love of his product.
—"Let me guess, Galmount. You've fallen off the wagon, or should I say your chest is feeling better, and you wanna get yourself a little herb for the evening?"
—"Got it in one, Dreck. Can you sort me out for a quarter?"
—"Step into the hall, mate."
Grudge crossed the threshold into a narrow hallway that smelt of cooking.
—"Wait here. I'll be down in a minute," Dreck said.
The girlfriend appeared at the top of the stairs, looking as mean as usual. She flashed a scowl Grudge's way and said something to LeBlanc about dinner as he climbed the stairs to fetch Galmount's deal.
Grudge stood waiting, happy at the efficiency of the transaction, excited to know that he'd soon be back in the rathole getting stoned.
After two or three minutes, LeBlanc came back down smiling.
—"Here you go," he said, handing Grudge a thumb-sized block of fresh and potent hashish. "Happy smoking, hope your lungs can hack it."

—“I’m sure they can,” Grudge replied, taking the hash eagerly, sniffing it and placing it in a secure pocket inside his coat.
He handed LeBlanc a twenty goldmark note in payment.
—“I’ll be heading now, Dreck. Thanks for your help. You’re as smooth as ever. I know where to come if I need any more.”
—“Exactly. Just keep to the hours. Six to ten. You know what she’s like otherwise. Throws the head.”
LeBlanc opened the door to see Galmount out.
—“Thanks again,” Grudge smiled. “Talk to you soon.”
With that, he was on the street and quickly caught a tram back to the Lie District. Forty minutes later he was sitting on his rickety bed removing a cigarette paper from its packet and preparing to blaze. First up he put a match to the lump of hash and burned it for a moment. Having sniffed it previously in Dreck’s hallway, he wanted to get a further idea of its strength; LeBlanc’s gear was known for its potency. A thin plume rose from the lump and its acrid scent told Grudge just what he wanted to know, namely, that his purchase had real punch. Hastily now, his anticipation at its height, he put the Rizlas together, added tobacco from a torn cigarette, burned the hash some more, and as it softened threw large hot lumps into the joint. He rolled it up, licked the paper, stuck it together, put the spliff in his mouth, and lit it.
After a couple of drags he felt the drug seize his system. The sights and sounds of the room intensified. He was aware in a deep sense that he was a human being alive on a tiny planet in the midst of vast interstellar space. He was also keenly aware that the clock on his mantelpiece had been missing a battery and stopped for several weeks now. I must get that sorted, he thought, and the concern became a matter of great urgency. The urgency soon grew to paranoia and Grudge found himself immobile on the bed worried sick that if he didn’t get a new clock battery he’d be late for a shift and fall deeper into trouble at the coffin factory, forgetting all the while that he’d been doing fine waking by his body clock every morning since the battery ran out.
He lay back on the bed with this enormous worry seemingly overwhelming him, but the drug was so strong and the colours in his room so intense now and the euphoria surging through his system so unstoppable that he couldn’t stay paranoid for long.

He sat up again, relit the joint and smoked it down to the end, stubbing it out in the ashtray, the last vestiges of its fire singeing his fingertips. He stared around the room. His anxiety about the battery was forgotten. Lust now overtook him. Sally's body, in particular her perfect ass. He considered masturbating, but Ann-Marie rattling round in the hallway, deterred him. Each evening and throughout the night she checked the front door.

So instead he rolled another joint and put on some music. Some gentle pop from the last century. He was a cauldron of emotion at this point: love/lust for Sally, hatred for his job and the Party; fear for his future, regret for his past, and above all euphoria, blitzed out of his mind on LeBlanc's dope.

After several hours of this tomfoolery—involving several more spliffs and eventually a wank—Grudge hit the lights and fell asleep. He woke once during the night to the sound of Ann-Marie coming out of her room to check the door. He remembered with a start that he was back on drugs—his groggy head and the smell in the room told him so.

He went back to sleep quickly, thinking he was going to need a lot of hash to numb his pain; either that, or quit the weed altogether—one more time.

***

Exchange Street was in an upmarket area not far from Revenue Road. Younghead College, where many children of Party officials studied, was nearby. The residents of the street were captains of industry, rich capitalists, wealth creators—those new gods!—business and shop owners riding the wave of Runway Four's economic surge, bankers, accountants and media personalities. There was also a sizable cohort of students, the rich-kid sons and daughters of Politburo members and suchlike. For all these people, life was one of privilege and entitlement.

Midway along the street was the aptly named Middle Building—a luxurious apartment complex built with funds from Younghead and used as accommodation for its pampered students.

Barry Martin, one such student, whose father, Finbarr, was on the Standing Committee, was alone in his bed sleeping off a heavy night's drinking and drugging. His girlfriend, Jessie, had stormed back to her mother's house some hours earlier following a violent argument between the pair over Barry's substance abuse. The argument had been brewing for weeks as Barry's habits got steadily out of hand. Jessie had had enough after a night of what was supposed to be a couple of beers and one or two joints. Things had turned quickly to mayhem with a sprinkling of farce into the bargain. On his fourth beer in the student bar, Barry had started to verbally abuse all around him and was forcibly ejected by a bouncer and a bartenderette. Jessie followed him outside and sat in an alley with him. They'd smoked a joint. She had hoped that this would calm him down but it only made things worse. He became obnoxious towards her, calling her a slag and a cunt. She brushed it off in her head as just his drunken ramblings, not wishing to confront him and provoke him further. Nonetheless, deep inside, Jessie was extremely hurt by his words.

The farce began in the takeaway they stumbled into upon leaving the alley. Barry rudely ordered a burger, chips and a brimming tray of curry sauce. Staggering towards a seat he dropped the sauce and slid all over it on the floor. He toppled to the ground and was lucky not to receive a nasty concussion landing on his elbows and ass instead. Jessie helped him to his feet and somehow or other they made it back to the Middle Building.

Once there, they'd argued some more and the shouting match was on the verge of turning physical—Barry was in a complete rage at this stage—when Jessie had an epiphany and mustered the good sense to tell him to fuckoff, grab her things and storm back to her mother's.

Now sobering up in his sleep, Barry woke and smiled to himself thinking she'd be back. It was four a.m. He'd slept quite a while. He sat up in his bed, lit the half-finished joint that lay in the ashtray, and thought about grabbing a beer from the fridge. He was full of defiance over his drink and drug habits and as far as he was concerned Jessie, the silly little cow, could go and fuck herself. As a matter of fact, he didn't care if she stayed at her mother's forever. He walked out to the kitchen, popped open a beer and returned to bed to drink it. He switched his radio on low and the relaxing music from his favourite station took his mind off things. He felt reasonably okay considering the drinking and arguing of earlier. He would, he thought, have to contact his father—a top politico if ever

there was one—later in the day to hit him for a loan. The beer and the joint now in the quiet of the early morn had him feeling good again.
There was a loud thump on the ceiling and then quickly thereafter a similar thud on the floor below. What the hell was that? he wondered, and turned the radio down and listened closely to the night. The sound had startled him for it seemed louder than neighbours, many of whom frequently hammered on his walls when he was partying hard. But Barry's party was over now, his radio was playing low and his woman had fled. Ah, fuck it all, he thought, and turned on the music again. The powerful woofer he used on his sound system brought the decibels up in a flash. He knew he could never be evicted on account of his father's position on the Standing Committee. If that was his neighbours banging hard on his ceiling and floor, he would, in his maliciousness, give them something to complain about. He cranked up the volume some more and flicked from the radio station to a cacophonous mixtape.
He felt nice and high again and grabbed another beer from the kitchen. On a table by his bed were the accoutrements of a mini-party. He eyed them lovingly. Even though dawn was approaching, he was not to be deterred. He had hash, cigarettes and beer, and from a miniature beer barrel—bought in a drug paraphernalia shop on a trip abroad—Barry laid out two fat lines of a synthetic cocaine substitute to which he was addicted. He was buzzing, and he wanted to keep on buzzing till the break of dawn. The fake coke would do the trick.
By means of a straw, he hoovered the lines up his nostrils. The mephedrone kicked his brain with a ferocious wallop; instant elation, and the higher he got the further Jessie went from his mind. If he thought about her at all it was just with the certainty that she would soon return. She always came back even after their worst rows.
Suddenly, the loud banging sound startled him again. It was ear-splitting despite the awful music he had on. He thought it must be a neighbour complaining, but then remembered that when he'd heard it the first time he'd had the radio on low. Barry was puzzled and unnerved. Frightened, too, for this time the noise seemed to come from the wardrobe in the room, mere feet from where he sat, self-medicating on his sad spree. A riotous angry din came forth like some god that needed pacifying. The fact that he was far from sober

didn't help in the least. It only served to freak him out the more, not knowing the cause of the sound and hearing it now for a second time. Still, he sprinkled himself out another line, wanting to get higher and if possible silence the awful noise for good. As he snorted, to his great relief, the din ceased.

The lights in the bedroom started to blink for about thirty seconds or so, stopped, and then started again about a minute later. This happened several times. Barry sobered up, never mind the drugs he had ingested. He had a really bad feeling about the disruption in his room, the lights flashing and the intermittent racket.

The sound struck for a third time. Painfully loud and coming it seemed from beneath his bed. Terror grabbed him like an animal clawing prey. He knocked off the mixtape to be sure he wasn't hearing things. He wanted to get to the street. At that point, it was the only thing that mattered. He threw on his pants and trainers and headed for the bedroom door. It slammed shut before he could go through. He tried to open it but it wouldn't budge. His heart raced from a combination of dope and fear. He found it difficult to breathe. This was something far worse than his drug-addled mind playing tricks on him. All the while the diabolical din continued.

He started to cry in pity for himself and his life. Something alien and vicious surrounded him. He felt his end was nigh, and what hurt most was the unfairness of it all. He was only twenty-one years old. Surely, he was destined for a long life ahead.

He pulled on the door handle, trying desperately to open it, and shouted for help at the top of his voice. It dawned on him as he sobered rapidly that nobody could hear his screams. A disgusting smell hit his nostrils like something from the pit of hell.

An acute pain struck his midriff as though he was being punched in the stomach by the fist of a devil. Confused and terrified, he hollered in pain.

The lights kept blinking on and off and when they came on he could see no one else was in the room. But he knew he was not alone.

The pain moved from his trunk to his extremities. He wondered if he was having a heart attack. He had heard one of the signs was sharp pain along the arms. He certainly had that. He knew, though, that this was no heart attack. Something outside of him was attacking him. The noise was deafening and the lights blinked off again. He could see nothing.

He sensed the malignance. His whole body was now in excruciating pain. The feeling travelled to his neck and brain. He felt simultaneously as though he was being strangled, and that an ice pick had been thrust through the centre of his skull. He was frightened out of his mind. Then he heard the words, words he knew would be the last he'd ever hear: the voice that bellowed them was chilling.

—"Now you are dead," it said, and the lights of Barry Martin's life extinguished.

In a sense for Barry it was a blessed relief, his throes had been so painful.

Some of the neighbours—hearing the ongoing rumpus coming from Barry's flat, though the noise was not as loud to them—had come down to knock on his door and complain. When all fell silent and they got no answer, they assumed he had passed out from drink. They returned to their rooms relieved by the peace.

Jessie found him the next day at lunchtime when she came round to try and put their relationship right. How she screamed at the ghastly sight of his mutilated corpse nailed upside down to the wall.

Being the son of a Standing Committee member, Barry's death caused the Party to sit up and cast an even closer eye on the murders in the land.

***

As soon as he heard about it, the newspaper editor Jeff Kern informed Sally about the murder of the top official's son. He phoned her that afternoon. He had a lot of faith in this Popplewell kid. The freelance stuff she'd submitted had been superb. Jeff had to admit, too, that the photo she sent in along with a brief bio was bloody gorgeous. Still, that wasn't his primary motivation in asking her to write a piece on the Goat Park murders and to incorporate this savage killing of Barry Martin into her article. Something—he knew not what—whispered in Jeff's ear exhorting him to help Sally gain a foothold in the trade. He believed she was marked for greatness. To this end, he inveigled an influential police friend at headquarters to grant her entry to the Middle Building.

Once she got off the phone to Kern, Sally made her way to Exchange Street. She felt blessed to be asked her investigate this latest killing

and to include it in her Goat Park article. She was blown away by the fact she'd got access to the crime scene. Talk about breaks! Kern was supplying them big time. She wouldn't let him down.
She was almost finished her Goat Park piece. It was turning out better than she could have imagined. When composing it, she was white hot, she was burning. She didn't know where the skill and inspiration were coming from, but she wasn't going to question their appearance. Fortune was bald at the back of her head, she would grab her upfront.
In her fantasies, she dreamt of her article being syndicated globally and her journalistic career taking off into the stratosphere. Mixing this new killing into her piece would be just the thing to spice it up further.
Standing on Exchange Street, she checked out the lie of the land. A strong police presence around the Middle Building was a clear indication of the victim's status. Police tape was in place and the men in blue were on the case. For Sally it was the same routine as Goat Park. Flash her ID and cross the line. She approached the building and for the second time that week handed her credentials to a youthful sentry.
—"Ah, the journalist," he said. "We've been told you were coming." The lad lifted the tape to let her in, adding: "Go on up. It's the seventh floor."
She took the bespoke elevator to level seven and stepped out to a frenetic scene: police photographers, detectives, uniformed officers, toing and froing in the corridor, trying to get on top of the crime; all giving the impression, nevertheless, of chickens without heads. The perpetrator, whoever they may be, had certainly bamboozled everyone.
The apartment itself—a proscribed evidentiary area—was cordoned off with more police tape. The photographers snapped away. A detective ran towards Sally and introduced himself.
—"Julian Brannigan. Are you the Popplewell lady?"
—"Yes, that's me," Sally said.
They shook hands.
—"Well," Brannigan said. "I don't know what strings you've pulled to get up here, but I've been told to let you take a full look around. The victim is Barry Martin. His father's a real tall guy if you know

what I mean. Finbarr Martin. A member of the Standing Committee."
—"That's tall alright. No wonder there's so many of you fellows here. Do you think his daddy's position had anything to do with his winding up dead?"
—"Too early to say, but naturally it's one line of our investigation."
—"Very well then. Let me see the room where he died first. Was it a bloodbath like Goat Park?"
—"Not as bloody, but quite a scene. His girlfriend found him in inverse cruciform tacked to the wall above the bed. Some kind of super strength nail gun in all probability, though there's no trace of it. Talk about a notch on the bedpost."
—"How's the girlfriend?" Sally asked
—"She's had to be sedated. She's not a suspect by the way. This is some heavy duty freak we're looking for. It's quite a work of art."
—"Can I see it?"
—"Afraid not. The body's gone to the morgue. There are photos and video we can send on. You seem to have all the permissions. I hear you're writing some big article about Goat Park and now this."
—"Wow," Sally said. "You know a lot of my business, detective. You can help my article by telling me: what's your initial hunch on this?"
—"Hard to say. We're pretty baffled to be honest. But it's only day one. We'd be hopeful of some kind of breakthrough in the coming days. The poor fucker. The expression on his face looked like he was scared shitless. I imagine he died in considerable pain. The Party are going to want this one solved, that's for sure."
Brannigan brought Sally across the threshold into Barry's apartment.
—"You wanted to see the bedroom first," he said, and led her through a wide, plush living room to the chamber where the brat had died.
This is how the other half live, Sally thought, drinking in the fixtures and furnishings.
The place put the home she shared with her parents to shame.
Brannigan told two of the forensics team and a photographer to leave the bedroom.
—"I'll let you have the room to yourself for a few minutes," he said. "It's completely against the rules. Not all the evidence has been

gathered. But your clearance comes from the top. I hear you like to get into the zone and record your thoughts on your phone."
—"My, oh, my," Sally said. "You really do know a lot about my methods. You're quite the detective."
—"It's not as sinister as you think. I just asked the chief how much freedom to give you. It was he who told me about your methods. He'd heard it from some gossoon who was standing sentry the other night in Goat Park. Oh, and Jeff Kern, too, of course. Jeff tells us lots of things. And we return the favour."
—"A real boys' club," Sally said. "Now, if you don't mind, Detective Brannigan, I'll be about my business."
He left her alone in the bedroom and she surveyed the scene. As with Celia and Martha's house, she saw blood splatter on the walls. The upturned bed told its own tale of violent tumult.
Sally felt her calling and began to concentrate hard. She was open to any lingering sense of evil; felt strong enough to let them in, if supernatural forces were involved. Not that she believed they were. Grudge had hinted something at the tram stop the other night. However, she was convinced this murder, and Goat Park, were the work of human hands. The idea of a supernatural shortcut to solving these crimes seemed outlandish, but her mind was not entirely closed to such a notion. Sally was bright enough to know there were more things in Heaven and Earth than she could ever dream of.
The death scene was still fresh. The wall above the bed marked with Barry's gore. Who in the hell hung him upside down? She couldn't fathom it.
She took out her phone and launched *voice memos*, and began to speak her mind. Thoughts and descriptions flowed out of her like wine at Cana.
Her calling was strong. She was a witness to wickedness and would report back to the world. She believed in her soul, and got down some terrific material.
After ten minutes, Brannigan returned.
—"We've tested the whole apartment for DNA," he said. "The swabs will go to the lab. Hopefully, they'll throw up something from our database. Otherwise it's another dead end—pun intended."
—"I'll look around the rest of the apartment," she said, and left the bedroom.

Moving through the living room, hall, bathroom and kitchen, she continued to record her thoughts. She felt a sense of excitement and professional pride. This access she had been given would result in a brilliant article, of that she was sure.
Back in the living room Brannigan appeared again. Sally couldn't switch off and made a myriad of mental notes about the scene while the detective chatted away to her. She took everything in and looked for something the police might have missed; if there was to be a breakthrough, she wanted to discover it.
Her nose led her back to the bedroom. Brannigan followed.
The small table on which Barry had laid out his drugs and paraphernalia had, like the bed, been upturned. A cop was down on his honkers, protective gloves on, meticulously bagging the table's scattered contents into plastic pouches. Sally felt a twinge of fear, an aftershock from the killing that had taken place in the room hours before. The consequences of the mayhem were all around her. She wondered if Barry had had enemies. Pampered little rich boys could provoke deep resentments in those who lived on little. To judge from his living quarters, Barry had all the toys that ordinary folk could not afford.
The cop got up from his honkers and left the room with his little pouches full. Sally's ego waded in, brushing aside the twinge of fear. Would she get international syndication for her article? It was quite possible. If it's good enough (and it shall be), the government will sanction its release overseas. A well-penned incisive piece by a conscientious citizen of Runway Four would act as a perfect propaganda tool for Chairman Young and his generals. Look, it would say, at what the good people of our civilised country can produce. Look at how unhindered our investigative reporters are.
Sally felt supremely confident that her writing would excel. As though on cue, Julian Brannigan asked.
—"When do expect to have your article published? I'm looking forward to reading your take on these murders. Right now we could use every angle we can get. Though don't quote me on that!"
—"I reckon I'll have it out there in a week or so. Watch those newsstands, officer!"
—"I sure will," he said.
Sally was ready to leave. On the floor beneath the upturned table something shiny caught her eye. Strange, she thought, that hunkered

down cop ought to have spotted that, whatever it is. Brannigan had gone back to the living room and was speaking to colleagues.
She reached down to pick up the shiny object: a pentagram in pendant form. Holding it in her palm, she wondered from whose neck it had fallen? If it was a clue or a breakthrough she suddenly had no desire to keep it. The object spooked her and her fear returned. She was well aware of its association with evil.
She left the bedroom and handed it to Brannigan.
—"Your forensics guy seems to have missed this," she said. "I found it on the floor inside. I guess I've contaminated it now. Sorry."
Brannigan snatched it from her, pleased to hold a possible fresh clue.
—"Oh," he said. "A pentagram. Now that's heavy with symbolism. Did Finbarr Martin's son dabble in the occult? Or was his killer a Devil's disciple? I'll have it sent to the lab."
He bagged the pendant and handed it to a uniform.
—"Thanks for your help, detective," Sally said. "I have more than enough material."
—"No problem, Popplewell, you're welcome. Good luck with the piece. Like you said, I'll be watching those newsstands."
She rode the elevator down the seven floors and left the Middle Building. In the evening air of Exchange Street, she phoned Grudge to tell him of the break she had just got. She wanted to see him soon but also needed time in the next few days to finish the article. Grudge sounded pleased to hear from her and was delighted to learn of her scoop.
—"Look," he said. "Go home and get the article finished. That's the most important thing. Ring me when you have it done. We'll meet up then."
Sally hopped on a tram and headed for home. Looking forward to finishing her article and more so to seeing Grudge as soon as possible.

Chapter 5

That same evening—Saturday—was Grudge's payday. Work was finished and as he got off the phone to Sally he hastened to the rathole clutching a wad of cash in his fist. He was afraid to even put it in his coat lest he be tempted to keep it for himself. His aim was to rendezvous with Conan, the landlady's spiteful boyfriend. The notes in his hand—the sum total of his rent arrears—were hot and sweaty, grubby even, and he felt in no small way as though he was headed for an appointment with a prostitute, or something of that sort. Of course, when he thought about it, Conan was exactly something of that sort. Younger than Lydia Morten by perhaps a decade, it was well bruited about town that Conan was only with her for the money. He serviced the wrinkled crone regularly, collected the rent from her slum flats and attended social events with her—ever willing to be photographed by her side for what passed as the society pages in Runway Four. In return he got his bed and board at Lydia's mansion, was paid a handsome wage by her, and had access to a lifestyle his prole roots would otherwise have rendered unreachable.

Lydia was a singer by profession who had had quite a number of hits in her day; though her day was a good many years behind at this stage, at least in the West. Curiously, over time, she had become huge in the Far South, selling tonnes of records to fervent fans in southern realms. She travelled out there often for lucrative tours. For the rest of the year she lived in style and luxury in one of the finer parts of Bludgeon City. The profits from her music career—record sales, those tours, t-shirts and memorabilia—plus the rents from the slum flats, gave Morten an income that was the envy of many.

She had embarked on her property buying spree years earlier upon receipt of her first fat royalty cheque. Her mother had always advised her that bricks and mortar were a safe investment. And so it had proved for the slumlord Lydia Morten.

Grudge reached Rodent Street anxious to clear up the nagging business of his rent arrears. He wanted Lydia and Conan off his back for when the two were out to get you they were an evil double act. Homelessness held no appeal. Life was hard enough at his level in society but he saw around him every day how hellish things were for those of no fixed abode. Platoons of police and soldiers regularly swept through the city rounding up indigents and carting them off to camps where they were effectively worked to death. Not wishing to end up in one of those bastions of horror, Grudge was going to make it his business to pay his rent. Actually, when he was sober stuff like paying his rent was easy. He met his commitments. It was when he went off on one of his binges that all the trouble started.

Sure enough, waiting for him, a sullen gatekeeper, was the sleek Audi 4x4—the beast of a machine in which Conan and Lydia got around town.
Grudge hurried along just as Conan was climbing out of the car. Their paths met at the garden gate. Grudge squeezed the money in his hand reassuring himself of its presence—the sum that would get him over the hump of his arrears.
Conan stood there in his designer clothes, a haughty grin on his face, sneering at the loser Galmount. Lydia's lapdog spoke.
—"Grudge," he said. "Glad you could make it. I hope you've got our money? Lydia's losing patience with you at this stage. And the last thing you want is that, boyo!"
—"Yes," Grudge said. "I've got the money, I got paid today. I have all the arrears."
A bolt of anxiety struck him as he realised he would spend the next month close to starvation once he handed over the back rent. He would need at least a month to play catch-up following this dip. Subsisting on tins of peas for dinner was not a prospect he relished. He despised Conan and his rich clothes and his expensive car and the expensive cologne he could smell off him. The cunt was only in this position of wealth and power having prostituted his life to Lydia Morten. Grudge would rather be poor than live such a lie.
The two walked up the garden path and Conan opened the door of the building with his master key. They proceeded along the hallway to the back of the house towards Grudge's rathole. They entered the flat, this time using Grudge's key, allowing him *some* dignity. Grudge grabbed the rent book from the windowsill where it lay growing damp in the draught and handed it, with the money, to Conan's outstretched paw.
—"It's all there," Grudge said. "I hope that makes us all square?"
—"Well if you don't mind, I'd prefer to count it first."
Conan's thumb and forefinger flicked through the notes while his lips mumbled in an act that reminded Grudge of prayer. He's worshipping at the altar of his God, Grudge thought. At last Conan finished his checking and lolled his tongue as he did so.
—"Okay, that's all there. Fair enough. But let me warn you, Galmount, if you as much as fall behind by even a day again, we won't hesitate to fuck you out on your ear. Am I making myself clear?"

—“Absolutely, Conan,” Grudge answered.
It hurt him to have to kowtow to this parvenu upstart. He knew though that it had to be done as the alternative was too appalling to countenance. Grudge continued in the same obedient vein.
—“From now on, all my rents will be paid in full and on time. No more messing.”
—“We’ll wait and see,” Conan said, unwilling to be any nicer to Grudge. It wasn’t in his nature.
Conan left and Grudge collapsed onto the rickety bed. He was close to tears, despising the fact that he was under the thumb of so many awful people. He looked at the four walls and decided it was time to think his way out of this stinking bind.

***

Friday morning, almost a week later, and life had gone on as it always does.
In the centre of the city was Git Malone, a wheelchair-bound heroin addict with no legs. Although lots of people were using heroin, polydrug use was the big thing right now in Bludgeon City. It was mainly benadryl, diazepam, valium, antidepressants, sleeping pills, snow blow (mephedrone), and a whole range of tablets, often mixed with alcohol. There was a thriving black market for drugs; pills of every kind cost about a goldmark each. To support a smallish heroin habit required around forty goldmarks a day.
Git lived in a homeless shelter on Back Lane and attended a methadone clinic daily.
In so doing, he and numerous other addicts believed that the government was saving their lives. In fact, their lives had been sold off to Big Pharma as drug-testing fodder in a rotten deal between health officials and an amoral multinational. The addicts were dying weekly from toxic substances mixed in with their methadone doses. The multinational was getting cheap research, stats and outcomes. The users were too out of it to put two and two together. They blamed the deaths of their fellow junkies on what they called “the life”. Git, a curiosity of medical science, had managed to evade death up to now.
Polydrug use caused lots of confidence and bravado in the junkies, and made people less careful about hiding their addiction in public.

Around town and in the wider land there was no shortage of easily identifiable lab rats for Big Pharma's needs.
Each morning Git had to wheel himself two kilometres along Domina from Back Lane to the clinic on Worse Street. It was a tiring, difficult journey fraught with obstacles and danger for a frail man missing two of his most vital limbs. He made it from a desire to be fixed through the ingestion of synthetic heroin.
The routine rarely changed and he'd been on this junkie trail for the guts of a year.
You would think that a man with no legs would garner lots of compassion; not so. The staff at the clinic hated Git. He was a cantankerous self-pitying man.
He would wait in the queue and when his turn came he'd wheel himself to the hatch where the methadone was dispensed. In an obnoxious tone he would demand his shot. It left him feeling at ease, rid of the junk sickness which otherwise plagued him. Lately, he'd started dabbling with other drugs. He was certainly off his methadone programme. Valium was a favourite, it kept him über chilled and stopped him from thinking too much about the fact that he was in a wheelchair for the rest of his life. He took an array of other medicines, too. Klonopin for one thing, as well as a particularly strong schizophrenia drug called Clozaril. He wasn't prescribed any of these cures but purchased them on Bludgeon's black market. The boardwalk by the River Plur and a warren of lanes behind Secular Hall were particular hotspots of the drugs trade.
So, following the travails of Worse Street, Git would wheel himself a further kilometre to the boardwalk to buy his daily pills. He financed this lifestyle through begging, chiefly in the high-end Tourist District.
All the wheeling himself around had resulted in his upper arms becoming quite muscular. They were in fact the best feature of his tattered and bereft body. He wouldn't have said no to an electric wheelchair if one was offered him, but that was unlikely. The health department was particularly parsimonious.
Pushing on and on, he felt lucky to be still around, still alive. In the street the other day a policeman had threatened him with execution, calling him a useless leech—lower on the pecking order than a cockroach.

Anyway, after the boardwalk for his pills, Git went begging. Begging patches outside shops were the most lucrative. He had several regular spots. The shop owners despised him and were always moving him on, summoning police on the beat to upbraid him and shove him down the street. It was a miracle really that he hadn't been carted off by now to some incarceration centre or even shot on the spot. Someone was watching over him. His little life of drug-taking and mendicancy carried on apace.
This particular morning he was perched outside an artisan food hall in the Tourist District. The passing tourists, visiting R4 from their Western democracies, were a great source of coinage and at times notes for Git. They were also a great source of income for the state. The visitors came to see a moneyed dictatorship in practice.
Runway Four was seen as a niche and curious destination with good hotels and shops in its touristy parts. The government laid on trips to corrective thinking camps (the more palatable parts) as well as visits to plebeian suburbs and villages. Tourists came, too, to view the *ancien* architecture that had survived the bloody revolution that had seen Chairman Young installed as Supreme Commander.
Like so many folk around town, the proprietor of the food hall harboured a deep antipathy towards Git Malone. Not that he knew Git's name, he was simply *that* filthy beggar. Mr. Fallon, for that was the proprietor's name, and all of his staff, could not stand the sight of the impecunious cripple garnering free money outside their premises, while inside they went about their work diligently. It was so unjust, and they were at a complete loss to understand how the little fucker got away with it. Wasn't this supposed to be a garrison state? Mr. Fallon remembered fondly history lessons from his schooldays. AH, now there was a dictator. He wouldn't have put up with such effronteries. The likes of that rancid little wart would not have seen the light of day under AH's regime. The chambers of gas would have snuffed him out. The Party was losing its grip when a bum cripple could flit from shop to shop like a bloody busker.
Still, Mr. Fallon was not against many of the changes that Runway Four had seen in recent years. The increase in tourism and the (almost) free hand given to capitalism had certainly helped to fill his coffers. He slept far better these days knowing that his wife and children and (future) grandchildren were assured of prosperity going forward.

The cripple was aggravating him in the extreme, however—the cheek of the man. He had told him to clear off several times, which he did, only to return the next day. Clearly, there were rich pickings for cheeky beggars in the Tourist District. Mr. Fallon, looking through his big shop window, decided that the best thing to do would be to contact a vigilante friend and have something more serious done to the beggar than a mere word in his ear.

Git was high as a kite, sitting outside the food hall. The tourists traipsed past in large numbers. Every third one, or thereabouts, dropped money into in his begging bowl (an improvised Styrofoam coffee cup). At this rate, he'd have enough money to keep him in pills for a week. He was as happy as the proverbial pig in excrement. Speaking of shit, the foulest of foul stenches—a most mephitic hum—suddenly hit his nostrils. He thought it must be a sewer problem but could not be sure. High as he was, the stink threatened to overpower him. Time to move on, he decided, and, marshalling the forces of his frail frame, he pushed himself along the pavement.

Grudge Galmount came along at that point on a half-hour break from the coffin factory—more of an errand really. He, too, caught the whiff on the air. It reminded him of Goat Park the other week.

The two men passed one another. Grudge gave a small sympathetic smile to the beggar. Git, however, seemed preoccupied moving himself along and didn't acknowledge Galmount.

Poor bastard, Grudge thought, no legs and has to beg all day. Still, he handles that chair pretty niftily. He turned and watched the tiny stump of Git Malone scuttle down the pavement before vanishing in the throng of tourists.

Grudge was happy enough to have escaped the factory for a few minutes and his tormentor Mary Dawn. She was taking her recent instructions to watch him like a hawk very much to heart. She had imposed a ramped up surveillance regimen upon him, and was tracking his daily doings with oppressive precision. He needed the job, he needed the money, he kept telling himself, as an excuse for putting up with such bullshit. This is a one-party state, he reasoned, if I rock the boat I'm thrown in a camp or, worse, killed.

He'd managed to get out this morning through the sheer lucky break of having a cousin, Norman, who owned a hardware shop adjacent the Tourist District and who stocked a particular form of screw that the factory had run out of. A manager, Jem Corry, more senior to

Mary Dawn, had approached Grudge as Grudge was heading to his morning break and asked him to pop over to his cousin's store and pick up several boxes of the scarce screw. Corry's face had seemed to Grudge supremely sympathetic when he was making the request. Grudge figured that Jem knew the oppression he was labouring under with Mary and being a naturally compassionate man had engineered it that Grudge could get out of the factory for a spell. After all, *Wormwood* can just order things in if they need them. Kudos to Corry; he's not the worst of them.

The Tourist District was impressively packed. Grudge realised all the government's brainwashing was affecting him when he found himself thinking of the lovely tourist goldmarks filling the central fund—the lofty-sounding title that the Party gave to the coffers of the state. He shook his head in an effort to stop thinking like a dutiful little serf. Still, he couldn't help but be impressed by the success of this unique form of capitalism that the Party championed.

He left the Tourist District and turned on to Hard Road where Norman's shop was situated. Norman—one of Grudge's few living relatives—was particularly fond of a drink. Nonetheless, he managed to keep his business ticking over and—like Mr. Fallon—was delighted with the way the authorities had opened up the market in recent years and allowed entrepreneurs and small business people to thrive.

Grudge was looking forward to seeing Norman as it had been a while. Jem Corry had phoned ahead and told Norm to expect Grudge and to have the screws ready.

Just as he neared the shop the legless beggar in the wheelchair whom he had watched scurry off some minutes before, came hurrying up behind him. Hearing the approach, Grudge turned around, startled by the beggar, surprised to see him again. The man looked agitated and scared.

—"Are you okay?" Grudge asked. "Can I help you?"

—"Mister," the beggar said. "He's coming for me. I think *you* can stop him."

***

The next day, coming up to lunchtime in the Popplewell household, Sally's mother Jane was preparing a fish pie. Her father Jett Popplewell, on a day off, sat by a window in the parlour reading his tablet. Every day was a stay-at-home day for Jane who worked as a seamstress from her kitchen table. Sally was in her bedroom writing. Jett loved to keep up with the government's line on all things political. Truth to tell it was the only line available in Runway Four. Dissenting voices, contrary opinions were not tolerated. Jett was an intelligent man and knew in his heart the perniciousness of the government's lies. He also knew, though, on which side his bread was buttered and therefore lived an outwardly loyal life towards the state. He did so for the sake of his wife and daughter both of whom he loved more than anything else in the world. Now that she was at that age, he wanted Sally to carve out a good life and career for herself. The secret as far as Jett was concerned was to play the game and toe the Party line.

The scent of his wife's fish pie wafting into the parlour was delicious. He loved to have her cook for him and to share this home with the two most important women in his life.

He fingered the tablet in his hand, flicking page after page, viewing pictures of what the government was calling an abject famine in an enemy land. He winced at the graphicness of some of the photos, emaciated souls clutching clumps of grass, some stuffing the grass into their mouths, as well as other unfortunates collapsed in fields with fat flies crawling round their eyes. The voiceover accompanying the photographs outlined the failure of the other regime to protect its citizens from starvation and spoke—stridently—of the superiority of R4's protection of her people. Well it certainly looks bloody awful, Jett thought, though I don't believe half of what the government puts out. I wouldn't be surprised if the whole thing was computer-generated.

Jane came in to the parlour. In Jett's view she was still as beautiful as the first day he'd laid eyes on her. Their marriage was genuine and loving. Sally was the issue of parents who wanted to be together. They weren't just in it for breeding reasons like so many R4 married couples were.

—"Well," Jane said. "Aren't you the right little lord of the manor? Sitting there reading the news while your food's prepared for you." She walked over to him, laughing, and tousled his hair.

—"C'mon, buster," she said. "Lunch is ready. I've made your favourite: fish pie."

—"I know. I can smell it from here. Where's Sally, is she joining us?"
—"She's been in her room all morning. She's finishing off some writing. I think it's that piece she's been working on for the last couple of weeks. She said she'll come out for lunch. That's why I made the pie. She loves it, too. I'll go call her."
In her bedroom, Sally was in a state of considerable excitement bordering on elation. At her desk, she had a laptop open side by side with a desktop computer. In its own way this was her version of a cabinet war room or mission control of a space agency. The article on the murders, into which she had put so much writing effort, was on her laptop. On the brink of completion, it had turned out better than she could have hoped. Hence, she was on a high.
On the desktop a webpage on ritual killing was open, while several more pages were minimized. Last night and this morning had seen a final burst of research to bring the article to its skilful conclusion. She was reading and rereading it now—tightly editing—perfecting her unique voice that sang through the entire piece. She was alert to any glaring discrepancies and errors and pleased to have found none at this late stage. As she read, she really couldn't believe her luck at how well the piece had formed. She was aware that her judgement was hardly impartial, yet confident that others would see the greatness of the article, too. In her view it was professional, crisp, intriguing, and anybody reading it would be eager to read more of Sally Popplewell's writing.
The voice she had achieved was just what she wanted. All her research reminded her of a writer from another era called Robert Caro. He had written a prodigious biography comprising several volumes on a Freeland president. Caro took his research so seriously that he slept outdoors in the Cowboy Hills to get a feel for how the young president felt in his itinerant family as a boy. Sally hadn't been quite so thorough, but had certainly done a fair amount of research and produced something special. She was optimistic and dared to dream—intimations filled her—that this work would grab awards and set her journalistic career on a path to glory.
After a morning of fact-checking and fine-tuning, she was ready to press send and deliver the piece to Jeff Kern. It was an exciting moment. Her confidence soared. Her father will be so proud. He had been wary when she first said she wanted to be a journalist, fearing

her forceful personality would somehow incur the wrath of the authorities. But when no trouble came, he grew encouraging of her ambitions. He read and relished the pieces she sent to the papers. His girl was blossoming into a writer. The same girl to whom he'd read difficult works of literature as bedtime tales, going out of his way to source banned books from contacts in the underground. This early tuition had given Sally a terrific command and facility with language.
Her mother came into the bedroom.
—"Sally, are you coming out for lunch? I've made fish pie. You've been typing all morning."
—"Yes, Mam, I'm starving. Just give me two minutes. I'm about to send off this article. It's going to be a game-changer for me."
—"Well hurry along, dear," Jane said, oblivious to Sally's bullish talk.
Now, with the computers humming round her, and tense from a morning's concentration, Sally decided that that was that. She had done all she could to prepare her work, devoted endless hours to its creation, even put off meeting Grudge to write it. The time had come to let it go. She took a last look at her words on the screen, felt a surge of pride, and pressed send. What a relief. It was done. Publish and be praised.
She went to the kitchen to join her parents.
Three place settings lay waiting. The pie had been carved up and put on plates. Jett was already sitting with a beaming smile upon his face. Jane sat down and poured everyone a glass of mineral water. Sally slid into her seat, feeling secure and loved, among the two who had brought her into being.
Jett was in great form. He loved these girls so much and felt blessed that the Lord had sent them to him. Of course, in R4 there was no such thing as the Lord—only Chairman Young. Jett, nonetheless, kept a Bible beneath his floorboards and read it often. He believed it fervently and called himself a Christian. Never in public, though, as it would have meant certain death.
Scientists traced Christianity's lineage to an ancient desert tribe, but Jett believed it was something far bigger than that. In the safety of their home and never too loudly he, Jane and Sally debated the subject on many nights and were filled with wonder. The girls

considered themselves Christians, too, and like Jett theirs was a secret devotion.
—"Well," he asked Sally. "Did you get that article written? It took you over for a while."
She smiled. Her father's encouragement and love was the reason she had become such a well-rounded young woman.
—"Yes, Dad," she said. "It's finally done. I just sent it off to the editor about five minutes ago. I gave it my best shot. Think I came up with an interesting angle on the murders and what's behind them."
—"Really?" Jane chimed in, her curiosity aroused by this statement of her daughter's.
—"I don't want to say anything just yet, Mam. Wait until the article is published—fingers crossed."
—"Let's respect Sally wishes," Jett counselled. "I'm delighted you got it finished. I'm sure Kern will put it into print."
—"Very well, dear," Jane said. "I'm just intrigued about your theories, but I'll wait till I read them on the page."
—"Let's say grace," Sally said, eager to change the subject. She was tired from her morning's work and just wanted to eat lunch and forget about the article for a while.
—"Good idea," Jett said. "I'm famished, but let's thank the Lord first."
The Popplewell family linked hands around their kitchen table and whispered a low prayer in gratitude for their food. They always whispered when praying. You could never be too sure who was listening.

***

Sunday rolled round and a walker between worlds arrived in town to give a concert with his band The Dudes. Steve Spirit checked into the Northbury Hotel in the Tourist District, one of the poshest in the city, offloaded his gear in his room, showered, and hit the shopping streets for some pre-gig flâneuring.
As well as being a gifted songwriter, Steve was also quite a talented shutterbug—indeed he was nothing if not obsessive about photography. Leaving his hotel, he turned onto Sudbury Street—Bludgeon's premier thoroughfare—and by means of his iPhone began snapping many of the things in sight.

Often called the embodiment of The Dudes (as in Steve Spirit *is* The Dudes) he ambled along the street shooting here, shooting there. As he did so he blended, chameleon-like, into the crowd. Nobody recognised him, even though he did have a certain degree of fame and notoriety. With his 8-megapixel iPhone camera, he shot random strangers, buskers, shop window displays; everything and anything really. Once taken, in a process known as tweeting, he would upload the pictures to the micro-blogging website Twitter—banned in R4—for the pleasure of his thousands of followers. Steve paid a fee to a company in Ireland that enabled his phone to use Twitter even behind the great firewall of Runway Four.
He was incessant about tweeting. He frequently took selfies, too, with quirky slants—his face beside a first edition of Finnegans Wake was a case in point. Also, it was not unheard of him to tweet a picture of his shadow resting on a wall or pavement somewhere. His Twitter followers loved it and their number rose loyally by the hundreds week on week.
Occasionally, Steve would rant on Twitter and those followers would catch a glimpse of a temperamental pedantic man a world removed from that gentle spiritualist who had penned such gems as *On My Way to Abbeyfeale* and *This is the Mountain*. He would rail against department stores over spelling errors in their promotional brochures, or tweet for all to see the various typos in books he was reading, lambasting the publishers royally. Still, he was a good man and a great artist and this pedantry and obsessive tweeting were but offshoots of genius.
The Dudes were one of a select group of bands who came to play in Runway Four. They were given the run of a Bludgeon stage because several senior Party officials happened to be fans. The band played at least two R4 concerts a year and had a large number of devotees. Two of their biggest fans were Grudge and Sally. They had discovered a mutual love of The Dudes in a late night text exchange—a courting correspondence where taste was discussed: music, books, film, etc.
With the concert coming up, Sally bought two tickets as a reward for finishing her article, and as a way to bring her and Grudge closer. Grudge was chuffed. He was practically penniless having cleared his rent arrears. Sally understood and had offered to buy dinner, too, before the show. How could he refuse?

On Sudbury Street Steve Spirit retreated back to the Northbury Hotel having tweeted seventeen times. In the hotel, he launched into pre-concert mode. This entailed yoga, meditation and a macrobiotic meal, plus a short nap.
Prior to hitting the concert venue—Chairman Young Hall—Grudge and Sally were in a Tourist District burger joint. The place was themed on nineteen-fifties Freeland.
—"Nice decor," Grudge said, sliding into a red leather-upholstered booth. "Have you been here before?"
—"Several times," Sally said, settling down opposite. "I hope you're hungry. The burgers are great."
—"I'm starving. Let's order."
He beckoned a waitress nearby who came over promptly. Her name card said Rosa. She wore a fifties Freeland diner uniform and a warm, seemingly genuine smile.
—"What'll it be, folks?" she asked.
They ordered a slap-up feast: garlic fries, onion rings, burgers with big buns and blue cheese, all to be washed down with strawberry malt milkshakes. Rosa wrote the chit remarking as she did that they were going to *love* the food.
—"I've eaten here before," Sally told her. "So I know I will."
Always an intuitive fellow, Grudge caught a look in Rosa's eye that implied she had something more to say than mere pleasantries about the food. Quickly, though, he let the notion go, putting it down to his overactive imagination.
—"Can't wait for the show," Sally said. "They were brilliant last year. Spirit really gives it his all."
—"Yeah, I was at that gig, too. We probably passed each other like ships in the night."
—"Well, we're sailing together now," Sally laughed.
—"So you got your article about the murders finished?" Grudge said. "You must be pleased?"
—"I'm bloody delighted. It took a lot out of me, but I think I've produced something special. I sent it to Jeff Kern yesterday. I'm waiting to hear from him."
—"He'll love it!"
Rosa arrived all smiles with a tray piled high with food. Again, for a moment, Grudge was puzzled by a knowing, pleading look in her eye behind the smile. Once more, he dismissed his hunch.

—"Enjoy," she said, and fled.
Grudge and Sally tucked in without delay.
—"She's all in the colours of Freeland with that uniform," Sally said, between bites.
—"The owner of this joint obviously has a real thing about that country. The place is decked out in homage. I must say, it's a land I'd love to visit."
—"Me, too. Who knows, Grudge, maybe we'll go there someday."
—"Wouldn't that be something."
—"Freeland's made for someone like you. You're wasted in that coffin factory. A sensitive, artistic type, you'd fit right in."
—"Artistic type?" Grudge pleaded. "What have I ever created but trouble?"
—"You just need to find your groove, Grudge."
He took a slug of milkshake and pondered Sally's words. She was right: he was sensitive and artistic, but he was stunted. Most days he felt he'd never get a chance to grow. Still, what a fillip Sally was to his glumness.
—"If journalism works out for me," she said. "I'm going to go to Freeland at the first chance I get. It's where all the action is, it's the most powerful country in the world. If I can cut my teeth over there, anything's possible."
—"Would you get a visa?" Grudge asked. "And would the authorities here let you go?"
—"Yes, I've looked into it. Working visas are pretty obtainable from the Freeland government. Obviously, there are terms and conditions but no hurdles too big. And R4 is opening up, too. Chairman Young now speaks of his wish to export 'our best and our brightest', so they can gain experience abroad and return to R4 as better citizens. Not wishing to sound vain, but I think I could qualify as one of the best and the brightest."
—"You sure look best and bright to me."
—"Aw thanks, Grudge, but if it does come to pass and I get to Freeland, I'll try my darnedest to bring you, too. I'll get you out of that coffin factory somehow. I'll buy you a second hand SLR and say you're my photographer and that I need you on assignment. I've seen the pictures you've taken with your phone. You've got a great eye."

—“That sounds like a cool plan. And now that you mention it, I do take a decent photograph when I put my mind to it. Nothing would thrill me more than to travel to Freeland as your photographer.”
Grudge let his mind drift for a moment to a pleasant daydream in which he and Sally were holed up in a Freeland hotel making love and calling room service afterwards to send up treats.
—“We’ll aim to do it, so,” Sally said. “Why not?”
Maybe dreams come true, Grudge thought.
The meal finished and they stood up to leave, both nicely full.
—“Okay,” Sally said. “The venue’s a fifteen-minute walk. No point in getting a cab. Let’s hoof it. It’ll burn some calories.”
—“Good idea.”
They approached the cash register, handed the chit and their money to a young man there, thanked him, and were about to leave when Rosa appeared once more, sidling up to say goodbye. Grudge and Sally accepted her good wishes with grace and headed for the door. Sally went through into the street. As Grudge was about to do likewise, Rosa tugged his elbow.
—“Yes?” he asked, turning round.
She looked frightened. Her smile was gone. That strange look he’d detected in her eye was now fully apparent.
—“He likes you,” she said. “He sees something in you. Do what he asks and your reward will be great.”
—“Who likes me?” Grudge said, taken aback.
But Rosa didn’t answer, just ran away into the depths of the restaurant.
—“C’mon, Grudge. We’ll be late for the concert,” Sally shouted from the street.
Grudge caught up with her but his mind was elsewhere. Rosa’s words had unnerved him. He tried to forget them as he fell in line with Sally and they began walking to Chairman Young Hall. He knew though that her words would reverberate in his skull, for whatever length of time, until their meaning was revealed. He was reminded of the legless beggar who had spoken to him in the Tourist District on Friday. That poor chap had been equally obtuse. Grudge had dismissed him as simply out of his mind on drugs. Now he wasn’t so sure. Rosa and the beggar, singling him out and speaking of a mysterious ‘he’, all in the space of a few days, was there a

connection? Ridiculous as it seemed, Grudge felt a spawn of some sort had sprung up from a putrid swamp and was shadowing him.
He looked at Sally and it eased his mood. She is lovelier each time I see her, he thought. He longed to consummate their burgeoning relationship—quite possibly after the show—though the idea of bringing her to the rathole was an embarrassment.
He couldn't wait for the concert. The Dudes always delivered a blistering set.
Many fans were on the street tonight. These gigs were a big event. As much as it was possible in an oppressive state, there was a carnival atmosphere around town. The authorities lowered the pressure and let people have a modicum of fun. Steve Spirit deserved credit for this mood change in Bludgeon City. The crowd would give their thanks with rapturous applause once the show kicked off.
Grudge and Sally reached the venue. The street outside Chairman Young Hall was buzzing. There were ticket touts, t-shirt sellers, hotdog vendors, plus a lot of security. The Dudes had brought some of their own people and the authorities laid on the rest. There would be no crime, public drunkenness etc. at this event. The heavy-handed security was actually unnecessary—nobody in the good-natured crowd wanted to tangle with the police; getting arrested was almost a fate worse than death. Still, the powers that be had left nothing to chance.
Grudge and Sally joined a big queue that stretched along the pavement. Everyone seemed to be in good humour, happy with their lot, at least for tonight.
When they reached the top of the queue, they were frisked and had their tickets scanned. With that, the couple surged into the auditorium.
ABBEYFEELZ! read an outsize sign above the stage; a gentle play on Spirit's famous *On My Way to Abbeyfeale* lyrics.
—"I hope he plays *Thud on the Nose*," Sally shouted into Grudge's shell-like.
—"A great track. I'm sure he will. It's one of his biggest hits."
She took his hand and a rush of joy filled him. It was the youngest, most sugary stage of their relationship and he relished every minute. She walked them through the crowd to a spot near the stage where they stood waiting eagerly for the band to appear.

After fifteen minutes or so a whoosh went up from the crowd as Steve Spirit and his merry men entered stage right. The house lights went down.
The wild thin mercury sound of a fiddle—performed by key Dudes member Fiddler Fred—pealed forth. The crowd burst into applause, cheering wildly, as the familiar opening strains of *Washerwoman's Blues* began. Spotlights lit up the stage, one in particular outshone all others. Beneath it Steve Spirit, looking, for all the world, like a young Dylan in his amphetamine phase. Age had been kind to the great spiritual folkey, the hair was still thick, the body lithe. As he bopped about, his barnet bopped with him. The place was electric.
—"I wish I was a washerwoman," he howled.
—"Mangling out my smalls" the crowd sang in unison with the bardic Spirit.
Happy and in love, Grudge and Sally danced around. The band sounded fantastic, easily as good as Glastonbury, 1986. They were as tight and as up for it as ever.
The gig continued at a rollicking pace.
—"May she live to be a hundred, may she always have a roof over her head!" Spirit sang, and the crowd roared approval.
On and on it went, hit after hit. Newer material was introduced and lapped up, too, by the adoring audience. A Dylan cover version—*Workingman's Blues* from 2006—was thrown into the mix. After that, Spirit hushed the band and put his hand out in a downward motion, to indicate that he wished to address the crowd. The fans complied, quietening quickly. Spirit was in full control. In an echo of his speech at Glastonbury all those years earlier he spoke in his soft Celtic burr:
—"That was a Bob Dylan song."
At the mention of Dylan's name, the audience whistled and cheered. Spirit went on.
—"It's a privilege to sing such a beautiful song in this the most fashionable place in Runway Four in this year of our Lord ____ …"
The crowd loved these remarks. Spirit was on thin ice referring to a Lord other than Chairman Young but he got away with it in the buzz of the occasion.
His reference to the most fashionable place in Runway Four was entirely apt. Chairman Young Hall was close to Younghead College in a golden triangle that stretched from Exchange Street up to

Sudbury Street and took in most of the Tourist District, as well as several other pockets of affluence along the way.
The sombre notes of *Terracotta Blues* made their menacing appearance in the acoustically pitch-perfect auditorium. The slow ominous drumbeat set the crowd to a state of high anticipation. It was one of The Dudes' greatest hits and audiences loved to hear it. It was a miracle that its lyrics—so close to the bone in the context of Runway Four—could be sung on a Bludgeon stage; testimony to Steve Spirit's popularity, drive and ambition, not to mention the troubadour's sheer chutzpah.
The show was nearing its end now. The band had been on stage for almost two hours. *Terracotta Blues* would be a key facet of a most satisfying climax.
Then to people's surprise Spirit stopped strumming his guitar and started waving his arms violently from side to side in order to silence the musicians and the crowd. Steve wasn't a democrat when it came to leading his band or indeed when it came to entertaining an audience. Everyone obeyed.
Whoever was operating the house lights took instant notice and brought every light down except for an intense spotlight illuminating Spirit's head. A hush enveloped the hall. Sally looked at Grudge, who looked back at Sally; with near musical timing their eyebrows raised. The audience scratched its collective head.
Steve Spirit took an iPhone from his pocket and spoke:
—"This gig is so amazing. I simply must live tweet about it to my followers."
Several people actually booed at that point. A surprising development in light of the fact that the show was going so well, with everyone—band and audience—getting along famously. Clearly, there was resentment that Spirit had chosen to contact his followers in the virtual realm and thereby disturb the flow of the live music.
—"Get on with it!"
—"Hurry up!"
—"For fuck's sake!"
Angry shouts abounded as the singer took a picture of the crowd and began tweeting it, along with some explanatory text, into cyberspace. His thumb pressed the phone's keypad with alacrity.

—"This won't take long," he assured the crowd in a jocular voice, trying to make light of the annoying holdup. Members of the band, in particular Fiddler Fred, looked pissed off, too.
Then, with anger mounting, someone threw a plastic bottle at the stage skimming Spirit's head.
—"Whoever threw that was a bloody idiot!" he said.
There was edge in the Celtic burr.
In the space of a few minutes the atmosphere soured. It seemed half the crowd was booing.
His tweet complete, Steve signalled to the band to start playing again. Clearly, though, stopping the show to go on Twitter had been a big mistake. More bottles hit the stage, several of which connected with Steve and The Dudes. It started to look like Steve Spirit and The Waterbottles up there. It was fortunate that the offending missiles were made of plastic. Had they been glass, some serious harm would have been done.
The crowd was in a near riotous state by now stamping its feet and ready to surge forward. The lighting man lit up the stage and quickly thereafter he brought up the lights in the entire hall. It seemed that the show would not go on. Grudge and Sally looked at one another with worry. There was a sense that violence could break out at any moment. It was the pressurised atmosphere of the police state that made people so volatile. Sensing the game was up, the band exited stage left as the security stewards around the auditorium drew their guns.
An announcement came over the loudspeaker telling the crowd that the concert had stopped and would not be resuming. People were told to leave the hall in an orderly fashion. The message ended menacingly with the following words:
—"Any persons disobeying these instructions will be detained by the security agents. Any persons deemed a physical threat will be met with lethal force."
The information was relayed at an ear-splitting volume and it seemed to have the desired effect. The whistling, booing and stamping of feet ceased. People knew the score and that the regime did not make idle threats. The country was governed by a one-party state without free elections and these forces would do anything to maintain law and order and thereby their hold on power. If it meant

shooting dead some rowdy concertgoers, so be it. There were never repercussions for the state.
It looked like this riot would not get past its initial labour pains. People who had been so emboldened moments earlier and had been shouting and roaring in defiance of any form of authority—Steve Spirit, or the government—and egged on by their sense of safety in numbers, now began to shuffle, cowed, towards the exits.
What a transformation, Grudge thought, it serves to prove how powerful this regime is.
—"Well," Sally said, as she and Grudge shuffled out, too. "That turned out to be a bit of a damp squib. I thought for a minute there was going to be a full-on ruckus."
—"It could have been another feather in your journalistic cap," Grudge laughed. "Sally Popplewell's eye-witness account from the great Dudes riot."
She joshed him in the ribs and told him not to be so stupid.
—"Let's go get a coffee," she said when they finally reached the street.
The crowd was dispersing in several directions under the beady glare of the police, well-armed soldiers and the private security guards hired by the band.
—"Good idea," Grudge agreed. "The security round here is too much. They really don't want anything kicking off. How about Sudbury Street? There're some lovely cafés up there?"
—"The Tourist District's a bit pricey, Grudge. Let's just skip down to the Lie District. It's got some nice places, too. I'll walk you home!"
At this suggestion of hers, Sally burst out laughing; so did Grudge. He was being walked home from a near riot by a beautiful girl who obviously liked him. All his other troubles melted in this moment as they ambled in the evening air.
Half an hour later they walked in the door of the same café they'd gone to on the night they'd met; the shabby chic place near the library.
—"What an end to a Dudes show, eh?" Grudge said, settling into a chair with a frothy latte in front of him. "We won't forget that one in a hurry."
Across a small table, Sally stirred a cappuccino and looked at him with dreamy eyes.

—“We sure won’t,” she said. “It was a great show, though, until the crowd turned ugly. Don’t think Spirit will be sending tweets again during R4 shows. It was so good to have you by my side, Grudge.”
At her warm words a wave of pleasure rolled over him.
The way she looked at him caused his heart to flutter. Concupiscence stirred in his loins. He detected a large hint of desire in her tone. He had never seen her looking so up for it in the couple of weeks he had been dating her. If I play my cards right, he thought, this could be the night.
—“Hey thanks, Sally. That’s very kind of you. Aren’t I the lucky guy having a gorgeous girl like you telling me such things?”
—“It’s only what you deserve. I felt really safe in your company tonight. When the trouble kicked off, it was so reassuring knowing you were there.”
She reached across the table and took his hand. He stared at her soft and sexy mouth. Although the lips moved, he didn’t hear her words. He was entranced by this girl and felt an intense desire to make love to her. Luckily for him, she was thinking along the same lines.
—“So, what do you think, Grudge, will I call them?”
Grudge snapped out of his reverie.
—“Eh, I’m sorry, what was the question again? I lost my train of thought there for a second.”
—“Will I call my folks and tell them I’m staying with friends? I want you to show me this rathole of yours.”
She let go of his hand and leaned back in her chair, adding playfully.
—“Of course, you can be a gentleman and sleep on the floor. Give your bed over to your visitor.”
Grudge was flabbergasted. Sally wanted to come to the rathole, and, what was more, she wanted to stay the night! He didn’t know whether to laugh or cry. Laugh because she wanted to stay, and cry because of the squalid state of the place.
With a poker face, he weighed up his options, concluding that there was no way he was going to pass on the chance to have Sally sleep in his flat. The place wasn’t as bad as he thought. He could do a quick clean-up when they got there.
—“Yes, sure, call them,” he said.
—“At last, an answer,” Sally laughed. “I thought you’d gone into a trance.”

—"No, my mind just wanders at times. I think the coffin factory has me prone to daydreaming. Sometimes it's the only thing that gets me through a shift in that shithole."
—"You're not saying that having a coffee with me is equivalent to a shift in the coffin factory? That's a bit harsh, Grudge."
—"Not at all. You've picked me up wrong. I'm just saying sometimes I break into daydreams no matter what the circumstances. It stems from my line of work. As it happens, having coffee with you is the nicest thing ever."
He turned on one of his best smiles. Sally seemed to love it.
—"Thanks for the compliment," she said.
—"I'm only saying it because it's true."
He felt dizzyingly close to sleeping with Sally. The condition of the rathole, however, remained a cause of concern.
—"But, listen, Sally, I don't call my place the rathole for nothing. It's an absolute kip. I've got this landlord—have I mentioned her before?—Lydia Morten, she's more like a slumlord, owns a stack of houses around Bludgeon, nice little earners the lot of them, she's a singer. You've probably heard of her?"
—"You've mentioned her several times," Sally said. "And I've seen her in the press."
—"Well, as I say, slumlord just about sums her up. She repairs nothing, maintains nothing, spends nothing on the house. It's just take, take, take with Lydia."
—"If you'll pardon my French, she sounds like a cunt."
—"She is," Grudge said, laughing at Sally's use of the C-word. "She's got this boyfriend, too, Conan—her henchman. About ten years younger. He's plainly only with her for the money. A bit of muscle to send around when a tenant acts up. I've been that tenant."
—"Yes, I've seen Conan and Lydia in the society pages," Sally said. "So, what did you do to rile Conan?"
—"Rent arrears," Grudge said, sheepishly, not wishing to come across as a man who didn't pay his way. "But they're cleared now. I paid him right up to date the other day."
—"Well, that's a relief. I wouldn't like to see you turfed onto the street."
—"No, I think I'm safe for now. But, Sally, getting back to the condition of my flat, be prepared, it's no five-star hotel. There's a Harold Pinter quote that sums it up: 'I have filthy insane digs, an

obscene household, cats, dogs, filth, tea strainers, mess, rubbish shit scratch dung poison, deficient order in the upper fretwork, roll on!' I memorized that quote when I first read it. It always gives me a lift."
—"They're colourful words alright," Sally said "But I'm afraid I'll have to use the search engine to see who Harold Pinter is."
—"An interesting cat. You'll find it worthwhile. I don't think he's been completely censored."
—"I look forward to reading up on the man. As to your flat, Grudge, you don't have to be embarrassed about it to me. It's sickening though to think that that model citizen, Morten, gets away with her slumlord activities. I'd like to expose her. No doubt she's Party-connected through and through. Anyway, I'll call my mother, shall I, and tell her I'll be home tomorrow? I'll say I'm staying with a girlfriend. It's no problem."
—"Whatever you think is easiest, Sally. I mean, I don't want to get you into any trouble."
Grudge tried to sound nonchalant. Inside he was flying.
—"Actually," Sally said. "My folks are quite liberal and wouldn't mind me staying over in a boy's flat if they knew you. It's just they haven't met you yet and might get a little worried."
She took out her phone. Grudge heard her tell her mother of her plan to stay with a girlfriend. The conversation—at least from the one-sided version Grudge got—seemed to go well and Sally closed her phone with a smile. Grudge's excitement was building, lust and love swirling about, though he kept his outward appearance calm.
—"That's settled then," Sally said. "Mum's okay. Now take me to your rathole!"
They finished their coffees, settled the bill and headed out into the Lie District. Holding hands they hurried in the direction of Rodent Street. Within minutes and in the throbbing glow of their ardour they were pushing in the front door of Grudge's building. They traversed the hallway and reached the door of the rathole itself. Grudge thought he heard Ann-Marie moving about in her flat. Ever the faithful listener, he suspected she had her ear to the door.
Grudge turned his key, telling Sally as he did so.
—"Be prepared, I told you, it's no palace."
—"C'mon," she whispered. "Just let me in."
They went inside.

Grudge looked anxiously at Sally who surveyed the scene with a gimlet eye.
—"It's actually fine. Cosy," she said. "I think you've made it out to be worse than it is, Grudge."
He wasn't sure if she was just being kind. His place was plainly a dump. The peeling wallpaper, the worn carpet, the rickety bed all said as much. He would love to see the back of it. Maybe move in with Sally? What a dream.
She got him thinking, though. Perhaps it does have a certain coziness. Familiarity breeds contempt after all. Could it be I'm being too hard on my living quarters? He wasn't quite convinced, however, and believed that the flat was as bad as he thought it was.
—"Thanks," he said. "But, Sally, there's no need to pretend. You won't hurt my feelings by calling it what it is. I know it's a rathole. I'm ashamed that it's my home. I always hoped I'd end up somewhere better than this."
—"Shut up, Grudge. Do you realise how self-pitying you sound? This place is fine, and I'm glad that I'm staying here for the night. From what you were saying before, I thought you were living in an actual rubbish dump."
—"Okay, if you don't think it's too bad, I'm relieved. I trust your opinion. Now let me get you some clean sheets for the bed. I've got some in the cupboard over there. And I'll make up a little nest for myself on the floor."
—"You'll do no such thing," Sally said.
At that point the several weeks of courtship between them reached its climax—almost the climax, that is, for that would come shortly. Grudge stood with an ecstatic grin developing on his face as Sally, making the first move, threw her arms around him like a necklace and placed her mouth upon his, seeking a kiss. In this endeavour she met no resistance. Galmount kissed her eagerly, and she him, in a quintessential passionate clinch. Intense happiness coursed through his veins. Sally too tingled with delight as their tongues locked and the tonsil tennis played. She felt gratitude that she had chosen this man to give herself to in spite of his strangeness, his isolated existence and the hints he had given of a history of addiction problems. She sensed the solidness of his soul and felt safe to embrace him. He was quite the kisser at that and she drank of him like a parched prisoner given water after days of thirst. It was sweet

and it was exciting and a raft of thoughts went through her mind. She remembered that first day when she had met him in the library and they had gone on that kind of date, and her mind travelled to an indeterminate time in the future when she and he had loved and lived long years together.
It had come to this point; a point of extreme passion. In a moment, to Grudge's utter joy, they were on the rickety bed having shed their clothing, greedily exploring every nook and cranny of one other. They made love and—in answer to that proverbial question—it was wonderful for both of them.
In fact, in Grudge's case, he could genuinely say that it was the best sex he had ever had; ditto, Sally. She lay on the pillow afterwards, her hair spread out behind her like a queen's fan and a dreamy faraway look on her face. She felt a spiritual connection to Grudge. In truth, to quote the cliché, they were made for one another.
Outside in the hallway Ann-Marie shuffled about checking last-minute things as midnight turned. Street sounds, too—cars, sirens, the cries of the damned—breached the rathole's thin walls.
None of these noises disturbed the lovers, joined as fate commanded. Sally and Grudge, at rest in one another's arms, slipped gently into a deep sleep.

Chapter 6

Intangible malignity. The seven-storied heavens. Long-pampered Gabriel, Michael, and Raphael. Imagine no religion, famously postulated in song; no heaven, too. Well, think about it.
A throne in a far kingdom, aglow with wondrous light: the King of Hell, the Prince of the Night; the ineffable light of divinity. This is not Freeland, nor is it Runway Four. It is one of the higher galleries beyond the sun.
Around the throne, seraphs—no, scratch that, nothing angelic about these fellows. Little winged beasts malevolent in the extreme. Only malice in what passes for their hearts. Ad infinitum, they sing the praises of their Prince.
His throne is golden. His face—no, not blank and pitiless as the sun—rather, sharp as an axe and with a high degree of beauty. It's a face that has won many a fair maiden down through the centuries;

won her, ravaged her and—her baubles lost—killed her as a matter of incontestable fact.
It's a face well acquainted with issuing decrees by means of a mere glance; a face that can inspire fear immediately in all whom it looks upon. A face too that can blend in anywhere in any situation and affect kindness, goodness and warmth; all masking a deep, underlying evil.
Unadulterated wickedness emanates from the throne of the Prince. In a place like Earth he controls millions of minds; a veritable legion.
The Prince has focused a lot of energy of late on that far-flung spot: the sublunary sphere. Murder, mayhem and terror have all accompanied this fresh focus.
Infinitely superior to the Prince in every conceivable way is the King of Heaven. They have been at war since time began in a constant battle of wits and will. Heaven generally prevails. Though not before the Prince has snared another million souls along the way give or take.
Every couple of centuries, the battlefield shifts to the soul of one individual, unbeknownst—until it's too late!—to the accursed person themselves. There, in one mere human body, good and evil fight it out, invariably killing the host in the process.
The handsome face assumes a new intentness. The little winged beasts hover, ever singing their evil songs. The Prince sees a chance to snare a new host in a satanic bind. This potential new host is lying with a woman in post-coital bliss.
The King of Hell's anger is great. He will not put up with this. He will tear apart all that is good in the man's world; rob him of life itself.
In short, the Devil is looking for Grudge Galmount. To this end, he's sending one of his strongest henchmen.

***

Morning came to the rathole and with it all the responsibilities of life in an autocratic state. Sally and Grudge stirred from sleep and smiled at one another. They knew their relationship had reached a higher level. For Grudge, the future contained more hope than despair. Sally for her part was shocked to find herself thinking of having Grudge's babies.

At five a.m. Grudge climbed out of bed. The drudgery of another day at the coffin factory lay ahead. As he stood on the threadbare carpet blinking into wakefulness he felt all too keenly he was falling from the dizzying heights of last night's love-making.
Sally sat up on the pillows and asked.
—"Any chance of a breakfast around here?"
—"I'll put some coffee on," Grudge said. "But I'm afraid my presses are rather empty. You might have to get breakfast in one of the cafés. I've got to get to work but I'll walk you down if you like."
—"No, I'm only kidding with you, Grudge," she said "Don't even bother with the coffee. I've got to go home and check in with Jeff Kern. See how my piece is doing, if it's out on the wires yet. I'll just use the bathroom."
While she was there Grudge counted his blessings at not having to send her to some squalid communal loo at the top of the stairs. The luxury of his own crapper never failed to please him.
She finished in the bathroom and then it was his turn.
At about ten to six they set off from the flat. Anne-Marie's curtain twitched as they left the house.
The morning was clement. They were happy of heart. They parted with a kiss at the spot where Lie became Truth and Grudge started walking to *Wormwood.* He took it slowly as he was early for his seven o'clock start.
After a few minutes his phone rang. He recognized the Spanish number. Christ! It was Beatrice.
—"Hello," he answered, keeping his tone even.
—"Hi, Grudge, it's Beatrice!"
Her tone, on the other hand, soared.
—"Jesus!" Grudge said. "This is a surprise. How the hell are you?"
He was less than thrilled to hear from Beatrice. It had been several weeks since she'd phoned; well before the entry of Sally into his life. Her bothersome letters, too, had ceased. Now she was back. Could it be she somehow knew about Sally? He dismissed the idea.
His feelings for Beatrice, once so strong, had definitely waned. How awkward to have to talk to her.
—"I am fine," she gushed down the line. "Very well indeed. And guess what? I am coming to visit you."

He swallowed hard. Before meeting Sally, news that Beatrice was to pay him a visit would have lifted his spirits no end. Now it just filled him with worry.
—"You're coming to visit?" he asked, feigning a degree of enthusiasm at the prospect. "Did you get another tourist visa?"
—"No, Grudgie, a work visa."
—"What?"
— "A work visa. I'm a journalist now. I have completed my studies here in Spain."
Grudge had forgotten all about her studies and her journalistic aspirations. His current focus was firmly on Sally. Nonetheless, being a consummate liar when the need arose, he feigned further interest in all things Bea.
—"Good for you, Beatrice! What's the assignment? Why are you coming to Runway Four?"
Inwardly, the thought of seeing Beatrice anytime soon appalled him.
—"The assignment is you my darling!"
—"I'm flattered," he said. "But what did you tell the authorities?"
—"Those fascist pigs."
Grudge hoped his phone wasn't being monitored.
—"Steady on, Bea," he said. "The R4 government doesn't take too kindly to that sort of language."
—"Okay, okay. I get the message, my little paranoiac. Anyway, your government says I can come and write about their 'economic miracle'. That's my official assignment. My real mission is to get you to change your life, Grudgie. I am arriving in one week. Isn't that great?"
Grudge was shocked.
—"Fantastic," he managed to reply.
His brain worked fast. He needed to end the conversation. Beatrice visiting Bludgeon was most undesired. How fickle he was. Up to recently he thought he was deeply in love with this woman. However, it seemed those strong feelings were nothing but an illusion.
—"I'll tell you what, Bea," he said. "I'm just getting to work now. Let me call you on this number later and I'll get all the details from you."
—"Okay, big boy. Ring me tonight!"

***

Revenue Road, *Wormwood*, another day in the coffin factory.
Grudge clocked in, the conversation with Beatrice still ringing in his ears. Measures would have to be taken. His heart was fixed on Sally. He would discard Bea like an old coat. He had the day to devise an exit strategy and have all the right things to say by the time he phoned her that evening. It wouldn't be easy, though.
He headed down the corridor to the factory floor in a stream of his fellow drudges.
He noticed an unfamiliar man walking in the opposite direction. Tall and handsome, with a Mephistophelean grin on his face, the man looked at Grudge intently. Grudge had the eerie impression he had met him in the past. Why is he looking at me, he thought? Grudge turned his head to double-check the stranger but the man was gone.
Suddenly, a commotion started up ahead and screeching workers began fleeing the Fabrication Hall. They ran past Grudge in the corridor.
—"What's going on?" he asked a terrified girl.
—"Séamus Cronin's head!" she cried. "It's been chopped off!"
—"What the fuck?" Grudge said.
Stunned, he ran towards the hall.
Workers continued to flee. Quite a few more—the gore fiends of the workforce—stood round a spot in the centre of the room where Cronin's dome had rolled. The lopped head looked up at them. The face wore an expression of shock and terror; something Grudge was unaccustomed to seeing on Séamus's normally cocky jib.
Grudge stared at the severed head and if the truth be told felt happy. He saw the rest of Cronin's body slumped in a heap by the industrial saw at his workstation. Several medics and ambulance personnel—they had been summoned by Mary Dawn—pushed through at this point in what could only be a clean-up operation. They'd come fast. R4 public service at its best. Charirman Young would be so impressed. Grudge kept thinking of the stranger he had seen on the way in. He spotted Mordechai Levy in the crowd. He looked calm; the circumstances not affecting him at all.
—"Mord," Grudge asked. "Did you see a guy around here a few minutes ago? Tall, good-looking, with a weird smile—looked a bit like a priest?"
—"Nope."

—"Well, there was something about him. What the hell happened anyway?"
—"Well," Mordechai said. "The way I heard: Séamus was kneeling by the wood checking the incisions. He nodded off or passed out and his head flopped into the path of the saw which was coming back along the plank. Pole Wallace shot around from his side but it was too late. His head was severed clean off at the neck."
—"I don't understand it at all," Grudge said. "How come he just passed out? He wasn't a druggie. He wasn't sick. It doesn't add up."
—"People can take a turn anytime, no matter how healthy they are," Mordechai said. "As my brother-in-law the doctor always says: you're only as good as your last blood test."
—"Are you sure you didn't notice that guy I described?" Grudge pressed him.
—"No, Grudge, I didn't. It could have been anyone, a maintenance guy, somebody in for a meeting with Bowe. Tell the police if it makes you feel better. Here they come now."
Following on from the medics, a detective and two uniforms appeared.
Then from the Tannoy, like an unappeased god bellowing from a volcano, Noel Bowe's voice was heard.
—"This is Mr. Bowe. Due to the fatal accident in *Wormwood* this morning, all workers are exempted from labour for the next few hours. You are to leave the factory and return at two p.m."
Grudge watched as Cronin's head was placed in a wicker basket and the police spoke with the medics. Séamus Cronin: basket case, Grudge laughed inside. Two male nurses put the rest of Séamus—the bloodied heap—into a body bag.
All his life Galmount had been an intuitive chap. Right now his instinct told him that the tall stranger he had seen in the corridor had something to do with Cronin's death. He didn't take Mordechai's advice, though, to tell the police. He decided to keep his hunch to himself. Part of his brain was lit up with joy that Cronin was dead. He wasn't in the humour of talking to the cops.
—"No sign of Bowe down on the floor," Grudge said.
—"You know what that lily-livered mammy's boy is like," Mordechai said. "He's far too squeamish to show his face down here. Not when Séamus Cronin's corpse is lying around."

Following Bowe's instruction, those workers who hadn't fled in the initial fright now started to leave. Levy and Galmount needed little prompting to depart.
—"You heard what Bowe said, Grudge. We don't have to come back till two. I'm going to go over to the Tourist District, have a ramble and grab some lunch. Do you fancy tagging along?"
—"Thanks but no thanks, Mord."
The casino had opened in his mind and like Neil Young in a basement he felt like getting high. The lights were flashing; all the sevens.
He could scamper back to the rathole, smoke some spliff, get high, daydream, sober up, and still be in a fit state to show up at two. Of course, it was a reckless plan and one that could easily go awry. What if he couldn't sober up in time? Coming in stoned to the coffin factory would be the last straw for his employers and would see him carted off for a dose of corrective thinking. But he was seized by an overwhelming compulsion and all his misgivings about it were swept aside by the strength of his urge.
—"Gonna head back home and catch up on some reading," he lied.
—"Fair enough, bookworm," Mordechai said. "What a morning, though. Poor Cronin. I know you didn't like the fucker but nobody deserves to die like that. Talk about a freak accident."
—"It looks like more than an accident to me. There's something fishy about it, Mord. But anyway, I'm off home. I'll talk to you later."
Grudge left the factory. He hopped on the first tram that came along. The intensity of his drug craving burgeoned. He was in the grip of a fever that a large part of him despised. Nestling into his seat, he consoled himself with the thought that the gaps between his drugging were getting ever longer. Surely that was a good thing in itself?
The carriage was half full with a motley crew of the elderly, the insane, the sick and the idle. Grudge kept his eyes stuck to the floor: *Think, Think, Think*, as the slogan went.
He made a vow to himself to get back on the straight and narrow once this latest smoke was finished. He believed he was now in the process of winding down his drug habit. Though his thoughts were the rationalisations of an addict, Grudge couldn't see it like that.

The temperature in the tram soared suddenly. He snapped out of his reverie and looked around at the ne'er-do-wells hanging thereabouts. To his amazement the stranger from earlier in the factory—the tall, priestly, handsome man—was sitting directly opposite him. It was like the guy had appeared from nowhere. He frightened Grudge. The stranger gave him the same deep look he'd given him in *Wormwood.*
—"Do I know you from somewhere?" Grudge asked, despite his fear. "You were at *Wormwood* earlier."
The stranger's eyes widened, his bushy eyebrows lifted and a broad smile flooded his face. He did not answer however and just kept staring at Grudge, who felt compelled to ask further.
—"Do you work at *Wormwood*? What were you doing there today?"
Still the man said nothing. Grudge went on.
—"My name is Grudge Galmount. I work at the coffin factory. There was a death there this morning. An accident they say."
At last a response came.
—"Oh that was no accident, Grudge," the stranger said.
The man addressed Grudge like they were old friends.
The rest of the passengers in the carriage—six souls or so—now sprang to life as though on cue at the sound of the stranger's voice. This ragbag of the old, mad, ill and malingering was all ears.
—"That man, Cronin," the stranger continued. "He bullied you for several years, Grudge."
Grudge was gobsmacked that the guy knew these details. He played it cool though and said simply.
—"We didn't exactly see eye to eye."
One of the newly attentive passengers—an elderly man not unlike a goblin—harrumphed at Grudge's tactful understatement.
—"Sally is a very beautiful girl in body and mind," the man said apropos of nothing.
It startled Grudge to hear this creep bring up Sally but his tongue was tied and he could only listen.
—"She is exactly the kind of girl who follows me."
—"Who are you?" Grudge managed to say.
—"My name is Puck Hellson," the stranger said. "There is one coming after me. I am not fit to unzip his flies."
At this remark, the six passengers chuckled. Grudge was mystified.
—"I'm not exactly sure what you're getting at, Mr Hellson," he said.

He was beginning to feel outnumbered. He was on edge. It looked like the passengers were travelling with Hellson. Puck and his entourage might be a force to be reckoned with. Grudge thought it best not to upset them. He sensed that the situation could turn nasty in an instant. He opted to let the man speak and to listen politely.
—"Whatever you want, Grudge," Hellson said, his blue eyes burning a hole in Galmount's soul. "You can have it. He will give it to you. He will make your enemies a footstool for your tired feet."
—"Hear, hear," the entourage chimed in.
—"The only thing you must do, Grudge, is what he asks."
With these words Hellson finished his speech, put his hands together as though in prayer and stared at Grudge.
Grudge was taken aback by the biblical language. He pictured Cronin's severed dome looking so piteous on the factory floor. Fear, confusion, anger, even; all these feelings filled him.
—"Who is *he*? What are you talking about?" he found himself shouting at Hellson.
But it was too late for an answer. The tram pulled into the Profane District, two stops from Lie and, without another word, Hellson and his ghouls got off. Alone in the carriage, Grudge felt defiled.

***

Following her night of passion with Grudge, Sally arrived home to some good news. It came from her mother the moment she walked in the door of the apartment.
—"Your article about the murders just got a mention on the state news!" Mrs Popplewell said.
—"Are you serious, Mam?"
—"I've never been more serious in my life. Your father's been on from work. He was called into the boss's office. He was worried. No one likes to be called into the office. Anyway, the boss just wanted to tell him he'd heard about you on the morning bulletin. Dad was so proud."
—"But what did they say, Mam? Why was my article mentioned?"
—"Well, I was sitting in the living room, your father was gone and I had just made myself a cup of tea and turned on the news to hear the latest as I always do at that time of the morning."
—"Okay, Mam. Tell me but don't turn it into a novel."

—"I see, I see," she said, getting a bit flustered. She knew she could be longwinded at times. "There was an item about the murders. Party bosses were said to be concerned over the lack of progress in solving them. Then the newscaster namechecked Sally Popplewell and her article in *The Inquisitor*!"
Jane Popplewell was beaming by now; her pride in her daughter boundless.
—"But what did it actually say?"
—"We can look back at it online in a minute, Sally. The gist of it was that the Politburo is pleased with the quality of your writing and research. They have decreed that all citizens are to read it posthaste in the hope that it will help to solve the crimes!"
Mrs P was cock-a-hoop.
—"Jesus, Mam, that's fantastic news. I had a good feeling about the article the moment I started writing it. Even when I came up against obstacles, I'm so glad I persevered. Remember I kept saying to you: this could be my big break? Well, it really could. I'll go get my laptop. I want to see this bulletin."
She scampered off to her bedroom and a moment later came back, laptop in hand, smiling like a lottery winner who's just got the all clear on his prostate into the bargain. Mother and daughter sat on the sofa giggling like a pair of schoolgirls playing truant in a pool hall as they waited for the computer to boot up. The machine came to life. With the artistry of a ballerina, Sally summoned the news show on a rerun. They watched it again with broad smiles.
—"The Politburo," the newsreader intoned. "Is heartened and impressed by the efforts of one loyal citizen, Sally Popplewell of the Truth District, to shine a light on these dark events."
Jesus, Sally thought, this is almost hagiographic. No wonder Dad was called into the office. Jeff Kern had told her it might go like this if she worked hard. She was so glad now she had done what he told her and put in all that research and read and reread and edited and altered bits here and there and eventually hammered out the article into the absolute best she was capable of. For here she was on the national news being praised for her writing by no less than the Politburo itself! It was hard to credit, yet it was true. The evidence was before her eyes in high definition on the laptop's screen.
Her mother tickled her in the ribs.

—"My daughter, the journalist," she said. "You're going all the way, Sally, to the toppermost of the poppermost!"
—"I love the way you believe in me, Mam."
Sally dared to believe her career was about to take off. She was ready to soar. She would contact Jeff Kern this minute to thank him for his help.
—"Have you had breakfast?" Mam asked
—"No, actually."
—"I'll make you a nice fry," she said, and headed to the kitchen.
Sally took out her phone and called Kern. He was at his desk, his ear to the ground as ever, listening for a juicy story.
—"Hi, it's Sally Popplewell."
—"Sally, my protégé! I was just about to call you. I heard you mentioned on the news. It doesn't stop there. There've been some amazing developments on foot of your article. The powers that be are really taking notice."
—"Wow, Mr Kern. It's thanks to you that I wrote it at all. I can't believe I was mentioned on the news. What do you mean by amazing developments?"
—"Well, Sally, it's happening on several fronts this morning and it's not even ten o'clock."
—"Go on."
—"For one thing the office of Standing Committee member General O'Flaherty telephoned after the broadcast and asked if you would come to Government Buildings with a view to writing a puff piece on the Politburo."
—"Are you serious?" Sally said. "That's incredible."
—"I'm serious as cancer, dear. You'll be heading to Centaur Street shortly to meet party bigwigs and paint gushing pen portraits of them."
Sally sank into the sofa in a swoon of her own good luck.
—"And it doesn't end there," Kern continued. "I hope you're sitting comfortably?"
—"I've just flopped into the sofa."
—"Okay," he said. "It's like this: your article has sparked interest in Freeland. I received a call from Clement Topcliffe the editor of *Money* magazine in Town Island City. He was so impressed by your piece he suggested you travel to their offices and spend a week working on crime stories. Town Island throws up plenty of murders

every year. This is a huge break for you, Sally. The way your article reached Topcliffe it's viral. He wants you to travel the week after next. They'll put you up in a nice apartment. I said it shouldn't be a problem. You're flavour of the month with the Politburo. Travel permission and a visa can all be sorted quickly."
Sally was speechless. Luck came not in single spies but battalions.
—"I'm going to need a couple of hours to take this in," she said. "To be honest I'm in shock. You always said there was a lot riding on my article. But I didn't realise how much. My mother's making me breakfast. Can I call you back later this afternoon?"
—"Of course you can. I'm very proud of you, Sally. This is your time. Now off you go and enjoy your breakfast."
The call ended. Sally's face beamed. Freeland! These were the kind of breaks young writers dreamt of. She couldn't wait to tell Grudge.
Mother reappeared.
—"I've breakfast ready in the kitchen, dear. Come and eat. Was that Mr Kern on the phone?"
—"It was. And wait till you hear what he told me!"
They waltzed to the kitchen still excited like those pool hall schoolgirls.

***

In his rathole lair on the rickety bed Grudge rolled a joint and worried about several things at once: firstly, Puck Hellson, the man on the tram, had rattled him with his enigmatic and sinister words. The ghouls who travelled with Hellson spooked him, too.
Secondly, there was the phone call he had received from Beatrice and the messy business of her coming to Bludgeon in a week's time.
Thirdly, Grudge was traumatised by the events in *Wormwood* that morning when he'd seen the decapitated head of Séamus Cronin on the factory floor. As far as Grudge was concerned, Hellson's presence in the building at the same time as Cronin's death was a sign of dark forces at play. While he had always hated Cronin, the violence of his death sent Grudge's anxiety levels soaring.
All these worries plagued him as he put the freshly rolled joint to his lips. He was banking on the drug to calm him down.
He took several deep drags in quick succession and felt Le Blanc's knockout hash seize him again. He finished the joint and threw it in the ashtray, lay back his head and let his mind drift.

At first his daydreams were pleasant and he was glad to be rid of his anxieties. But his addled psyche soon brought him to nightmarish ground. High as the proverbial kite, his imagination lurched to a dark, hellish spot where hope was gone. He became convinced that his newfound relationship with Sally was doomed. Masochism and pessimism had the upper hand with him. The drug's power strengthened these emotions. Thinking it might help things he sat up and rolled another one. It only made matters worse. He went to the kitchenette and demolished an entire packet of chocolate biscuits he was lucky enough to have in his press. Then he lay on the bed again with his racing mind chockfull of worries and bliss. He lost all track of time and embarked on a bout of wild reverie. When he eventually snapped out of it and looked at the clock it was half past two. Jesus Christ, he thought, I'm late!

***

While Galmount wrestled with his demons indoors, out on the streets Git Malone's day was going downhill fast. As was his wont, he had left the methadone clinic on Worse Street with a large dose of synthetic heroin inside him to set him up for the day. In his mind it was a normal morning.

As the drug took hold he started to feel stable again. He buzzed nicely. There had been trouble in the shelter the night before and his sleep was disturbed. A group of homeless young men had arrived late to the door and following some debate with the night porter and several other staff the boisterous fellows were granted admittance. High when they arrived, they spent the rest of the night getting even higher. The commotion they caused brought staff to their room, the burliest of whom—Alonso and Kieron—threatened them with immediate eviction if they did not pipe down, which they did when they saw the size of Alonso and Kieron. However, the part of the night that really got to Git and caused him the most stress and the biggest loss of sleep was when one of the buckos crossed the landing to take a leak and spotted Git trying to sleep, sitting upright in his wheelchair with his head tilted to the side. The stoned lout considered the sight of Git to be absolutely hilarious.

—"Check out the freaky cripple in the chair," he told his mates.

They all came to gawp; laughter ensued. Poor Git was mortified, and obviously couldn't run away. His night was ruined by becoming a freakish exhibit.
So it was with great relief that he wheeled himself onto Worse Street, his methadone taking effect and his troubles melting like lemon drops. He headed back along Domina, hit the boardwalk for his pills, before ending up in the Tourist District tapping outside a convenience store. He spent the guts of two hours watching his Styrofoam cup fill with goldmarks.
Following their encounter with Grudge on the tram, Puck Hellson and his creepy cadre had sneaked around the Profane District for a spell until they felt like a change. They came now like raptors in formation—Puck leading the procession—along the same street where Git chased alms.
For his part, and he didn't know where it came from, Git's mood began to alter for the worse. It was like the methadone had stopped working, and what had begun as a groovy high a couple of hours earlier now turned to a dreadful downer. His favourite pills which he'd been swallowing all morning had no effect either.
He could only liken it to a similar experience he'd had a couple of days before, also in the Tourist District. Then, in what he subsequently put down to a dastardly variant of delirium tremens, he had felt like his life was about to end and that Satan himself was coming to destroy him. The feeling had got so bad that he'd latched onto a passing stranger believing the man was some kind of angel who could protect him.
The man/angel had simply said: "You'll be fine, mate, go easy on the drugs", but it seemed to work and Git had felt better immediately.
Now, sadly, Grudge Galmount was nowhere near Git, as noon rolled round and malaise swamped him.
Puck and the others moved along the footpath, a flock of fearsome fiends. Orders issued silently, everything communicated and understood without the need for words. Eye contact and telepathy were enough. It was well understood that the invalid was the target; his days were numbered and today was his final one.
Git's last donor passed and threw chump change into his cup. The paltriness of the donation was a fitting end to Git's small life on the streets.

He hoped his ill feeling would pass quickly. *This Too Shall Pass*, he remembered, the slogan from the meetings he'd attended from time to time at the behest of a parole officer. Early childhood memories flooded his head and then like a movie his teenage years and his first steps into adulthood flashed before him. He had a moment of shocking clarity and knew that his addictions had all been driven by self-centredness above anything else.

God, he felt awful! He thought it might be a side effect of the Clozaril. That feeling of low level anxiety that plagued him every day of his life was now ramped up to a brute terror.

Still, unbeknownst to Git, the flock moved forward.

Fifteen years before when Git was eighteen and still in possession of his legs, he had staged a daring robbery of a public house that netted him a large sum of money and enabled him to feed his habit for many months thereafter. Unfortunately for Git, in the course of the robbery, the son of the landlord was shot dead by the coked-up young thug that was Git Malone at the time. Killing the landlord's son marked Git's card.

From that throne in a far kingdom, the King of Hell, the Prince of the Night, had singled out the landlord's son for greatness in the shadow realm. Git's murdering of the son put paid to these malevolent plans. Git's demise was prolonged, designed to inflict maximum pain. A decade back he'd lost his legs when they went gangrenous from injecting heroin. His career as a criminal was cut short. With no money he descended into a life of begging and drugging. Today was the culmination of a long-drawn-out plan of vengeance.

Puck and the flock drew near.

They were twenty feet away by the time he spotted them and he knew instinctively that they were the reason he felt so bad. They were coming for him. Deep down he'd always known they would. He was almost resigned to the fact.

Their leader, a tall man with a devil's grin, looked straight at him. Git wanted to cry but was unable to do even that. He sat frozen with a fear in his gut that no human should ever have to feel.

Git's final moments would be swift. The fiendish flock knew exactly what they had to do. Reaching the cripple they swooped. There was a hint of Munch's *The Scream* to the look on Git's face. He was lifted from his chair, his cigarettes and pills leaving his pockets like passengers fleeing a doomed train. A taloned hand covered his

mouth to silence his cries. Puck Hellson did not partake in the attack itself. He stood watch, commanding the commotion with his eyes. His foot soldiers devoured Git Malone like a wolf pack scrapping over a kill. Out came his eyeballs, plucked violently, clumps of his hair, too, along with most of his teeth. Somebody or something mustered the strength to penetrate his chest cavity and reach under his ribcage to tear out his heart. He was dead within two minutes. The destroyed stump of his body was then discarded back into his chair and the cadre and Puck Hellson moved on; their job done with ruthless efficiency.
For an hour or two it was as though Git (what remained of him) was invisible. No passers-by paid any heed to his sorry corpse, slumped like a sack of offal in his wheelchair. Eventually a young girl on an errand to the store had her eyes opened to the dreadful scene. She screamed like the banshee. People came running and the authorities were alerted.
Grudge Galmount hurried past bleary-eyed, fretting and late. He looked at his second dead body of the day. He hardly recognised Git but the clothes and the chair were the same. That's the beggar who wanted me to save him, he thought, and he grew afraid.

Chapter 7

Beatrice Marcos pottered around her mother's apartment in Madrid. Watering plants out on the balcony she observed several marucas in conversation at the door of an apartment complex opposite. Maruca was Spanish slang for an embittered, gossipy, wrinkled, poisonous, shrewish crone. Beatrice saw the marucas most days and was adamant she would not end up as one. Twenty-seven years old, an only child, with a string of university qualifications, she nevertheless found it difficult to find work and could only do so for periods of weeks at a time. The Spanish economy was pretty much on the ropes and had been for years. Fortunately, her widowed mother was not short of money. Papa Marcos had fixed his will that mother and daughter were comfortable.
Beatrice was keen to work and had no intention of living idly off an inheritance. Invariably, the work she did find was beneath her skill level but she took it if only to be doing something. She was never afraid to roll up her sleeves and turn her hands to any task. She

believed in the dignity of work: menial restaurant jobs, getting down and dirty as a cleaner, door to door tedious legwork selling household appliances from catalogues or insurance policies or cable television subscriptions. Each year the Spanish government devised a national survey to be conducted and Beatrice would sign up as a state employee and travel the barrios of Madrid gathering data from citizens and being paid peanuts in the process.
Although extremely outgoing and sociable by nature, she was also a diligent and studious girl when need be. For the past few months she had knuckled down and gained herself a qualification in journalism. As she told Grudge on the phone, she was now a journalist.
She was on a high at having landed a writing gig in Runway Four—having spent six months there as a coffee shop waitress, going back as a journalist would be a real step up. She was thankful to her mum for encouraging her to travel. It had introduced her to the weird and unforgettable world of R4.
It was during her first stint there that she had fallen for the charms of Grudge Galmount, smitten one day serving him a coffee. She loved the boy but, *Dios mio*, such problems! In time, his struggles with drink and drugs drove her back to Madrid.
She could not forget him, however, and was bent on rekindling their spark. The journalistic course and the writing gig were a means to that end.
She had detected a note of hesitancy in his voice this morning. It was quite a change from the last time they'd spoken on the phone. It was some weeks ago but on that occasion he had pleaded with her to come back to Bludgeon.
Now, sitting in the living room of the apartment, eating an apple, with the street sounds floating in from outside, she put Grudge's hesitancy down to tiredness, it being early when she phoned and he was not a morning person.
She was sure that when she spoke to him later he would be more responsive. She worried at times that Grudge might have another girl in his life. It would be perfectly understandable. He was a good-looking guy. Any number of girls would be interested in him. But what could she do? She had fled back to Madrid when she could no longer deal with his behaviour. She missed him terribly, though, and was determined to reunite with him and shove any other girls out of the picture when she did.

She finished her apple and put it in the bin by the balcony window, and pottered still. She was not interested in watching television today. She liked the news channels but had watched so much lately while doing her course that she needed a break. Ditto the internet. It was a research tool she had to put aside for a spell.
She was suffering a bit from information overload and needed to stay unplugged and disengaged for the sake of her mental health. Otherwise she felt good and was quite content to lounge indoors. The curtains fluttered in the light breeze and the warm air of Madrid from the open balcony door kissed her face. It was a great relief to have finished the journalism course. There had been study days when the apartment felt like a prison. She was free of that feeling now and soon to be on her way to Runway Four as a genuine journalist. She planned to spend the next couple of days visiting friends and saying her goodbyes. She could be gone for a quite a while if things went the way she planned. Her self-esteem was soaring, and life was good.
Her mother would be back from the shops shortly and Beatrice looked forward to some Spanish omelette mum had promised to cook.
The apple she'd just eaten had perked up her appetite. She stepped through the balcony door and looked down onto the street to see if her mother was coming yet, but there was no sign. I know what she's like, Beatrice thought, once she gets down to the shops she spends an age chatting with people. I might be waiting a while for that omelette.
Across the street up the road slightly in the direction of the public park she noticed a tall man wearing a conical Asian hat. Even from afar she could tell that he was handsome. Strangely, the hat actually suited him although it was not the kind of headgear you'd expect to see on a Western man in the middle of Madrid.
As she looked over he appeared to smile. He was about twenty feet away. His smile was warm and to Beatrice's surprise he began to cross the street and walk in her direction. She grew alarmed. Her apartment was on the second floor, not high at all. Is he actually coming towards me, she wondered? Then the man waved at her. She guessed that maybe he was signalling to someone else nearby. But that couldn't be. The angle was all wrong. He signalled to her. Puck Hellson—fresh from killing Git Malone.

Bloodlust and death walked with him unseen. Outwardly, he was like nothing more than an eccentric uncle waving to his niece following an absence of seeing her.
A mean-eyed crow landed on the balcony railing and startled Beatrice. A part of her wanted to retreat back inside to the cool and safety of the apartment. The crow turned its head and stared at her. She grew giddy with fear. Something else inside her felt compelled to stay in the stranger's line of sight. It was as though he had rooted her to the spot.
He now stood directly below her balcony—a perverse Romeo to her Juliet.
—"Yes?" she called down to him, mesmerized. "What do you want?"
The street was busy enough. It was a normal working day. Time stood still, though, in this little scene: Beatrice on her balcony and Puck Hellson beneath.
From nowhere others flocked to his side, his cadre of loyal malefactors working for their king. They would do whatever Hellson asked.
Beatrice did not even know why she had questioned the behatted man. She felt like she was losing control of her actions. She still clung to the idea of going back inside, shutting the balcony door, and forgetting all about the goings-on in the street. But that careful side of her could not gain supremacy in her mind. It was like the time she once took LSD and was consumed with fear from a sense of losing control, but had dropped a second tab after an hour nonetheless. Now, perched on her balcony, drawn to this sinister man, that feeling of powerlessness returned with force—as did her fear.
She noticed some six or seven bodies had appeared around "Romeo". What an ugly bunch they were. Her tongue wagged furiously inside her closed mouth. She was seized by an uncontrollable urge to talk. The words came from somewhere else, they were not hers.
—"Wait there," she said. "Let me come down and join you."
A battle raged in her head. One side repulsed by the man in the street and his ugly band of followers. On the other hand she was drawn irresistibly towards him.

She wished her mother would come home. She cursed the fact that she had stepped onto the balcony in the first place. If she hadn't done so she would not be caught up in this drama now.
Hellson spoke.
—"I am Puck Hellson, emissary of the King of Hell."
She heard him loud and clear though he made no effort to shout. His cadre sneered and hissed.
—"You will not join us, Beatrice Marcos," Puck continued, his words piercing her brain. "You have no luck in this world. You love a man who shows no loyalty to us. Your closeness to him has cost you your life."
The hissing of the ghouls reached fever pitch.
Beatrice, rigid with fear, understood all too well.
She leaned forward on the railing, hoping to plead for mercy. But just as she couldn't stop her tongue moments earlier, now her footing defied her. She toppled over and hit the street. Her skull cracked. Death was instant.
Puck Hellson and his crew flew to another world.
Beatrice's mother arrived. Dropping her groceries, she screamed.
—"My daughter, my beautiful daughter!"
Six eggs in a carton became a mess of shell and goo.

***

It was just after three when Grudge re-entered the doors of *Wormwood* for the second time that day. Late and dishevelled, coming down hard from his high, the man was a mess.
He punched the clock and heard the shrill sound it made when a worker was late. The Shouting Judge from Nazi Germany came to mind. In R4 there were tyrants even in the machines.
He ran past security, startling the porter who lifted his eyes from his tablet tabloid and raised them further to Heaven at the sight of Grudge Galmount, the loser/loner, darting by.
That fellow's in a lot of trouble, the porter thought, carrying on like that he's going to bring a whole bucket of shit down upon his head.
With Grudge out of his sight, the man—a stalwart prole—returned to his reading: the gossip, tits and football of the gutter press.
Poor Grudge, he was his own worst enemy. Everyone else had obeyed Noel Bowe and returned promptly at two p.m. They were

busy working. The messy matter of Cronin's corpse was swept away.
Grudge burst on the scene, breathless and red-eyed, and attempted to blend in; an impossible task considering his condition.
He tried to calm down and take some deep breaths. He could tell it wasn't working, though, from the pounding of his heart inside his chest cavity. Short of breath from running, the effort to breathe deeply made him look demented. Colleagues noticed. He slotted in on the line beside Mordechai and Pole Wallace.
He had his own brand of charisma whether high or sober. Many in the room hoped that this was the start of Galmount's downfall.
He moved around the workstation with the lumbered gait of a drunk walking the line before an audience of nightstick-wielding lawmen. He felt all eyes upon him. The pressure made him act more intoxicated than he actually was.
Watching, too, from her corner desk was Mary Dawn. Her blood boiled at the sight of Grudge. Despite being on his last chance, he was up to his old tricks, showing a blatant disregard for the rules and regulations of *Wormwood.* He was making a holy show of her turning up in that state—and late into the bargain. It could have harmful repercussions for her. After all, she was his line manager and to judge from this performance she could not control him.
Mary was only short of emitting smoke from her ears. She would nail his ass to the cross. This was it. He had just used up his ninth life. There would be no more chances, no more trips to Bowe's office to get Galmount to reform.
She picked up her telephone and dialled Noel's secretary. She just needed final clearance from the boss to undertake her plan. The secretary listened attentively.
—"This is quite serious, Ms. Dawn," she said. "You do know that Galmount will have no comeback? Once he goes for corrective thinking, he's locked into the programme for life."
—"Yes, I'm perfectly aware of that," Mary answered curtly. "But, believe you me, it's what he bloody well deserves. We've been adopting the kid gloves with this bucko for far too long."
As she spoke, hanging Grudge out to dry, Mary felt a frisson of joy in her loins. As well as loathing Grudge for so long, she had lusted after him, too. Crushing him now, ensuring his demise, was proving quite a thrill.

—"Very well, then," the secretary said. "You seem determined. I'll see to it Mr Bowe makes the committal request. It shouldn't take long. He's got plenty of contacts in that department. Expect the police to just sweep in and take him away in a matter of, oh I'd say, half an hour."
—"Excellent," Mary said. "I'll contain him till then. Any problems or hold-ups let me know."
Mary put down the phone, checked her makeup in her pocket mirror, applied a fresh layer of lipstick, licked her lips, got up from her desk, straightened her skirt, and—with the eyes of the workforce upon her—waddled towards Grudge to administer a bollocking.
The factory floor had become a theatre with the Mary and Grudge show as the main act. Productivity would surely slump this afternoon on foot of this performance. It seemed everybody had downed tools and was watching raptly the line manager and her unruly beast.
Grudge was more or less sober at this stage. Coming into *Wormwood* had the effect on him of water to flame. His fire was gone out. In actual fact water to flame was too mild a comparison, the sensation was more like drowning in a bath of vomit. That was how the place affected him. The rules, the (mostly) awful people, the fact he was under the disciplinary cosh more than anyone else, days spent manufacturing receptacles for the dead—those cold final boxes—all these factors combined had been steadily crushing his spirit for months.
He knew he was in big trouble today, and also that almost everybody on the factory floor was looking in his direction, anticipating his next move. He tried to handle his tool correctly and set about creating a new coffin, but his heart simply wasn't in it. Le Blanc's strong dope—he had had so much of it earlier—had opened his eyes to the futility and ridiculousness of his standing in this factory and in the world in general.
By not cooperating with *Wormwood's* rules, he knew he was putting his life in danger. The police wouldn't hesitate to haul him away. But he had to make a stand.
He saw Mary Dawn come into his field of vision. He was crouched by a brass handle doing a passing good impression of a diligent worker. But his rebelliousness was simmering to boiling point and just as Mary reached him he hurled his tool to the ground and cried out.

—"Enough! No more!"
The passing good impression of a diligent worker was over. The real Grudge Galmount stood up, his expression wired, and faced Mary Dawn who stood before him like an angry dog let loose from its kennel.
The room was agog with everybody hoping for a good old scrap culminating in Galmount's departure to Runway Four's own version of Siberia.
—"Grudge Galmount," Mary barked. "What are you doing, throwing your tool on the floor like that? Why aren't you working, and why were you late?"
Mary's fusillade of questions incensed Grudge. He was mad as hell and he wasn't taking it anymore.
—"What am I doing?" he asked, opening wide his arms.
He circled the spot where he stood.
Sensing Grudge was about to go on, Mary tried to gain the upper hand.
—"Yes, Grudge. What are you doing? Don't you remember our visit to Mr Bowe's office? You're under special observation. You have to prove you are a good worker."
—"You know what, Mary? Fuck that!" Grudge exclaimed.
At this, a collective gasp filled the Fabrication Hall. Mary's features warped into a hideous mask. She opened her mouth to speak but Grudge cut across her.
—"I've had it up to here with *Wormwood* and your fucking regulations."
He felt like he was stepping outside his body to watch his physical self vent this rage. He knew he had crossed a line and that by talking thus he was closing a chapter of his life.
The atmosphere in the factory was tense enough as it was. Some muttered darkly that Cronin's death had not been an accident. Everybody was expected to knuckle down and help the company over this rough patch. It certainly wasn't a time to start railing against *Wormwood*. Noel Bowe's connections in the Party were rock solid, and if you crossed him he could see to it you were finished. Grudge knew all this but he wasn't going to hold back. Mary spluttered but failed to actually speak.
Grudge continued despite the danger. He felt strangely liberated.

—"I've given seven years of my life to this place, day in and day out, trudging to my workstation and delivering the best coffins I could make, and, for what? To be treated like a cornered rat, watched over like prey by you Mary Dawn and all the others of my so-called higher-ups and all the fucking surveillance equipment in this godforsaken place, and all the fear spread around here and all the threats of corrective thinking if somebody doesn't toe the line. I'm a young man, I turned up drunk one day, I had a tough childhood, what's my sin? Where's the compassion? Where's the understanding? Instead it's the gun to the head, the over-monitoring. You've labelled me a problem and now you think you're going to solve me. Well, once again I say, *fuck* that!"
Mary's hideous mask slipped. Now she just looked worried. Fearful Grudge might turn physical. There were plenty of objects near to hand that could be used as weapons. She wished the police would get here. Half an hour seemed an eternity.
To her relief two of *Wormwood's* own security showed up and started to placate Grudge. At first he ignored their pleas to calm down, but settled somewhat after a while.
—"Grudge, you're clearly very agitated," Mary said, as though addressing a dementia sufferer.
She turned and spoke to the whole floor.
—"Everybody, back to work immediately. This is not a show. Galmount isn't well. The company is dealing with it. Now get on with what you're doing!"
The obedient drones did what they were told.
The security porters spoke softly to Grudge—they actually liked him—and told him to take it easy and not make it hard on himself. They knew his fate was bleak. The police were coming. In his heart Grudge knew it, too. That's why the steam had gone out of his rant when he saw the porters appear. They were the precursors to his hellish destiny, the lesser angels so to speak.
—"Okay, okay, guys," Grudge said, waving them away from his elbows and ears. "I hear you, I am *calmed* down."
—"Galmount," Mary said, maintaining her authority. "You'll soon find out what a mistake you've made by acting like this today. Your display has most definitely been noted."

Grudge knew what she meant. His *Wormwood* days were over. He was going away to camp. The agents of the state would be here any minute. He stood there breathing slowly, keeping his courage up.
He said nothing further to Mary. The drones hammered away at their workstations. He'd given them enough scandal to keep them going for a year.
Presently, a pair of police appeared full of purpose and menace. They flashed their badges at Mary and did their best to instil fear in Grudge. It worked for, suddenly, he was gripped with terror. The workers at their caskets stole glances in his direction and thanked their lucky stars it wasn't them in his shoes.
Without further ado, the police manhandled Grudge and hauled him away.

Chapter 8

A week later Sally was at home preparing for her audience with the Party bigwigs up in Centaur Street. For several nights beforehand she'd been laying the groundwork, staying up late reading reams of information on the Politburo, the Standing Committee, Chairman Young, the foundation of the state, and the laws of Runway Four. She would have liked more internet access to contextualize things, but she'd made do with what she had. She was ready to go up there today and give it her all, ask the right questions (nothing too probing), and write the puff piece the powers that be wanted. She was unhappy about the craven tone she would have to adopt, but Jeff Kern, who'd been on the phone to her several times throughout the week, assured her that a forelock-tugging attitude was a necessary step on her road to greatness. Kern the old radical quoted an ancient poet to her, a man who had never gone out of fashion, saying she must *"try to change the system from within"*. She was, he said, her very own sleeper cell of one and was being afforded, on the strength of her talent, unprecedented access to those at the top. "Use your time well, Sally. Ingratiate yourself with them and the world is your oyster. Afterwards, when it comes to writing the piece just let your talent shine. God knows you have enough of it."
Kern said such nice things.
The obsequiousness she would have to display towards the Party bosses bothered her as she gathered up her things and set about

saying goodbye to her mother. Thanks to Mam, every neighbour in the block knew of Sally's good fortune and the important business she was embarking on. Sally reasoned with herself that it was best to get the piece written no matter how craven its tone if it meant getting access to Centaur Street. The insights she would gain into what goes on up there were invaluable and would help in the writing of future (less glowing) work. Kern was right, she was a sleeper cell of one. Still there was a niggle; actually, a running sore. Mordechai Levy had phoned Sally with the news. Grudge was incarcerated; a victim of the very system Sally was on the brink of eulogising. How was she going to square that particular circle?

***

The past week had been, to put it mildly, difficult for Grudge Galmount.

When the police had dragged him out of *Wormwood*, he was handcuffed and blindfolded and thrown into the back of a prison van on Revenue Road. Once inside he knew he'd entered a particularly fiendish circle of Hell. Initially, he hoped to be left alone to acclimatise as the vehicle wound its way to wherever it was they were taking him—somewhere awful he imagined such as the headquarters of military intelligence. But instead, right from the outset the police were in his face, hitting and spitting at him.

The back of the van contained a bench on one side for the guards, not that Grudge could see a thing—they had royally blinded him with their oh-so tight fold. He stood helpless like a sick man brought to the x-ray room by hospital orderlies. His captors though were infinitely more hostile than anything one might find in a house of medicine.

—"What's happening? Where are you taking me?" Grudge had asked.

One of the guards slapped him hard across the head and told him to shut the fuck up.

The slap brought home his predicament. He stayed silent.

He heard the sound of a creaking metal hinge. His elbow was grabbed and he was pushed forward by the back of his neck.

—"Get in, scum!" the guard barked.

Grudge stumbled into a standing cell, two feet square at most. Designed for maximum punitiveness, it was known in the system as a coffin cell.
The van drove on. Grudge was scared, sore and shocked though not surprised really that this day had come.
He was right about the headquarters of military intelligence. It was the first port of call at journey's end. The HQ was a national processing centre. It fed inmates to prisons up and down the land. After processing, where they'd taken his fingerprints, photographed him and dressed him in austere prison garb, he spent the night in its grim basement. The screams of torture were all around.
The next morning he was brought to another van. He was cuffed and blindfolded once more, and put in a coffin cell again. The van sped up country to a corrective thinking centre. It was hell, and it was where he had been for seven days now.

***

"Beloved, be not ignorant of this one thing, that one day is with the Lord as a thousand years, and a thousand years as one day" 2 Peter 3:8

The throne in the far kingdom: the King of Hell, the Prince of the Night, sits satisfied over the fate of Grudge Galmount, knowing his suffering will be great, sent by coffin cell to a place of no return. The winged beasts sing as Puck Hellson is out in the world—that benighted orb—doing great work. There have been many gruesome deaths. Waves of grief swamp the Earth.
Galmount has dug his own grave. He could have chosen to walk with God but instead fell into snares. A weak-willed man, a slave to his appetites, he's blown any chance of a happy life. The Prince of the Night knows this and his joy is great.
Puck Hellson flits across borders doing evil all the while. His trusty demons aid him. Hellson, though, is not all-powerful. Often, he is thwarted by the Father of Heaven.
The King of Hell is strengthened by humans using their free will. Wicked deeds feed Satan.
In his mind: a worry. Galmount is unique, and although confined there's no saying he won't break his chains.

Puck Hellson must pay a visit. For this is the crux of the matter: the battle has been joined in the soul of that one man. Evil must conquer. The afternoon can last for months. This particular one has dragged on for the guts of a year. Night is approaching and the long sleep is coming.
The winged beasts are in full voice. The Prince focuses on Galmount's suffering.
The afternoon continues. The story continues.

***

Sally had dressed in a smart suit for her trip to Centaur Street. She looked the part of a hotshot reporter. A composite of Connie Chung, Dorothy Lucey and Melissa Lee, and more attractive than all three. Though Grudge's misfortune was never far from her mind, she focused on her image with pride. She would be a professional today. Still, he haunted her; learning—through corrective thinking—the true extent of Young's powers. No matter how grim and nasty life was on the outside, it was nothing compared to the inner workings of R4's penal system.
Sally put on a finishing layer of lipstick in the hall mirror. Her mother stood by, a guard of honour of one. Sally said her goodbye and headed for the elevator. Jane's parting words rang in her ears.
—"I love you, Sally. Your father and I are so proud!"
This is the big one, Sally thought. The elevator arrived. Other tenants were already inside. They seemed to be smiling at her. She looked straight ahead thinking of Grudge first and foremost.

***

Jett Popplewell's line of work was totally unsuited to his intellectual ability, but such were the breaks in Runway Four. His days were spent cleaning the bloodied drains in a chicken slaughterhouse. His beloved girls, Jane and Sally, motivated him to keep going when work was a burden. No two people meant more to him and he often found himself buoyed up by the thought of them whilst down on his knees scrubbing the fowl blood. The other thing that got him through this repulsive labour was his faith in God. The fact that faith in God was outlawed did not deter Jett in the least—as it happened, the proscription of religion emboldened him all the more to pray and believe.

The only thing differentiating Sally's father from a serf of old hunched over his hoe in a rocky field was the fact that he did not wear an ankle chain.
He had been employed in the factory for over twenty years. He'd married Jane, she'd got pregnant straightaway, and suddenly they had a young baby to feed. Jane worked at her sewing and sold dresses and did repairs. The junta were consolidating their power base in R4 at the time and the luxury of becoming a rebel was not an option for Jett. He took whatever measly menial job he could find—which happened to be in the slaughterhouse—and he set about raising his girl and loving his wife selflessly.
All through the past twenty years as Sally matured into a beautiful young woman, he had prayed for a better life for her. He knew that the child of proles would always be at a disadvantage when it came to finding a career. But she seemed to be doing just that. Thank Jesus, he thought, as he hunkered down scouring a latrine that was essentially a river of chicken blood. Today, her trip to Centaur Street, was the culmination of everything she had worked for. Popplewell's colleagues knew all about his daughter's success. Word got around quick.
He realised how lucky she'd been in meeting that fellow Kern. He had opened doors for her.
This morning—well before Jane or Sally stirred—Jett was up. His long shifts began early. It didn't bother him. He leapt out of bed like a lark. He'd lifted up the floorboard and retrieved his Bible. He leafed through the thin pages, pausing at certain passages. The book never failed to comfort him; to inspire him in adversity.
In the cold dawn, he'd touched it reverently and murmured its weighty words. He'd prayed for Sally. Her task was great.
Whenever success comes for anybody in this world, or, in Jett's case, success by association, there is always at least one—and often dozens—of begrudgers, riddled with jealousy, who will try to denigrate that success any way they can. The slaughterhouse contained many such types, bitter about the toughness and futility of their lives. They couldn't bear to see Jett Popplewell so happy at the lift his daughter's career was taking of late. This is the guy who cleans the drains, for fuck's sake, the lowest of the low.
Sure enough, a bunch of these bitter wretches had got together the previous night and placed several shards of glass in a drain

Popplewell cleaned. People really were that awful. Jealousy is a poison that sickens the heart.
The plotters busied themselves with other things—wringing chickens' necks, plucking feathers, gutting birds—but watched all the while for him to enter the drain. The general consensus among the wretches was that Popplewell was getting above his station. They hated to see Sally's ascent. She'd been named on TV, publicized in print, and was clearly going places. To them, Jett would always be, and should always be, a little man.
The day's second batch of fowl entered the production line. Intensively reared, these birds were plump and scared. To save money, the animals were not stunned before slaughtering. The men and women of the plant set to work. Many birds died in quick succession. Blood flowed. The wretches waited for the proud dad to get hurt.
He was up above the drain in great form, at one with his Lord and delighted about his daughter. He knew he was an intelligent man doing a job that was beneath him. However, he had long ago reconciled himself to this fact.
He could see the drain filling quickly with the spilled blood of the birds and knew that he would have to jump in pretty soon.
It was then that a hot young angel showed up. "She" looked about nineteen, a seraph of delightful proportions, not seen by anyone except Sally's dad. She spoke to him telepathically. He would remember none of it later—his hard drive wiped clean. That's how these higher beings roll.
Do not go into the drain, she told him. Plead illness. Say you need some water and to get off your feet for a few minutes, that you're feeling faint.
He did just that. On autopilot, like an activated sleeper in a spy cell, he proceeded to the foreman and said he felt unwell. He was excused and went off to the changing room to lie down. The wretches were thwarted. In fact they were reduced to taking remedial action, fishing out the shards with rubber gloved-hands before another cleaner jumped in. Saved by an angel; Jett would never know.

***

Freeland's most famous city—Town Island City—with its skyscrapers and its yellow cabs; its teeming streets of harried

pedestrians; its hotdog stands; its homeless war vets begging for change; the smell of burning flesh from those same meat stands; the stairways down to the subway on every street corner; the crush of commuters.
Today, a cobalt blue sky burnishes over Town Island.
The magnificent views of that same sky if one looks up between the buildings; the world famous department store opened in 1902; the constant honking of car horns; the Indian shops; the Chinese shops; the black men on the corner at Barge Street trying to entice passersby to buy counterfeit goods; the infinite number of restaurants from the most basic to haute cuisine; the ever present tourists from out of town and abroad; the constant photographing and filming of the skyscrapers and the street scenes and the famous landmarks by those same tourists; the public parks; the squirrels; the cops; the commuter ferry travelling from one borough to the next, commandeered by visitors as a cheap and cheerful means to view the downtown cityscape and the bay; the street performers—*"the jugglers and the clowns"*—the street poets, street artists, penniless creative types and buskers; the panhandlers on the subway, shuffling through the carriages spinning sob stories; the occasional musician who gets on board and plays a tune for chump change.
Those famous landmarks: the Fanning Building—a Gothic apartment complex from 1880—outside which its famous resident, the world-renowned wizard Winston Stanley, was shot dead; Stanley was returning from a séance downtown when it happened. Even to this day devotees come to pay homage to their dead idol.
Naught Ground: site of the world's most spectacular terrorist attack 8/10.
The Suspension Bridge, with its towers recognizable the world over.
Brimful of boats, Rock River, wider and purer than the River Plur.
The Domain Building, so long the tallest in the world, till beaten into second by a monstrous carbuncle in the Middle East. George Harrison ascended it in 1963 and shot 8 mm footage from the top.
The Domain Building is in midtown, close to the action. Puck Hellson has been hanging around it a lot of late. He has hatred in his heart, and a lust to devour the innocent.

***

Lydia Morten got word quickly that her tenant Galmount had been hauled away to jail. The police had called to her home and told her. They requested access to Galmount's flat informing Lydia that they were impounding Grudge's earthly chattels. They might well prove evidential, the good cop of a good cop/bad cop routine had explained to Lydia as he stood in the sumptuous hallway of her mansion. She informed the cop that it was her boyfriend Conan who looked after her flats and he would meet them there the next day and furnish them with Grudge's things.

Lydia explained everything to her lapdog when he arrived home and off he went the following morning to meet the police. They arrived, five of them, burly and menacing, conveying an air of torturers. Conan showed them the flat and they got on with it quickly. They found nothing incriminating as they took away Galmount's stuff. It would be held in storage for a spell and then destroyed. It was not envisaged that Grudge would ever see the light of day again. He was a nuisance to be dealt with forcibly by the State.

The flat was to be let out again. Lydia left it in Conan's hands to spruce it up, which was quite an exaggeration considering she specialized in dives.

Conan was fine about it. After all this was the kind of handyman work that he excelled at. He appraised the rathole and decided that a lick of paint and a sweep of the carpet would do the trick.

He also had a private idea for the place between tenancies.

Lydia kept a number of dogs. It wasn't so much she was an animal lover, but she thought it did her image good to be seen caring for pets. Truth to tell she didn't care for them at all and had the help tend to the curs' needs. It was enough for her to be seen in public stroking a Pekinese. Not to mention stroking Conan for the benefit of the gossip columnists.

Anyway, Conan had a particular perversion that nobody knew about: a taste for bestiality. Lately, he had taken a shine to one of Lydia's Pekinese.

With the rathole vacant he saw it as a perfect chance to get to know the dog better.

He drove to Rodent Street in the 4x4 with the animal on the backseat in a basket. The coast was clear—even Ann-Marie was nowhere to be seen having gone for her weekly grocery shop—and Conan smuggled the Pekinese into the cleared out rathole. Once inside he wasted no time undressing himself. He lay the dog face down on the rickety bed and after some initial foreplay he tried to insert his penis into the brute's anus. He had some trouble achieving his aim. How the dog wriggled! But finally he did. Then, Lydia walked in. She had decided on a whim to swing by and had hopped into the runaround. The shock nearly killed her. She and Conan as an item ended right there.

***

The elevator hit the ground and Sally dashed into the street excited and ready. She was a little unsettled that her mother seemed to have told all the neighbours about her business. Then again if my aim is to be on the national news, she thought, I'd better get used to it.
Jeff Kern had told her to take a cab and charge him for the expense. "It's one of the perks of the job, Sally," he'd laughed. She was chuffed with the chance to ride in style. Cabs were generally the preserve of Party officials and those on the top tier.
She stood on the street corner, stuck out her hand and hailed one.
—"Where to, lady?" the driver asked, a swarthy type who turned his radio down when she got in. His aural diet consisted entirely of news and military marching music.
—"Take me to Centaur Street. Government Buildings."
The cab moved off and Sally sat back checking her phone, and preparing questions in her head.
Seeing his passenger didn't want to talk, the driver turned up the radio. The sound of a rousing march came forth.
They reached the imposing gates of Government Buildings. The cabbie lowered the radio once more and turned in his seat to take his fare. He scrutinized Sally's face.
—"I know you, don't I? You're a writer?"
—"I'm a journalist," Sally said. "I'm freelance."
—"That's it," the cabbie said. "Now I know. My wife was reading your article last night in bed: the one about the murders."
—"That's me alright," Sally said, and she thrust the fare at the driver, anxious to get away, yet thankful Kern had used a good photo of her along with the article.
—"Thank you," he said. "And very nice to meet you. You are going to be famous!"

Sally got out of the vehicle frazzled by the man's enthusiasm, yet thinking if that's the price of fame, some questions from Joe Public, it's not too much to pay.

Chapter 9

She stood outside Government Buildings on the cusp of great things. She told the sentry in the box her name and walked unmolested into the complex.
She made her way past several more checkpoints to what she took to be the *sanctum sanctorum.*
There a soldier greeted her and having verified her credentials—this was about the seventh check she'd gone through—he released the large bolt by hitting an electronic code and allowed her enter the Great Hall.
Chairman Young was not meeting Sally but had sent two of his key generals—O'Flaherty and Scully—to deputize. The Chairman was interested keenly in the meeting and wanted a full report on it once it was over. The young lady, Popplewell, had caught the Politburo's eye and Young had almost to draw straws to select the two generals he'd sent to meet her.
Generals O'Flaherty and Scully sat in the Great Hall on throne-like chairs large enough for their ample rears. They were dressed in full military uniform. The hotshot young reporter would be arriving shortly and a servant had set out a chair for her, too. A teapot, china teacups and fresh scones lay on a table beside the chairs. Large versions of R4's flag—a black jackboot on a white background—along with flattering portraits of Chairman Young adorned the hall. The servant retreated and the two generals were left alone in the echoic room awaiting Sally.
—"She's a good looking one this," General O'Flaherty said. "She had better make sure Young doesn't take a shine."
—"She might never leave Government Buildings again if that's the case," General Scully laughed.
Chairman Young was known to keep sex slaves in the basement of the complex.
After some minutes the massive doors of the hall opened and Sally Popplewell made her entrance. She looked terrific, a woman truly on the up.

The generals straightened in their seats, impelled to do so by Sally's stage presence. Her heels clicked on the tiled floor.
She reached them smiling. The men stood to greet her, unusual for ones so powerful.
—"Good morning, Ms. Popplewell," General Scully said. "Welcome to the Great Hall."
—"Yes, welcome, young lady," General O'Flaherty added. "I'm sure you realize how privileged you are to be granted this interview at the behest of Chairman Young. We trust you will use your time here with us wisely and productively."
She shook hands with both men.
—"Thank you, noble generals. I'm so honoured to have been invited here today. I fully appreciate the chance given me to enter Government Buildings and write about the Politburo."
The generals nodded. Despite their power and stature, they found themselves listening deferentially to Sally. She had that effect on people. Both O'Flaherty and Scully thought how attractive she looked and how likely it was that Chairman Young would want to bed her. Yet they also felt—and this was the strange part—that this girl with the authoritative air would not become just another victim of the licentious Young.
—"Let us sit," O'Flaherty said, indicating the chair provided for Sally. "These scones and this tea will fortify us. Then we can talk."
—"Talk in great detail," Scully added. "The Politburo is anxious to be open with its citizens."
Sally laughed inwardly at Scully's comment knowing how secretive the Politburo was and the contempt it had for the people. Still, she would play them at their own game. Pretend to swallow all the crap they fed her. Not to mention swallowing the delicious scones, the scent of which reached her nostrils as she took her seat.
She buttered one, as did the generals, and poured tea for the three of them. The scone tasted heavenly and it made her think of the gulf between the food the Politburo ate and what the ordinary folk of Runway Four lived on.
At several points around the walls guards stood watch. The security in the place was paranoid. Plainclothes roamed, too. She was reminded again of Grudge. He was constantly on her mind. Locked up and suffering right now as she sat in the Great Hall taking tea with two regime bigwigs. She would have to pull something out of

the bag to help him. Oddly, though, and it felt like a kind of obsessive compulsiveness, a hidden part of her mind took an almost sadistic pleasure in Grudge's suffering. She didn't know where these thoughts came from, and they made her feel ashamed.
—"That's great to hear," Sally lied. "The citizenry are always curious, indeed hungry, for news of the workings of the Politburo." She kicked herself for this reference to hunger. She hoped the generals would not think she was taking the piss. The citizens were indeed always hungry—but for food, not for news of the reviled government. The generals' smiles indicated, however, that they had not taken Sally's hunger reference to heart. She went on.
—"As you know, I'm here today to gather material for an article on the Politburo. I want to show it in the best light possible. Of course, the only light from the Politburo is good light. Everybody knows that. But I need to hear from yourselves your mission statement so to speak so I can relay it to the people."
—"It is true. The Politburo's light is good," General Scully said. His eyes lit up with the fervour of one who had been indoctrinated from a young age. He was delighted with this chance to expound. Particularly to such a sweet young thing as sat before him brushing crumbs from her blood red lips. Her mouth reminded him of a vagina. Scully was aroused and the interview was only a few minutes old. He had to check himself and try to cool his lust. Enjoy the view but don't do anything, he told himself. Young, if anyone, will have first taste.
He continued with his hollow robotic spiel.
—"The Party believes that the collective is infinitely superior to the mere individual. In fact, it is the citizen's duty at all times to contribute to the collective. Should a citizen harm the collective in any way, society *must* eliminate that citizen."
Scully noticed Sally's mouth opening and closing, as though a question hovered. He stopped speaking and went into listening mode. Her mouth was beautiful. The vagina comparison remained strong.
A hovering flunky approached and set down a fresh pot of tea. The trio was being waited on hand and foot.
—"Can a citizen ever come back from having offended the Party?" Sally asked.

She saw the eyes of the generals widen at this odd question. She knew she was getting sidetracked and really ought to keep it non-offensive. Nonetheless, she had Grudge in mind, ever conscious of his current plight.
General O'Flaherty looked with fatherly reproach at Sally.
—"What is a human life?" he asked. And he answered his own question.
—"A human life is nothing. The collective is all. Even possible threats must be eliminated. We have a country to run and thousands of citizens to feed."
Sally decided to broaden her questions. These generals were wily old devils. No doubt they'd had a background check run on her and knew all about her relationship with Grudge. Sally had the stardust, though. Normally, the lover of a known criminal wouldn't get within an ass's roar of the Great Hall. She positively glittered and the two old birds of the Politburo had fallen under her spell. They sat there smitten in their pristine uniforms waiting for the captivating girl to go on.
—"Okay," Sally said. "I think you've made it clear that in all cases the state takes precedence over the individual. Runway Four functions excellently with this policy in place. How do you see the future of our great land? Are you both confident going forward? Is Chairman Young confident?"
Scully cleared his throat and spoke.
—"Young lady," he said. "That is a rather silly question. The Politburo and the Standing Committee are powerful entities and Chairman Young is supremely so. He holds all the cards. It is not a question of him having confidence in the future. He creates the future."
—"Therefore," O'Flaherty interjected. "It is actually quite ridiculous of you to ask about the confidence of Party officials going forward, given the fact of the Politburo and the Standing Committee's power and Chairman Young's supremacy in all things. If he decrees that the sky is red, then the sky is red. I hope you can see that, Ms Popplewell."
—"Of course I can," Sally said, starting to worry she may be upsetting the generals. She made a mental note to be more flattering.

—“Chairman Young is our Godhead,” she said. “You generals are as his saints and we the citizens are his people. He makes the world for us.”
—“Very good, girl. It’s clear to you now.” This was Scully. His fat lips and shifty eyes full of arrogance and lust. Sally found him repulsive but maintained a polite demeanour.
—“My piece will be broad in scope,” she said. “I want citizens to understand the efficiency of the Politburo, the majesty of Government Buildings, and just how lucky we all are to be under such a dispensation. But I will narrow the focus down on one thing and that is the utter supremacy of Chairman Young.”
Sally couldn’t help but think how useless Young and the Politburo had been in catching the murderer of Martha Murtagh and Celia Sellers, as well as Barry Martin, and several other unsolved murders before them. She had also heard of the gruesome butchering of a legless beggar in the Tourist District only a week ago. All these crimes were hardly being dealt with efficiently. She hoped that somehow today she could meet Chairman Young, the great systematic falsifier of history, but she didn’t want to push her luck.
O’Flaherty and Scully smiled in unison.
—“The whole of the Politburo awaits your piece with great excitement,” Scully said. “We all loved your article on the recent murders and have no doubt you will come up with some sparkling prose regarding us.”
—“The people await it eagerly, too,” O’Flaherty said. “You are becoming popular. Remember of course that Chairman Young must be central to the piece. He will be reading it with keen interest. Someday, you may get to meet him.”
Sally’s heart quickened at the thought that she could meet the Chairman. She would definitely bring up Grudge if she came within his orbit. The poor fellow, for all she knew, he could be dead at this stage. Once more a weird OCD gripped her and she found herself taking a strange delight in Grudge’s pain.
—“Let’s tour the bureaucratic wing,” Scully suggested.
—“Permit me to ask?” Sally said.
—“Yes?”
—“Does Chairman Young work from Government Buildings, or from his residence Chairman’s House? It’s often hard to tell when he appears on TV.”

Both generals looked irked by her question. O'Flaherty spoke.
—"You've been given access to Government Buildings, Ms. Popplewell. Don't take advantage by exceeding your remit. Questions about Chairman Young's comings and goings are completely out of bounds."
Whoa! Sally didn't know where to look following this rebuke.
—"Certainly," she answered. "I never should have asked such a detailed question about the Chairman. Thanks for pulling me up on it."
—"Well, now that's clear," Scully said. "It's time to take a walk. Feel free to ask further questions, as long as they're within the rules."
—"Absolutely," she replied.
They got out of their chairs and headed for a large door at the far end of the hall. Flunkeys and plainclothes scurried ahead. The threesome reached the door and it was pushed open for them by a servant. They crossed the threshold and walked along a corridor lined with statues and busts of Chairman Young. Sally took it all in, impressed by the sheer adulation the scene conveyed.
—"These busts and statues of the Chairman enhance the corridor tremendously," O'Flaherty spouted.
Sally had to mind not to zone out, her natural defence against bullshit.
They turned into an open-plan office area. It was huge. There must have been a staff of at least two hundred on the floor. On one side were cellular offices for, Sally assumed, higher-ups. The generals explained the layout of the place to her and what went on there. The odd worker threw a glance at Sally, but most kept their heads down. In Sally's mind the article she would write was taking shape and she knew already it was going to be great—just like her piece on the murders. These dinosaurs could prattle on all they liked. It didn't matter anymore what they said. She had her own view of things and her own unique way of expressing herself, and that's what she'd put across. They'd get a puff piece alright, but it would be written in code. Somehow, she would speak to the people truthfully. Oddly, this aspiration felt hollow in her heart almost instantly and she was drawn to the wickedness of the regime like never before. Then that feeling itself passed as quickly as it had come on and she was back to thoughts of her writing career.

The threesome and their attendants moved out to a lush courtyard where the scent of flowers was beautiful and strong.
—"This garden is reserved strictly for Politburo members," O'Flaherty said. "You are privileged to be standing here, Ms. Popplewell."
Sally was beginning to tire of her trip to Government Buildings. In her mind she was already at home glued to her laptop composing the most exciting piece of journalese she'd ever written in her own inimitable, scintillating style. She didn't need to see any more of the complex. Her research was done. Coming through the open plan she had had something of an epiphany, and her role was now defined in her head: she would in the subtlest manner imaginable expose the fraud of the Politburo and Chairman Young for all its evilness and in the process she would engineer the release of Grudge Galmount. She didn't know the ins and outs of how she would accomplish this; only that she would.
—"You are so kind and good, both of you," she said, with the sweet scent of bougainvillea filling her nose, as cloying as her words. Towering angel's trumpets, present in abundance, seemed to nod as Sally spoke.
In itself, the courtyard was a sight to behold. To complete its tropical feel the gardeners had grown dozens of fuchsias, pelargoniums, canna lilies, hardy banana trees, windmill palms, cactus and succulents. The place brimmed with some of the most heavily scented plants on Earth.
—"I want to say how thankful I am to the Politburo and especially to Chairman Young for this chance to visit and learn about the workings of power in our fabulous country," she continued.
—"We've enjoyed having you, dear" O'Flaherty said. "You may go shortly. We detect you wish to leave and get to work on your writing. Lastly, however, let us take you past this flower-bedecked courtyard to the place of the machines: our Server Room."
—"I'd be delighted, General," Sally said, her curiosity aroused.
They passed through the courtyard, with assorted security still hovering, and proceeded down another corridor not quite as ornate as the last one. Sally could hear the thrum of the servers from behind an approaching wall. They turned left, O'Flaherty entered a code in a steel door, and they were in: a closed world. The heat in the room was palpable, and the humming noise of thousands of servers was

like a fearsome animal. Every flash of light represented somebody, somewhere going online. There were colourful cables everywhere. Computers and servers on floor-to-ceiling racks that stretched on infinitely like the stacks of the biggest library in the world.
As well as coming from the servers, the overwhelming droning sound came from air-conditioning units running constantly to stop the machines from auto-melting. There were aisles between the stacks to enable a worker to get at any machine, every cable connection, if needs be. Staff buzzed about.
O'Flaherty, Sally and Scully were greeted by a tall man who was the head computer scientist. In the midst of handshakes and introductions, and indeed smiles all round, Sally sensed how false it all was and detected fear on the face of the scientist to be in the presence of Politburo generals. His staff went on working, heads down, not wanting to convey any sense of idleness whatsoever. The scientist informed her that they stored and processed five zettabytes of data in the Server Room. Sally was impressed.
The little party walked the aisles. Red, blue, yellow and green wires ran like neural pathways in a brain; which, in a sense they were, only this was the mass brain of Runway Four (not unrelated in its own way to the long arm of the law). On these servers the fruit of the surveillance society hung ripe. It became clear to Sally that those in power knew everything about everyone.
—"We are working towards a scenario," the tall man explained. "Where, when a citizen has a thought, we can capture it for our records. It will do away with hidden dissent which we know is a real problem in society. We're not quite there yet, but it will involve the insertion of a chip into every citizen's brain."
Sally smiled, trying desperately to hide how appalled she was at the notion of mass brain-chipping.
—"Chairman Young is particularly keen to stamp out any discussion of what he calls the 'seven evil subjects'," Scully butted in.
—"And what are they?" Sally asked.
But before the general could tell her, a trumpet fanfare erupted close by. A commotion rippled through the room. Staff stopped what they were doing and jumped to attention. A flunkey approached and whispered in the generals' ears.
They seemed somewhat startled and began to nod and smile at Sally.

—"Well, well, Ms. Popplewell," O'Flaherty said. "You are quite the mini-celebrity. It is an honour indeed and quite a surprise that Chairman Young who is in the complex today has expressed a wish to meet you."
It was Sally's turn to be startled. Her eyes widened.
The fanfare died down and the people between Sally and the trumpets parted. Suddenly, before her was Chairman Young. She recognised him from television. He looked majestic in a uniform that would outdo Gaddafi. A scoop, she thought, I'm meeting the Chairman! Young had cut through the field of minions, bodyguards, soldiers, and servants, ignored the two generals, and stood by Sally with a beaming smile on his famous face. She could have reached out and touched his epaulets. She trembled a tad for she had seen him on TV so many times. He always appeared in commanding scenes: driving a tank, shooting game, inspecting a military parade. The natural reaction to him was to be intimidated.
—"Well, well," the Chairman spoke. "I am finally meeting Sally Popplewell. I've heard so much about you."
Sally was taken aback by this, not sure if it was such a good thing to be on the Chairman's radar. She saw O'Flaherty and Scully smiling manically. Their heads nodding like bobbing toys on the tops of pencils.
Young thrust out his hand and Sally reciprocated. A vigorous shake ensued.
—"It's an incredible honour to meet you, Chairman Young," she said. "I have had a wonderfully constructive morning here with your two generals. I'm quite confident I'll produce an excellent piece of writing as a result of my visit."
—"I fully intend to read it," Young answered.
This was a massive compliment to Sally. The respect the remark bestowed upon her was immeasurable. Everyone within earshot now knew she was a force to be reckoned with. She hoped to use this favourable tide to her—and more particularly Grudge's—advantage. Intuition told her that there was something to be gained. Still, her mind was beset by a new trickery and unkind thoughts of Grudge addled it. A lust for Young and all the perniciousness he represented began to fill her. She hid this inner turmoil well.

—“I’m so flattered to hear that, Chairman Young,” she said, smiling coquettishly, and drawing him in. He might have been the most powerful man in the land, but he was not immune to feminine guile.
—“I want to talk to you in private,” Young said.
This came as a surprise to everyone. The way was cleared and Chairman Young led Sally out of the Server Room to a plush chamber a short distance away.
General O’Flaherty worried for Sally. It would not be unheard of for Young to rape a girl in one of these chambers on a whim. His worry was unfounded. Young was genuinely impressed by Sally, and simply wanted to pick her brains rather than prise open her pants.
—“We are to be left alone,” Young told his minions at the chamber door, and extended his hand chivalrously to let Sally pass inside.
She sat down in a Queen Anne chair while Young took one opposite. She was thrilled to be sitting face to face with Chairman Young—in private!
—“I’m delighted you enjoyed your morning in Government Buildings,” Young said. “I read your piece on those infernal murders. I thought it terrific. Regrettably, despite the power of my government, the murders remain unsolved. It’s a source of extreme frustration to me, and reflects badly on my leadership of this great nation.”
Sally was surprised by his candour.
—“I still think the killings will be solved, Chairman,” she said. “I’ve no evidence to back up my belief. It’s just a hunch really. But I feel strongly that the culprit or culprits will be found.”
—“My police are working on it around the clock. I hope your hunch proves correct.”
The Chairman looked lost somewhat; all his power useless in the face of an unseen enemy.
Out of the proverbial blue, Sally was moved to say something the full import of which she could not grasp. She didn’t even know where the words came from:
—“The answer to the murders will come from outside our world.”
Young’s eyes twitched. Sally worried. Had she overstepped the mark? It was hard to read the Chairman’s expression. It was naturally stern. It was not forgotten by Sally that officially there was only one world: Chairman Young’s. He may have been curious about what she said, or he may have been angry.

To her relief he seemed to mellow. His look softened.
—"An interesting suggestion, Sally. Between you and me, I've had similar thoughts myself recently. I've been thinking about Ree, my late wife. Today would have been her fifty-fifth birthday had she been spared. But even all my power could not protect her from the grave."
Again, his openness was stunning. The vulnerable Chairman becoming emotional about his late wife. Sally kept schtum, wanting him to go on. He did.
—"Something numinous is afoot in the land. If my security services can't solve the killings, what else can it be? This is the most surveilled society in the world. Our punishments are brutal. Only something supernatural could slip in here with impunity and carry out such deeds."
Sally couldn't resist the chance to ask an impertinent question, on a subject never to be broached in Runway Four least of all with the Supreme Leader. Then again, she thought, it might be the only chance I'll get.
—"Do you pray, Chairman Young, and to which god?
The Chairman looked startled.
—"Well, Sally," he said. "You certainly are a brave girl. No one else would dare ask me such a question. There's something about you makes me willing to give you an answer rather than have you carted off to jail."
He laughed, and so did Sally, nervously.
—"*I* am God," he said. "I pray to myself."
She was struck by his breathtaking egotism and feared he actually believed his own words.
—"Thank you for that answer, Chairman. I'm noting everything and will include it all in my article. Could you tell me a little about the 'seven evil subjects'?"
—"I want all discussion of them stamped out: universal values; freedom of the press; civil society; civic rights; historical mistakes of my government; crony networks; and judicial independence."
Sally wrote everything down.
—"I'm taking you into my confidence, Sally. Not all of this can go into your writing."
—"I understand, Chairman."

A silence ensued that wasn't awkward. They sat well together despite the disparity in their stations. It had the feel of a long married couple at ease in their quietude.
Once more Sally thought of Grudge. Now might you do it, Sal, she said to herself. Broach the topic. Bring Grudge up. And again a nasty compulsiveness seized her, and she pictured with some pleasure his sorrows.
It turned out she didn't have to bring him up. Lady Luck did the work for her. Chairman Young spoke with emotion about his deceased wife Ree.
—"I wish she was here today. I wish it everyday but the pain is pronounced on her birthday. She always loved her big day and we would celebrate it in style. Today I feel like doing something kind in her honour. I've been studying the file on you, Sally."
Sally nodded, wondering where this was leading.
—"I saw a lot of references to a Grudge Galmount."
She tensed hearing Young say Grudge's name.
—"He's my boyfriend," she said. "He was taken away to prison recently."
—"By prison I take it you mean one of our corrective thinking centres? They work very well. Perhaps Galmount will find his time there beneficial."
Sally remained wary of Young. He might have come across all emotional about his dead wife, but he was still one of the world's most ruthless men. No point in rubbing him up the wrong way.
—"Of course," she said. "I'm well aware how the centres have benefited society. It's just that I don't think Grudge belongs in one. His incarceration is a mistake."
—"Really?" Young smiled. "I've looked at the file—my aides call it micro-managing—and your fellow seems to have sullied his bib entirely off his own bat."
—"I will admit, Chairman, that Grudge is a mixed-up man. But his heart is in the right place. He actually helped me when I was researching my article about the murders, the article that brought me the acclaim. Grudge came with me to the horror house in Goat Park. He was a calming presence as I went from room to room."
—"He's fond of drink and drugs, Sally," Young snapped. "You know how strongly that is frowned on in this country."

—“He’s not an addict, Chairman. He can take or leave those substances. Grudge is an artistic and creative person. He just feels the weight of the world more keenly than others, and he uses drink and drugs to escape those oppressive feelings.”
She thought she was going too far in explaining Grudge’s habits. A typical prole—as he was—had no time to get in touch with their feelings. The main thing was to work and keep your head down and not think, least of all about how you felt on an existential level. Sally sensed she got the Chairman on a good day. She didn’t like to think what he’d be like on a bad one.
—“My dear girl. Please don’t talk as though my subjects are allowed inner lives. Galmount is a boy from a coffin factory. You speak of him as if his feelings carry weight. His first and only duty is to the state, to work well and obey the law. Leave the inner lives to me, your Supreme Leader.”
—“Of course,” Sally said. “You are quite right, Chairman. I don’t know what I was thinking. Grudge is happy to work in the factory. He has got himself into some difficulty however by being locked up.”
—“In so many ways, Sally, today is a lucky day for you. You have come to Government Buildings to interview two of my top generals. You have got to meet me, the Eternal Chairman, the luckiest thing that can happen to anyone. And now, continuing your run of luck, and for the glory of Ree’s memory, Galmount can go free.
Butterflies danced in Sally’s stomach.
—“Thank you, Supreme Leader!” she gushed.
—“I will have my officials organise his release immediately.”
—“I am ecstatic. I can’t thank you enough.”
—“Thank me by writing an excellent article about your day here. Maybe bring Galmount to Freeland with you. I know you’re going there soon. There is nothing I don’t know. Don’t worry about travel visas, it can all be arranged. Now, Sally, I’m tired and sad. Our interview is finished. Good luck with everything.”
They stood, shook hands, and left the chamber. Young was ushered away. Sally was taken to the street by an aide. She hailed a cab and headed home, anxious to hear if Grudge had been released yet.

Chapter 10

Intensive Maoist-style re-education will stop the spread of detrimental information. The monstrous leverage of the R4 state machine applied to screwing down troublesome components. There are twenty to a cell here. Cells built for four at most. Prisoner comfort isn't high on the priority list. There's a hole for a toilet where you must squat to defecate. Privacy is dead. Most inmates have lice. They spread throughout the cells. Stretching out to sleep is out of the question. The best you can do is slide down the wall, pull your knees up to your chin, and try to catch some winks if you can, with one eye open all the while. An air of menace prevails. Prisoners are attacked in random acts of shocking violence. Homosexual rape is a frequent occurrence.

For Grudge it was a blessing of sorts he had been placed in solitary confinement away from these pestilent vaults.

The stint in solitary began after his first few days in the centre. During his initial interrogation sessions, he'd been bastinadoed, placed in stress positions, deprived of sleep, electrocuted and subjected to extreme noise and extreme temperature. Yet still they could not break him. The interrogations themselves were fiendishly pointless affairs born of fabricated allegations. What had Grudge done after all apart from disobey *Wormwood's* rules? But they threw everything they could at him, even the murders in the land they tried to pin on his spotless head. His interrogators had never come across his likes before. He refused to bend his will to their commands. The painful indignities visited upon him did not have the required effect. When told he could unloose himself from a stress position he would smile and mutter something gnomic like: "You can lead a horse to water but you can't make him think."

Grudge's smart-alecky comments incensed his tormentors, and the guards, particularly the lower ranked ones, grew more violent towards him. One loathsome little Hitler swore, while pulling on Grudge's hair: "I will personally cut your bollix off."

The commanding officer, Kuntar, learned of the prisoner in Unit 8 who was not responding to torture, who was in fact giving cheek during the sessions. It was as though a guardian angel was protecting Galmount. Every horror visited upon him emboldened him rather than broke him. The guards could not believe how little effect electrocution had. He barely flinched. Something was shielding him from the pain.

Kuntar ordered Grudge to be thrown into solitary until they could decide how to proceed. "We will break this guy," he asserted. "Stick him in the rubber room for now. Pipe Daniel O'Donnell in. Make him suffer while I think about it."
Grudge sat alone, naked, with a peaceful look on his face in spite of it all. The horrendous music they blasted failed to impact on his soul. He didn't know where he was getting his strength from considering everything he'd been through. He still felt reasonably okay.
Someone was carrying him. The pain of his wounds made him wince from time to time but he didn't think there'd been any permanent damage. He felt things would heal up eventually—if the interrogators didn't kill him first such was their zeal. But even the thought of death did not frighten him in his current frame of mind. Though, objectively, his circumstances were dire, he was at peace with the universe and his place in it, and if the time came for him to meet his Maker he was ready. The government of course and his interrogators acting on the government's behalf hated people to consider a higher being. The official line was that Chairman Young was God. Grudge had always had a strong belief in the Almighty. Gerard and Sarah's miracle baby had been born with it. At certain times during the torture sessions when the pain was at its most unbearable he had suddenly been overcome with a floating feeling. He had read of such things. It might just have been his body releasing hormones to help him cope. He believed, though, that it was something altogether more celestial.
He found Kuntar to be a nasty piece of work. He had participated in the torture sessions when he heard that Grudge wasn't bending, and took immense pleasure inflicting pain.
Grudge knew they'd be back soon to drag him out for more. He was calmly resigned to it, and felt it was his calling.
He had no idea of the time. The harsh neon began to flicker and he heard voices near. Fresh hell, he thought, as keys clanked on an outer door.
These past hellish days he had been thinking of his parents, Gerard and Sarah, even though he had never known them. A nurse in Arenta who had taken a liking to him had given him some of their story. They had tried so long to have a baby. Grudge arrived when Sarah was forty-five. He was their gift from Heaven. Ultimately, though, their happiness proved tragic. They had gone around telling

everyone they could that Grudge was a miracle sent by God. A neighbour informed the Secret Police. They were lifted and taken to Camp Thirteen. Grudge was put in the orphanage and from there had graduated to the coffin factory. He assumed his parents died in the end from hunger and overwork. But he could feel their presence this week. As an electrode was being clamped to his nipple he would travel in his mind to a blissful scene where Sarah kissed him and Gerard's hand held his, lessening all the while the torturers' inflictions. Such scenes were all the more strange for the fact that Grudge had no idea what his parents looked like, never having seen a photograph. Yet he was sure it was them, in his hour of need, sending heavenly aid.
He knew they'd help him now as a fresh round of torment was about to start. The voices grew louder. In amongst them and clearly holding forth was Kuntar's, the ringleader's. Grudge scurried up the rubber wall and stood on his feet. The key to his cell turned. Kuntar stood on the threshold with four grim-faced guards behind him. Here we go again, Grudge thought.
However, he noticed a change in the dynamic today. Normally, he was grabbed immediately and the scourging, mental and physical, would start without delay. They seemed to be holding their fire. Kuntar was annoyed about something.
—"What is it fellas?" Grudge asked. "I was just daydreaming when you called."
—"Shut up, Galmount," Kuntar said. "No one's in any mood for your wisecracks."
Grudge shushed. He saw the hatred in the eyes of the guards. These boys were not in the mood for banter. They would kill him in an instant if they could.
—"You must have nine lives, you little shit," Kuntar said. "No less a personage than the Respected Marshal Chairman Young has decreed that you are to be freed. Word reached our camp an hour ago. Apparently, you are considered a valuable aid to an up-and-coming writer by the name of Sally Popplewell."
Grudge was sceptical. Could this be true, or was it a cruel hoax on the part of his captors? Certainly, to judge from the guards' expressions, he was going nowhere. Nevertheless, something in the way Kuntar spoke gave Grudge hope.

—“Gather up that bundle of shit,” Kuntar instructed, referring to some articles of filthy clothing. “And come with us to the reception area. And for fuck’s sake put some rags over your body. You disgust me.”
Grudge began to believe it was true. They were letting him go. Sally, the little angel, had somehow engineered it. He threw a soiled and bloodied shirt over himself and pulled on a pair of pathetic pants, then slipped on his jail issue crocs.
Out he went into the corridor and all six of them marched along it. From cell doors Grudge heard the soft moans of tortured souls. What was it about them that their spirits sounded so much more broken than his, he wondered? Just who or what had propped him up and carried him through this experience?
He was elated now thinking he would taste freedom at any moment. The idea that Chairman Young had intervened! He couldn’t wait to ask Sally how she had managed that. He worried whether he would have to return to the coffin factory. He couldn’t bear the idea but he dared not broach the subject with the brutes accompanying him. He feared if he mentioned conditions about his release, the whole thing would be called off. So he marched along and said nothing, his fingers crossed. He just wanted to get through the processing and back on the street as quickly as possible.
The processing area was as busy as ever with cowed newcomers standing against the wall to have their mugshots taken, their retinas scanned, their rectums examined, and their fingers printed. Verily, this was no holiday camp.
It was an odd event to have a prisoner heading in the opposite direction. The guards on the desk had rarely seen it before. This was the kind of place once you came you never left.
Grudge got to the desk—was shoved in front of it by Kuntar, who knew this was the last time he would get to be cruel to Galmount and decided to make the most of it by pulling Grudge’s hair.
—“Hey, stop that,” Grudge said. “We might as well part on civil terms. Show some example to your men.”
The desk sergeant was amazed at Grudge’s insolence and the fact he was getting out.
—“Run him through quickly, Ned,” Kuntar said. “This little fuck’s getting released. Seems he’s got friends in high places.”
—“Lucky guy. I think you fellas were close to breaking him.”

Ned grabbed Grudge's wrist and steered his hand towards a computer that read his fingerprint and signed him out of the centre. Grudge was smiling full-on now, thinking of Sally, the rathole and the coffin factory, and the possibility that he might never have to see at least two of those three entities again.
—"Okay, he's cleared customs," Ned said.
—"Lads, take him out the back and clean him up," Kuntar told the four stooges. "Make it a last shower to remember, but leave no marks. And put some fresh clothes on him. There could well be a press photographer sniffing round when this wise guy walks."
The guards grabbed Grudge and took him to the showers. He was stripped, kicked and punched a little, though nothing as severe as in recent days. They hosed him with freezing water. Their abuse was more verbal than physical. They told him what a dog he was, and that he would not last long on the outside. They said his attitude to authority would get him arrested again and he would soon be back. They promised to torture him to death when that happened. The shower from hell lasted around ten minutes. Grudge took it in his stride.
When the hosing was done they threw him a towel and some surprisingly decent clothes. A prison doctor came and examined him quickly and pronounced him well enough to leave. He was taken back to reception. Ned the desk sergeant gave him a couple of goldmarks to see him on his way.
—"You've scrubbed up well," Kuntar sneered. "Ready for your public? I hear there's press outside. Your bit of pussy's there, too. Get going. I won't say good luck. I wouldn't mean it"
Grudge said nothing. He was feeling better already. Miraculously, his injuries were superficial. He knew that he would heal soon. The doctor had just said as much, joking that he must have supernatural powers.
He took a last look around. He said a mental prayer for the new prisoners filing in. He didn't know who he was praying to.
Then he walked through the main exit and down the steps to the open air. He hurried along the drive, passed the security hut and out through the gate. Nobody stopped him. There was a bus that ran from the city twice a day. He thought he'd have to wait for it. Once he got to Bludgeon he wasn't really sure how things would pan out. Turned out he wouldn't be catching the bus. Sally was waiting for

him. She'd driven straight here after a brief stopover at her parents' following her interview with Chairman Young.
Grudge's day just kept getting better and better. Amazing considering how things were earlier. Then, he had thought he was in for another torture session. Now, he was running towards Sally outside the walls of the corrective thinking centre.
There was a car parked nearby, a runaround with *The Inquisitor* logo on its side. Behind it a white van idled. Two men sat in the front. As Grudge and Sally embraced the man in the passenger seat trained a camera on them and fired away.
—"It's bloody great to see you, Sally. I can't tell you how relieved I am to have left that place."
—"My darling. I've missed you so much. Are you okay? What did they do to you in there?"
—"I'm good, girl. Nothing that won't heal in a couple of days. I can't believe you got me out—and with Chairman Young's involvement! How the hell?"
—"I'll explain in the car. By the way, have you noticed the photographer in the van? We've attracted some attention."
—"Yes, and the driver seems to be taking notes. What's up? Are you a celeb now? Am I infamous?"
—"Let's get in. Like I said, we'll talk on the way."
—"Cool wheels. Kern's been good. Are they going to follow us back to the city?"
—"Kern's been great. He helped get you out of jail by getting me into Government Buildings. Though, I feel a little guilty driving this car. So many people are deprived. We're going to be trailed all the way to my parents'. Success comes with a price."
They set off and sure enough the white van pulled out and started following them. It didn't bother Grudge. He had the feeling that from now on he and Sally were going to attract quite a lot of attention.
As the car headed towards Bludgeon, Sally filled him in on her visit to Government Buildings, her interview with the two generals, the Server Room and Chairman Young's arrival on the scene.
—"You're making this up!" Grudge said.
—"No, it's true!"
She told him of Young's suggestion that he accompany her to Freeland.

—“Me and you go to Freeland?” he exclaimed. “Yes!”
He felt like someone who had just taken an escalator from Hell to Heaven. As they reached Bludgeon, even the pain of his torture wounds had started to recede.
He told her of his meeting with the enigmatic Puck Hellson on the tram the day Séamus Cronin died. He thought it strange that Sally seemed overly interested in Hellson. She expressed a desire to meet him someday, and dismissed Grudge’s suggestion that he may have been responsible for Cronin’s death as pure flight of fancy.
—“I’m the investigative journalist,” she said. “And let me tell you there’s nothing to investigate there.”
Why was she so emphatic? Grudge wondered. And how the hell does she know?
At the Popplewells’ place she drove them into the small underground car park where the management committee had allocated her a space. Their pursuers in the white van halted on the kerb outside.
The runaround had been waiting for Sally when she got back from Centaur Street, a gift from Jeff Kern.
They took the elevator up to the apartment. Jett and Jane let them in, greeting them like prodigals.
Food was served and all four sat around talking long into the evening about the exciting turn of events.

***

Town Island City—midtown—the Avenue of the Freelanders: the headquarters of *Money* magazine.
The magazine occupied the top three floors of an enormous skyscraper. It was one of the most widely read publications in the world—though, needless to say, its popularity did not extend to Runway Four where it was on the banned list. It had a staff of about three hundred, from lowly cleaners to high-salaried columnists, and all types in between. The editor, Clement Topcliffe, was a larger than life fellow who ran a tight ship. A true micromanager, there was nothing he didn’t know about the goings-on at his magazine. Its name, *Money*, suggestive of a financial organ, did not tell the whole story. There was no topic out of bounds for *Money*.
Toplcliffe had a large penthouse office which he left often to go walkabout like the captain of an ocean liner surveying the decks. Despite this slightly annoying habit of sticking his oar in

everywhere, he was generally liked by his employees, and his opinions were valued. He was a prominent and respected figure in Freeland itself. Always found at the best social gatherings, he was sought out by politicians and captains of industry for his views, not to mention his great wit. A lifelong bachelor, he was married to his job. He lived in a luxurious apartment uptown north of the park and was chauffeured to the Avenue of the Freelanders each morning. He was the kind of man on whose opinions countries pivot, eminently knowledgeable on a vast range of things: sport, politics, the arts, entertainment, cinema, current affairs, economics, to name a few. He had a keen interest in the totalitarian society that was Runway Four, fascinated by and to some extent admiring of Chairman Young. The Chairman was always so "correct and glorious" and "sagacious and great" to quote two phrases Topcliffe had read describing Young. How does the dear respected leader keep it all running so smoothly, the editor was wont to wonder.

Clement was the closest thing any foreigner came to being a RunwayFourophile.

The launch some years back of a medium range missile by R4 got extensive coverage in *Money*. The sheer effrontery towards the international community impressed Topcliffe. Although the regime had been warned at the UN that the test would not be tolerated—they were threatened with all kinds of dire consequences if they disobeyed a UN mandate—nonetheless they just went ahead and fired the rocket. It was as though they were giving the two fingers to the world. It was Young's way or the highway. It didn't surprise Topcliffe that the people of Runway Four had never rebelled to any extent against their government. He believed it was down to the freedom they had in their economic lives. A sort of microcosmic, proxy capitalism reigned and nobody starved. Granted many subsisted on bare rations. However, people were even allowed to get an education. There would be no repetition of the grave mistakes of Mao in the Great Leap Forward. The generals knew their history and they wanted work, prosperity and enrichment for themselves and their closest family members. Food was produced efficiently and that's what kept the people pacified. They worked—some at private enterprise—and they went home, and ate and slept in frugal yet comfortable accommodation.

The recent murders in Runway Four were covered by *Money*. When the girl, Sally Popplewell, published her article, it was syndicated worldwide. Topcliffe based the *Money* article on the bones of Sally's piece. He had watched with admiration as her story gained international recognition. He knew he had to have her over, to meet her in person and let her write some stories, this talented girl from a fascist regime whose talent shone through and allowed her reach the world stage. Circulation had been flagging of late and she could be just the thing to boost it.

He went through all the correct channels and finally, working through Freeland's own State Department, secured cooperation from the Runway Four authorities. To his surprise they couldn't have been more accommodating. Clement put it down to a push on their part to improve their image abroad. When she arrived, he intended to nurture Ms Popplewell and get the absolute best from her. It was the Topcliffe way: hands-on.

Clement was in his office drinking his first coffee of the day. A steady stream of emails pinged to his inbox. He opened his mail. There it was, an official R4 communication confirming Sally's travel arrangements. It said that all the paperwork was cleared and she would leave Runway Four the following day for Freeland. She was to work at *Money* magazine, and would avail of their offer of an apartment for her stay. Accompanying her as an aide on the trip would be a man called Grudge Galmount.

It was excellent news. Clement was most pleased to get a chance to work with her. Her story was epic in its sweep, when one considered the oppressiveness of R4. He'd get her started on some meaty stories straightaway, team her up with the best crime reporters on his staff, and boost her profile to the highest extent. She was going to be working in Town Island after all, the place oft referred to as the greatest city on Earth, on a magazine with a superb reputation. Clement suspected that the Runway Four powers knew exactly what they were doing granting her travel rights. It exposed her and more importantly them to much favourable publicity. It was great for *Money*, too; a win-win situation.

He got up from his chair and headed to the floor where some of his brightest and best journalists plied their trade. He needed to tell them that Sally and a Grudge Galmount were on their way. He would also get Shawn Burns, his top crime reporter, in on the action. Burns was

the very definition of a grizzled hack. He had an office, less plush, across the open-plan from Topcliffe's.
Clement spoke to his staff. He told them to make the visitors welcome and to give them any help they needed when they arrived. The hacks were intrigued about the Popplewell girl. They had heard of her from the internet.
Clement headed over to Burns, who exuded confidence in everything he did even if it was just sitting at his desk making a paper aeroplane which was what he was doing when Clement walked in. Burns threw the plane into flight and straightened up in his seat.
—"What's the haps, Clement? Good to see you," he said.
—"Hi, Shawn. Nice morning out there. As you probably know, there's a girl coming the day after tomorrow. Sally Popplewell. I want her to work some crime stories. Anything meaty you might have. You know she's from Runway Four?"
—"Yes, I've heard all about her," he said. "People are wondering how the hell she got such a free rein. I mean it's Runway Four we're talking about, not Sweden. Is she boning one of the generals, or Chairman Young?"
—"Well I don't know about that," Clement laughed. "She's bringing a guy with her, Grudge Galmount. We're putting them up in a tony apartment uptown while they're here. If she's boning anyone, he's your man. She seems supremely talented. From a journalistic point of view, her piece on the R4 murders was a joy, leaving aside the subject matter. She laid out the situation, the evidence or lack thereof, the clues or lack thereof, and the guesses as to who or what might be responsible. It was poetic in its execution. Reportage is the new fiction."
—"You could be on to something there," Burns said. "I agree it was a great article. In all humility, even I'd have trouble knocking out something *that* good!"
—"Well," Clement said. "I want you to take her under your wing. You're the best crime reporter in this city. It's only fitting that her first introduction to working in the West is with you."
Burns grinned with self-satisfaction. Topcliffe had put him on a pedestal and he loved the view.
He loved the view, too, of the woman who now appeared on the threshold. *Money's* finest piece of eye candy, strawberry blonde Kathryn Harrington, breezed in.

Kathryn was the kind of sassy, successful lady journalist that Sally was shaping up to be. Although still only thirty, she had the air of a veteran about her. Famous to a degree, she'd worked on many notable stories. Clement Topcliffe was particularly fond of her and deferred to her opinion all the time. She was liked in the office even by the lady folk; surprising considering how bitchy women can be. Some people just have *it*, inspiring love and devotion wherever they go. And Kathryn Harrington had *it* in spades.
She had come in to ask Burns a favour, namely, would he accompany her upstate to Mountain Lion Correctional Facility to interview a perp for a piece she was writing on serial killers. The lifer in question, Archie Shaw, had killed seven women over seven months, and would have gone on killing had a flat tyre not intervened. Victim number eight had managed to jump from his van on a city street when a puncture forced him to pull over. The murderer had contacted Kathryn asking her to visit, saying he wanted to talk about his crimes; he told her he'd found God and needed to unburden himself.
Kathryn could be humble when the need arose. She wanted Burns to come along because of his vast experience in the business.
—"Hi, guys," she said. "Sorry if I'm interrupting. I want to ask you, Shawn, if you'll come with me on some field work?"
If Kathryn was involved, Clement and Shawn didn't mind being interrupted. Both men listened as she explained her proposed trip to the facility upstate. Watching her lips move was an erotic experience. She seemed to lick each word as it came from her mouth. The men were enraptured, and Burns quickly agreed to embark on the trip. He remembered the case and promised to bring whatever assistance he could.
Kathryn turned to leave. The men's eyes focused on her firm buttocks, its beauty accentuated by a tight pencil skirt. Clement had a brainwave.
—"Kathryn," he said, speaking to her back. "Could I just stop you before you go?"
She turned once more and faced them.
—"Yes, what is it?" she asked.
—"Well, I'm sure you've heard we've a girl coming from Runway Four. Sally Popplewell. She'll be here for a week or thereabouts. I think you guys should work together. This interview in Mountain

Lion, if she sits in on it it'd be great experience for her. How about if you, Shawn and Sally all head up there—and her boyfriend, too, a Mr Galmount?"
Kathryn didn't mind at all. Unlike more egotistical reporters, she was glad to share her time with the up-and-coming. This attitude contributed to her general likeability. Burns was fine with the idea. His priapic side rejoiced at the prospect of working with the young ladies.
—"You okay with this, Shawn?" Clement asked.
—"Absolutely, boss," he replied, a broad grin on his face. He winked and added: "I'll be delighted to travel with the girls."
—"She's getting great attention on the international wires," Kathryn said. "Having her over could do *Money* the world of good."
—"It sure could," Clement said.
—"It just puzzles me, though, and I'm sure it puzzles a lot of people. Why the hell did the R4 authorities treat her with such leniency? I mean, allowing her to travel and giving her such a free hand?"
—"It's a bit of a mystery alright," Burns said. "Clem and I were just wondering the same thing."
—"We can ask her when she gets here," Topcliffe said. "Now, come on folks, I've work to do. I'll talk with you crazy cats later."
With that he left Kathryn and Shawn behind. He headed back to his desk and checked emails, excited about the fact that Sally was coming. He had a good feeling on this.
Life in *Money* continued apace.

Chapter 11

Sally and Grudge had had a hectic time operating out of Sally's folks' place. Operating is maybe too strong a word. They didn't venture out. Rather, they sat round discussing their next move and enjoying a certain degree of newfound freedom and status. True to her word Sally presented Grudge with a second hand SLR camera for the impending trip. Their internet access improved. The government and their ever watchful watchers freed up a lot of the blocked sites on the Popplewells' line. Grudge and Sally checked out Freeland on the web. Airline tickets and apartment reservations (courtesy of *Money*) were couriered to their door. Clearly, the

powers that be were monitoring their every move and wanted to ensure it all went smoothly.
A doctor and nurse arrived and gave them full checkups. Sally was in fine fettle and pronounced fit for travel. Remarkably, too, Grudge was given a clean bill of health. He had suffered no lasting damage from his torturous week in jail. The doctor gave him pain relief medication, and told him it was a miracle he had not been damaged more. The doctor and nurse chatted freely and not to say a little enviously with Grudge and Sally about their upcoming trip. Sally's article on the murders was mentioned. The doctor said he hadn't read anything as good since Chairman Young's *Seven Steps to Good Citizenship*. Under a barrage of questioning the couple caught a glimpse of what it might be like to live a celebrity life and to be probed by reporters the livelong day. Sally didn't mind at all. Grudge was not so sure.
In another sign of the State's beneficence, a hamper of fine food and wine arrived compliments of Generals O'Flaherty and Scully.
Sally's father, with clearance from his boss, stayed home from work in order to be in on the action. He was so proud of Sally and he loved Grudge, hoping he would one day be his son-in-law.
There was an air of great excitement around the apartment and it permeated the whole complex. Chairman Young had seen to it that a security detail was posted in the corridors to ensure peace for the couple prior to their flight to Freeland.
What exactly was the threat against them was hard to gauge, but it seemed to be the fear that the killer or killers would get to Sally before her moment of glory on foreign shores.
When they needed a bit of time to themselves, the couple got off the sofa and went to Sally's bedroom. They kissed and canoodled but held off on full lovemaking. The closeness of her parents in the next room dissuaded them.
Grudge felt a sense of wonder, and a sense of duty calling. A powerful force for good wanted him to act. His moment of destiny had arrived and, without putting too much of a gloss on it, he was ready to do what he had to do.
It was in the lap of the gods really; or God for that matter.

***

Town Island City was a twenty-four-seven hive of activity. In this milieu Puck Hellson thrived. He slinked through teeming streets taking orders from the Devil. He eyeballed and terrified folk in the process.
He sensed the days, like the crowds, were passing fast. The voice in his ear said this was the year the showdown would occur. The woman and man were on their way. They were to be vanquished till Doomsday. Puck was expected to prevail. His crew of ghouls were on hand, too, ever ready to assist.
At a hotel bar on West 35th Street, Hellson rolled in, took a seat and ordered a shot of bourbon and a beer chaser. It was eleven a.m. There were no other customers. Darlene, the bartenderette, disliked him instantly. She handed him his drinks, turned her back, and continued doing what she was doing before he came in, lining up bottles and checking the optics. In the large mirror that filled out behind the bar she saw the creepy stranger knock back his shot in one gulp and then sip his beer. To her fright she saw he was looking straight at her. Who is that motherfucker, she thought, and why do I think that he wants to harm me?
She turned back around and tried to face him down, picking up a glass and polishing it in an effort to seem calm. Hellson licked his lips and smiled. She dropped the glass and it crashed to the floor. Her manager came rushing in from the back office.
—"What's the matter, Darlene?" he said. "Take it easy for heaven's sake!"
She stooped and swept up the shards with a dustpan.
—"Sorry, Hal," she said. "I don't know why I'm so clumsy today."
But she did know. It was the man at the bar. He had set her nerves on edge. She wondered if her boss sensed him, too, for Hal retreated at speed back to the office.
Darlene emptied the pan into the trashcan. Hellson's eyes were upon her all the while. She noticed that her hands were shaking, as though she'd overdosed on coffee or had been partying till the early hours. None of this was true. In point of fact she had gone to bed at nine the previous evening, and only drank decaffeinated coffee these days. The tremor seemed to spread throughout her body. Why the hell was she shaking like the proverbial leaf on a fuzzy tree? Plainly, the stranger was to blame. He called for more bourbon.
—"Fill me up another one, and make it fast!"

He was playing with her the way a kitten plays with a ball of string; or a cheetah with a gazelle after it has bitten the gentler animal's neck. Darlene jumped to attention, took his glass and filled it again. She set it down in front of him and backed away fast, like a circus performer dicing with a dangerous beast. Again Hellson knocked back the shot in one go. He continued smiling at her. He finished off the beer and got to his feet. He straightened out his jacket and looked admiringly at himself in the mirror.
—"Today's your lucky day, honey," he said. "I was toying with the idea of taking you off the board."
Darlene didn't answer. She was still trembling and knew she was in shock.
She wondered how he got away with speaking to her like this.
—"For whatever reason," he continued. "The quality of mercy is in me this fine morning. I'm leaving now and walking out into the sunshine."
He winked at Darlene, turned on his heel and left. To her shame she realised she had wet her knickers.
—"I'll be back in five, taking a toilet break," she shouted into Hal. When she reached the restroom she burst into tears.
Hellson made for the Avenue of the Freelanders and the offices of *Money* magazine. He patted his pocket and felt the letter still there. Sealed in an envelope the previous evening, the words had come to him automatically as though down a pipe. His task was to deliver this missive to the editor, Clement Topcliffe.
The alcohol he'd consumed had gone down well. He navigated the midtown crowds with ease. People blanched at times when he passed. He stopped at a food stand and bought a hotdog. The vendor sold lamb kebabs, too, and the smell of burning flesh aroused Hellson. He walked and ate, an automaton doing the work of the Devil. He had millions of friends; a legion. He mulled over the words of the letter he was about to deliver. He was a man possessed. The letter, which he hadn't signed, told Topcliffe that the prisoner, Archie Shaw—the guy Kathryn Harrington was going to interview—had information on the Runway Four murders. How the plot thickens, Puck thought, it's frankly incredible. They're my murders. Who is this impostor? What does he know?
He turned onto the Avenue of the Freelanders and started walking north towards *Money*. Their skyscraper was two blocks away. He

would drop the letter at reception. The city was beginning to bore him in spite of its bustle and the possibility it held of so many souls to steal. You would think this would make him happy. Not anymore. Having lived for centuries all he wanted now was to return to the bosom of his evil godhead. He would happily see out eternity in Hell. First, though, he had that last great task to complete.
After two blocks, the street opened into a plaza and there was *Money's* HQ. He stood at the base of the building and looked up to the top and to the blue sky beyond. The forces of darkness were out there calling him. It would not be long till he returned to the fold.
It bothered him that Archie Shaw might get the glory for solving the R4 murders. As far as Hellson knew, the guy was just some jerk who happened to have murdered seven bitches. What of it? Crimes like that were ten a penny. The whole thing irked him. But, he thought, I am just a messenger for the Prince of the Night. I won't question his plans. I'll just deliver the letter.
He took his eyes down from the sky and walked into the *Money* lobby.
He approached the desk and proffered the envelope to the porter there. The guy looked up, unhelpfulness on his face, long used to many days of being rude to people. His expression changed on sight of Hellson.
—"Can I help you, sir?" the porter asked meekly.
—"Give this to Clement Topcliffe, tell him to read it quick. It's urgent."
Hellson's tone brooked no refusal.
—"Yes, sir. Who will I say it's from?"
—"Don't. Just give it to him."
Errand done, Puck hit the street once more. He slithered towards Middle Park—that age-old oasis of calm. He was of a mood—it had suddenly gripped him—to go see the Fanning Building where Winston Stanley was shot dead. The wizard's death was a source of great pleasure to him. He remembered fondly the year it happened, a deep and dark December in nineteen eighty. The King of Hell worked through a Jesus freak called Davy Pease. When Pease blasted Stanley a dream died. Known as the Good Wizard, Stanley's premature death brought the curtain down on a life of great creative promise. The killing delighted Hellson, and saddened the good people of the world.

Hellson entered the park intent on cutting across it to the Fanning Building. Years on, fans and worshippers still flocked to the old gothic pile to pay their respects to Winston. Such idolatry nauseated Hellson. His bloodlust was up and he fully intended killing someone within the hour. The park was busy. Let's kill an animal first, he thought. He walked down a tree-lined slope to an open area where people sat around a lake in the morning sun. Nobody heeded him. He had that skill, that deft ability to almost obliterate himself when the need arose. He sidled towards the edge of the lake and stood invisible to the people nearby. At these moments when his lust to kill was at its greatest, Hellson entered a trance-like state akin to the peace experienced through meditation. The feeling was pleasant and intense with the thought that he would shortly take the life of something small, weak and helpless and not before instilling maximum terror into the creature first. He thought there was nothing on Earth, or anywhere else for that matter, to better this feeling.
His ability to blend in was perhaps not as good as he imagined. He noticed two girls on a blanket uneasy at his presence. They looked like the kind of kids he could have a fun time torturing. But he moved away making a mental note to return to them later if he got the chance. He left the lake area and headed up another tree-lined slope still in the direction of the Fanning Building.
He would go and stand in contemplation and pay his own perverse homage to the dead wizard. As he walked he grew dizzy from bloodthirstiness. It had to be slaked—and fast. Squirrels weaved in and out between his legs scurrying from one piece of foliage to the other. The animals, cute and furry, bugged him in the extreme. Without a second thought, he lifted one by its tail, swung it in front of his face to focus, and bit its head off. A woman of middle years passing saw what had happened and ran away screaming. Hellson tossed the headless body of the squirrel into the undergrowth and stood there, blood trickling down his chin, chewing on the skull, finding the gristle and bone particularly appetizing.
He walked on. Middle Park crawled with the lovable rodents. He grabbed another one and repeated the process of decapitating it with his teeth. Again he was spotted, this time by a jogger, who became a sprinter and fled.
Hellson felt more settled, happy in his head, his thirst satisfied. The tapestry of life unfolded: joggers, tourists, pedestrians, horse and

traps, skateboarders, buskers, drunks shipwrecked on benches, old folks, nannies walking prams, muggers on the prowl, drug dealers, nuns and priests, hookers, orthodox Jews, Sikhs, Muslims, the deranged; the park had 'em all; a dizzying array.
He knew he would have no difficulty finding a victim here. First, though, Winston Stanley's old home beckoned. On the west side of the park he scuttled out a gate. A block later he was across the road from the Fanning Building. The usual devotees were at the main entrance. Taking photographs or standing in respect. The two doormen from the security hut had a hard time keeping the more enthusiastic from crossing a red line only residents of the complex could cross. The security men had seen it all before. This kind of enthusiasm was a daily occurrence. Love of Stanley was still strong in the world. Look at them all, Hellson thought, what a bunch of dumb cocksuckers. I'll kill one of them. He crossed the road and walked up to the doorway, adopting the guise of an enthusiastic fan. He stood with a warm expression on his face, with just the hint of a smile. A girl—a prepossessing, big-boned, white-toothed out-of-towner—addressed him. She wore the prettiest smile on her gorgeous face. It's the kind of face I'd like to crush with a rock, he thought, but he smiled back as though he meant well.
—"Excuse me, sir," she said.
She seemed to be alone which pleased Puck. He would lure her away for coffee, and then take her to Hell on the scenic route.
—"Yes," he asked. "What can I do for you?"
There were black iron cherubs on the railings of the building and the big-boned girl was enamoured by them. She'd always had a thing for angels and believed herself well guarded. She wanted to have her picture taken beside a cherub, especially as it was outside the Fanning Building where Winston Stanley once lived.
—"I was wondering, sir," she said. "If you'd take my picture?"
She held her camera out to him.
—"I want to get that cherub in the shot," she explained, pointing to one of the black angels. "I'm such a fan of Winston Stanley. I wish the angels had protected him that awful day."
The way she talked made Puck's gorge rise, but he remained the picture of gentleness and politeness.
—"Certainly, my dear," he answered. "Just stand over by the cherub and I'll take a nice shot."

He took the camera and kept smiling. She positioned herself with one arm straddling the cherub's head and the other stretched over the sidewalk in a showgirl-style pose.
—"That looks fine," Hellson said. "Hold that pose, I'll take a few. You can keep the best ones."
He clicked away capturing the beautiful farmer's daughter on what he believed would be her last day alive. She looked like a flower in full bloom.
When he was finished she ran back to his side and took her camera.
—"Thanks so much," she said.
—"You're welcome, honey. What's your name by the way?"
—"I'm Kelsey, pleased to meet you. What's yours?"
—"Puck Hellson," he answered.
Kelsey thought she caught something less than sweet in his tone but she dismissed it.
—"Are you a big Stanley fan?" she asked.
—"I love the man," Puck lied. "I come here every year when I visit Town Island. It's in the paying of my respects that I can help Winston live on."
Hellson could certainly spout platitudes. He did a steady line in bullshit.
It worked. Kelsey was impressed. She began to gush about her own love of the wizard and how his writing had helped her overcome depression. Hellson loved depressed people. Sensitive souls were a joy to destroy.
The conversation went back and forth in this vein for a few more minutes. Winston Stanley was well-nigh canonised by the devil in disguise and the sweet country girl. Duly, they went for coffee to a nearby diner.
It was there, ensconced in a booth, Kelsey noticed a dramatic change to her new acquaintance's manner. She could hardly believe it. The nice man she'd met outside the Fanning Building was gone.
She felt trapped in her seat and though she yearned to do so she couldn't leave.
They ordered two coffees. Hellson got cheesecake. She sipped her brew glancing at him nervously.
The vibes he gave off were noxious. He stuffed the cheesecake down his throat.
—"Look at me!" he said. "Stop averting your eyes."

His tone terrified her.
—“What is it, sir?” she pleaded. “Why are you speaking to me like that?”
—“Listen, bitch. You don’t get to ask me anything.”
Kelsey gasped. She wanted to cry. An overweight black lady in an opposite booth took time out from her hamburger to stare at Hellson. Kelsey was quiet. Tears ran down her cheeks.
She thought about her pops. He was home on the farm tending to the animals. Mom would be setting lunch by the kitchen window with its view of the prairie. Something told Kelsey she would never see home again. She thought of the epigrammatic sayings of Winston Stanley and figured they were the right thing to think about as death drew near.
Suddenly, the black lady was out of her seat and waddling in their direction. She hovered at their booth panting for breath. Puck looked up at the behemoth of bad diet and tried to capture her heart with his eyes. He wanted to grip and control it. The woman was made of stern stuff. Kelsey was a rabbit awaiting vivisection. Hellson didn’t understand. His powers seemed diminished. Why wasn’t this lady responding to his stare?
She spoke in a strong voice and he was forced, despite himself, to listen.
—“Sir, stop speaking to that girl in that way. How dare you? Look at her. She’s trembling all over, the poor flower.”
It was true. Kelsey was shaking from head to toe. Though, the lady’s voice brought sweet and blessed relief.
—“Are you okay, sugar?” the woman asked. “What’s this man been saying to you?”
Kelsey couldn’t answer. She snivelled and wiped her nose with a table napkin.
—“Look what you’ve done, sir. You’ve rendered her speechless!”
Hellson was taken unawares by the woman’s intervention. He thought—and his nostrils flared at the notion—that he recognised her from somewhere a long time ago. Had he fought with her centuries back? It might explain his lack of power at this moment. His brain grew addled trying to remember where it was he knew her from.
She spoke to Kelsey again.

—"Honey, it's okay. Ain't nothing dramatic or dangerous gonna happen you today. Constance here's gonna see you're alright."
She smiled and for the first time in over an hour Kelsey smiled, too.
—"That's better," Constance said. "Now why don't you go on over and sit in my booth. I'll be right along to join you. We're gonna to have some pecan pie and strawberry malts."
Hellson was now the powerless one. His mouth hung open as Kelsey slid from her seat and made her way to Constance's booth.
—"That a girl," Constance said. "You just relax now and I'll be over in a minute."
With Kelsey out of the way, Constance redirected her attention back to Hellson who looked chastened. The sudden weakening of his powers alarmed him. Memories flashed. He had fought this angel seven hundred years before but failed to establish supremacy. Now at the most awkward time imaginable—when he was on the cusp of a killing—he'd been tracked to this diner in Town Island. I should have conquered her all those centuries back, he thought, now she's using some kind of higher power over me and it's working. He couldn't even stand up in his seat to meet her head on.
—"You know who I am, Puck," Constance said. "I can see the recognition in your eyes. I know you remember the battlements where we last locked horns. It must be all of seven hundred years ago."
—"Yes," Hellson said. "I remember you. I was hoping I could forget you and never have to see you again. Our last contest was rather inconclusive."
—"You bet," Constance said. "We're both still here. Though, if we fight again I think I'll get the upper hand."
—"I don't have the energy, Constance. I should have finished you off when I had the chance."
—"Now, now, Puck," Constance laughed. "Don't let your famous anger get the better of you."
—"I'm saving my strength for a bigger fight that's coming; for one who must be stopped. You're just a pesky interlude. Run on back to your Heavenly Father."
Constance could only grin at Hellson's rant. She might as well have had him in a headlock such was the hold she had on him. It felt good to be guided by the Lord.

Kelsey in the other booth had relaxed completely. She was under the angel's wings though she didn't know it.
—"Why don't you just drag your sorry ass outta here, Puck. There ain't nothin' else for you to do. That lil girl over there. She gonna live a long, happy life and forget about you from this moment."
—"I'll see you soon!" Hellson snarled.
He was angry with himself for backing down. Keeping his powder dry, he got out of his seat and left the restaurant.
Constance sat down beside Kelsey. They ordered strawberry malts and pecan pie.

Chapter 12

The landing gear was down. The seven-hour flight was almost at an end. Grudge and Sally fastened their seatbelts and held hands. Grudge's thoughts were all over the place. He was fired up; Sally, too. They were about to touch down on Freeland soil.
Their trip to the airport in R4 and the whole process of catching their flight had been a rollercoaster. Chairman Young arranged for motorcycle outriders to accompany their car from Sally's parents' place. A crowd of press and citizens saw them off at the terminal. The attention, the special treatment, the meeting of their needs; it was all enough to put you in a tailspin. It was only the fact that they had each other that kept them centred. Their feeling was that all would be well and that all manner of things would be well.
Sally saw the trip as nothing less than her destiny.
The air hostess came down the aisle wearing a practised smile ensuring that passengers were seat-belted and that the overhead lockers were secure. Grudge craned his neck beyond Sally's head to see the skyline of Town Island emerging in the window. He felt like an astronaut discovering a new world.
The city spread out before him. A warren of a billon stories, and his—important and true–had somehow led here. The pilot announced their impending arrival over the intercom and apprised them of the time and temperature in Town Island.
Grudge smiled at Sally.
—"This is it, honey," he said.
—"I'm so glad you're here," she said, and squeezed his hand.

The Town Island airport and the light rail to uptown were a thrill for both of them. The voices of the people, the obvious wealth of the land, differed so much from their own austere country, notwithstanding the false sheen of money in R4's cities.
Their first port of call was to the apartment house where they were billeted for the duration of their stay; a grand old pile in the west seventies, not all that far from the Fanning Building. A concierge introduced them to the head of the residents' committee, a friendly, nervous guy by the name of Job Spielberg. They had been expected and Spielberg showed them along quickly to their seventh floor apartment.
The place was a revelation. Its grandeur unlike anything they had experienced before.
—"Wow," Sally said, gazing across the parquet floor towards a balcony with panoramic views of Middle Park. "Look where we've landed. *Money* magazine talks!"
They unpacked and showered with the intention of heading out for a quick bite of lunch and then on to the offices of *Money* and their first meeting with Clement Topcliffe.
Job Spielberg called by to see if they had settled in and they thanked him warmly. Coming out of the apartment block and heading down the edge of Middle Park towards the Theatre District, the couple were filled with a sense of wonder. Their fiery vision was lifted. They passed the world famous concert hall, named for a philanthropist, and headed into midtown. They'd not eaten since the plane and were feeling peckish.
—"I want to sample some proper Town Island food," Grudge said.
—"I was thinking the same thing," Sally agreed. "There're plenty of places around here. You pick."
Grudge chose a bar on 54th Street with an authentic menu in its window. In they went. The food was great. They finished off with coffee and Town Island cheesecake.
Back on the street once more, they proceeded to *Money* for the important business of the day.

***

In Mountain Lion Correctional Facility, Archie Shaw sat by a small window in his cell looking at a view of a concrete wall. He pondered what he was going to say to the journalist coming to visit him. She

was due the next day and he felt he must have something big to tell her. He also wanted to speak about God.
He was two years into his life sentence. Despite being imprisoned, he would like to live for a long time. He likens life, even at its worst, to a wonderful party at which he is a guest and he never wants to leave.
Another guest at the party, so to speak, was the new guard who had started on his wing the previous week. The guy was a puzzle to Archie. He kept coming by his cell as though he had a message but couldn't muster the courage to blurt it out. Say what you've got to say, Archie felt like screaming. But instead he'd stayed quiet, believing he would hear the message in time.
Once, Archie had considered himself to be some kind of criminal mastermind. He had planned out the string of seven murders over seven months (and he would have gone on had he not been caught) with the intention of keeping the authors of true crime fiction busy for many years to come.
But he had been caught. That flat tyre in the Fruitpacking District was his downfall. He'd been hauled off to custody where he had remained ever since. He often wondered if potential victim number eight realised how lucky she was; he had had *such* indignities planned for her.
His court case became a cause célèbre. The victims' families all made powerful victim impact statements and the judge in his closing remarks more or less instructed the jury to pass a guilty verdict; not that they wouldn't have in any event such was the extent of the evidence against Archie. In the end he got seven hundred years; a century for each victim. He would never see the outside world again. Prison was now his home, and so it came to pass.
He stared at the concrete wall. He wished he had a better view. He missed human company, too, and engaged in long dialogues in his head with God. Most days he heard God's voice talking back to him. God forgave him his crimes and even allowed him to justify them in a sense. The girls he'd picked up in his van off the street and murdered, well, most of them deserved it walking around in public like that dressed like prostitutes. God told Archie he had done the world a service by cleaning up that filth.
When he wasn't talking to God he was contemplating his meals. They were markers in his day. He hated the prison food, though: thin

gruels masquerading as soups; rubber meat and two foul-smelling veg; cloying confections of cheapness and nastiness. All prepared in the jail's kitchen by other inmates. Archie was sure they added something special to his food each day; he prayed it wasn't powdered glass. He missed his mother's cooking. He hadn't seen her since the court case. He was royally shunned.
The strains of the radio from the guards' office reached his ears; a breezy tune out of keeping with the surroundings. The gate at the end of the corridor opened and footsteps approached. It was time for his luncheon of near-slop. A guard appeared at his cell bars. It was the new fellow again. He had an almost stupid look on his face, Archie thought, what's he smirking about? The guard carried a plastic tray with Archie's lunch on it.
—"Here's your food," he said, slipping it into the slot. "When you're finished I'll be back. We need to talk."
Archie was well and truly puzzled now. He supped on his gruel and thought on the matter further. It was the first time the guard had addressed him. All he could do was wait to see what the guy had to say.
He finished lunch and stared once more at his soulless view. He began to feel uneasy though he couldn't put his finger on the reason why. It felt ominous. He chided himself for feeling so pigeon-hearted. You're a man who has killed seven women, his inner voice mocked him, but at base you're a coward now that you've been caught. Archie believed he was getting everything he deserved.
The lights blinked of a sudden and went out completely. He was left in total darkness for a while. It all served to unnerve him further. Then, just as quickly they came back and the strange guard was in front of him with that same quasi-stupid look on his face.
—"You wanted to talk?" Archie said. "Please go ahead."
—"I'll keep this quick," the guard said. "Listen, Archie, as though your life depends on it."
By now, Archie was all ears.
—"When the lady comes to interview you, you will know what to say."
—"Is that it?"
The guard turned on his heel and disappeared back up the corridor. Archie was left staring at the concrete wall for the afternoon wondering what the devil it all meant.

***

On the Avenue of the Freelanders, outside the offices of *Money* magazine, Sally and Grudge were about to go in. Grudge, though, had come over all shutterbug with his camera. It irritated Sally. She was here on serious business, and focused. He was focused on the skyscrapers and snapping away. How touristy, she thought. Pedestrians, too, dashing past found Grudge an irritant. He blocked their path and several told him to "Move along, buddy." in that laconic Town Island style. One or two actually called him a jerk.

—"C'mon, Grudge," Sally called. "There's work to be done. There'll be time for photos later."

He finished the shot and caught up with her. They entered *Money* and made enquiries at the desk. The same porter whom Hellson had spooked directed them to Clement Topcliffe's office where Kathryn Harrington, Shawn Burns and Topcliffe greeted them. Following some polite questions about their trip, the five of them got down to work talk in earnest.

Grudge felt a little out of the loop being the only one with no journalistic training. They were discussing the proposed visit to the prisoner Archie Shaw. Topcliffe came into his own in the discussion: directing, challenging and encouraging. Kathryn seemed relaxed in Sally's presence, devoid of envy of the younger woman's success. To paraphrase Thatcher on Gorbachev, Kathryn could do business with Sally.

Still, Grudge's low self-esteem which had plagued him from time to time all his life reared its ugly head. To distract himself he gazed out at the Town Island skyline. He loved the skyscrapers. They had tall buildings at home but the Town Island ones gleamed with their own unique majesty. The Domain Building in particular caught his eye. It dominated the skyline. Grudge knew from general knowledge that it had been the tallest building in the world for many years till overtaken by some oil sheikh's vanity project. Looking at it now, its upper stories called to him.

—"Grudge, you seem distracted," Topcliffe said. "Is there anything you'd like to add to our discussion?"

—"Well I'm just admiring the city's skyline," Grudge said, to the bemusement of the others. Sally wanted to shake him to get him to pay attention, but his eyes were fixed on the Domain Building, its

architecturally perfect lines spellbinding him. That's the building whereon I'll make my name. This sentence swam into his head uninvited, and he sensed its momentousness.
—"You ought to take the time with Sally to go see some of the tourist sites," Topcliffe said. "You can venture to the top of the Domain Building, as many do. I can highly recommend it though it's been years since I've been up."
—"Can't say I ever did," Burns chimed in.
—"It's well worth a visit," Kathryn said. "The views are breathtaking. Shawn, you remind me of a cousin of mine in London. He's lived there all his life yet he's never been to Buckingham Palace. I was visiting a couple of years back and told him I was going to the Mall. He hardly knew where it was."
Grudge decided to focus on the work. The look on Sally's face told him he had better.
—"Alright, folks," Topcliffe said "I think we're straying off topic a little."
—"Well I'm okay about travelling upstate to see this guy, this killer of seven," Grudge said. "I just hope he feels like talking when he sees us. Is there any chance he'll feel intimidated with four people staring at him wanting him to speak?"
—"Good point, Grudge," Topcliffe said. "What's your feeling on it, Kathryn? Will he clam up at the sight of four people?"
—"I don't think so," Kathryn said. "If anything he'll love an audience, and the bigger the better."
—"Kathryn's right," Topcliffe said. "Most of these nuts enjoy the attention. Speaking of which, I received an anonymous letter about Shaw the other day. It was left at the front desk in the lobby. The porter says he didn't see who by. According to the letter, for what it's worth, Archie Shaw has information on the R4 killings. There's probably nothing to it, just thought I'd let you know. Somebody heard you were coming, Sally, and wants to stir things. Anyway, you people are in for a terrific interview. Sally, feel free to participate as much as you like. I know Kathryn is more than willing to help you."
—"We all wish you well at *Money*, Sally," Kathryn said. "I want you to take an active role in interviewing this degenerate, the abominable Archie Shaw."
Grudge surveyed his new surroundings. He was a hell of a long way from the corrective thinking centre. Who ever would have believed

it? Talking shop with journalists (and the editor, don't forget the editor!) at *Money* magazine in Town Island City!
—"Best of luck, people," Topcliffe said, wrapping things up. "To our newcomers let me assure you Shawn and Kathryn will see you right. And I know the four of you on this mission will do the good name of this magazine proud."
Topcliffe sat in his chair feeling pleased. This was the greatest job in the world in the greatest city in the world. He wouldn't swap it for anything. Something about the Galmount fellow played on his mind. He couldn't put his finger on it. He wondered was the guy suicidal the way he'd been staring out the window.
Meanwhile, Kathryn, Shawn, Sally and Grudge repaired to the *Money* canteen. People were friendly towards the newcomers, throwing smiles and making it clear *Money* was one big happy family.
They sat at a table with coffee and chatted.
—"Is it true there's no internet access for citizens whatsoever in Runway Four?" Burns asked, his tone indicating he could not countenance the idea of living without the web.
—"Not quite none, but it's extremely restricted," Grudge said. "We're literally the proles about whom George Orwell wrote so eloquently and passionately. I was (am!) essentially a drone, working as a drudge in a factory that makes, and you won't believe this, coffins."
Several years back Grudge had got a hold of a smuggled copy of *Nineteen Eighty-Four* and devoured it.
Kathryn laughed at his words and at the peculiar lilt in Grudge's accent so different to that of a Freelander. Sally shot Kathryn a warning look, anxious to prevent any flirting between Kathryn and her man. There was no real danger of that. Kathryn was interested in these Runway Four folk and wanted to hear about their lives. She found Grudge attractive but had no intention of making a play for him. She could see he was happily hooked up with Sally, and that was that as far as she was concerned. Catching Sally's reproachful look she smiled back gently to convey the fact that she posed no threat.
Grudge went on:
—"If it wasn't for Sally's supreme writing skills, I'd still be languishing in the coffin factory."

Sally smiled at the compliment. Her man was bigging her up and she was flattered.
—"It was Sally who saved my life," Grudge said. "She pulled me up out of a pit of hellishness and despair."
He had the camp in mind when he said this, more so than the coffin factory. The camp in which he had been brutally tortured only a few short days ago by Kuntar and his thugs. His mind boggled once more at the wonder of how far he'd come so quickly. He thought of the strange and gentle force that had helped through his period of incarceration, acting as a healing balm to his scourged flesh. That same spirit was with him now, of that he had no doubt, by his side in this new metropolis. Powerful, supreme and benign, it would see him through to victory. That much he knew; anything else he was clueless about for the time being. He continued to praise Sally.
—"She has the skill. I mean I know you have the skill, too, Kathryn, but Sally just has it down. And the party bosses knew it. They made the path easy for us to come to Freeland. I was released from jail only the other day."
—"Jail?" Burns said. "Tell us about that. What were you in for?"
—"Well, Shawn, I'll put it to you this way: it was no picnic. In point of fact the place I was held in—a corrective thinking centre—is one of the worst in Runway Four, a real living nightmare. I infringed discipline at work, blew my top and got hauled off. I was kept in solitary. I feel so blessed to be here today, still alive and speaking to you all."
—"Oh my God! You were in solitary confinement in Runway Four?" Kathryn said. "You should write a book about that. How did you survive? I mean, I've read Amnesty's reports."
—"To be honest with you, and I don't want to sound like a holy Joe, but my faith in a power greater than myself pulled me through," Grudge said. "I mean I was actually being tortured up until a few days ago. But the funny thing is my wounds which were immense have left no lasting scars on my body. I've healed up rapidly as though under the protection of God."
—"It's true. When Grudge got released, we went to my parents' apartment in Bludgeon and he was right as rain within a couple of hours. It's miraculous really."
—"These generals who rule your country," Burns said. "They've got all the power sewn up for themselves, am I correct in saying?"

—“That’s exactly it, Shawn,” Grudge said. “They rule supreme, with Chairman Young as godhead. This is why I’m so grateful to Sally for her writing. It was through it that we were freed and allowed to come here.”
—“Well it’s great that you guys are here,” Kathryn said. “We want you to have a productive and enjoyable visit. After this coffee, Sally, you can come down to my desk and we’ll go over some things. Shawn, why don’t you take Grudge out for a spell and show him some of the sights of the city? I’m sure he’d love that.”
Grudge smiled, thinking of the chance he’d get to take photographs. They finished up in the canteen. The girls headed to Kathryn’s desk to talk work. Burns and Grudge sauntered out into the midday midtown.
—“These are truly great streets,” Burns said. “I was born and raised on them. My late father owned a barbershop a block from here.”
—“I’m going to take some photographs as we walk,” Grudge said. “Don’t take it as a sign of rudeness. Please keep talking.”
—“No problem, Grudge, if that’s your passion.”
They skirted past the usual obstacles of a Town Island sidewalk, chief among which seemed to be food stands. The smell of the charred lamb and chicken flesh hit Grudge’s nostrils lighting in him a mix of sorrow for the animals and guilt for the fact that he found the smell entirely pleasant in its own right. While not vegan or vegetarian, he could certainly see himself becoming flexitarian—a word he’d come across in the in-flight magazine on the way over. Flexitarian: someone who, for health and ethical reasons, eats a large amount of vegetarian food but hasn’t quite crossed the line to a full meat-free diet, still taking a quality steak at the weekend, say, or a piece of corn-fed chicken. Yes, he could see himself becoming such a person were he to live in Freeland.
The idea of becoming a Town Islander was so appealing. Here he could reinvent himself. Sally could, too. They could be anything they wanted to be. He resolved to speak to her at the first chance he got about the possibility of defecting.
Burns talked on as they walked on. Grudge kept snapping with the SLR. A candid crowd shot here, a streetscape there. It was enormous fun, exhilarating. Burns’ company added to the mood. He was an entertaining old hack. A native Town Islander full of wit and charm.

—“Tourists!” Burns said. “We get so many of ‘em. Great for the city’s economy but they can be a pain in the ass. Clogging up the sidewalk, just like you young man, with that goddamn camera. I’m generally polite if they ask for directions. Couple of weeks back one of ‘em caught me on a bad day. I think he was a Kiwi—wanted to know the way to the Domain Building. ‘Do I look like a fucking map?’ I asked him. Like I say, though, I’m generally nice.”
Grudge laughed.
—“I see what you mean,” he said, as he dodged a walking party fronted by a guide. “They’re everywhere!”
—“The money they bring in is phenomenal,” Burns said. “We can’t be without ‘em, our taxes would shoot up, so I guess we gotta treat ‘em nice.”
Grudge stopped to photograph a plaque on the wall of a church. It commemorated the author of The Power of Positive Thinking who had preached from its pulpit for many a long year. Grudge was as prodigious a shutterbug as Steve Spirit was a tweeter. Such obsessive levels of the one activity could well annoy others. Burns was a tolerant guy though and put up with all the snapping. He found the visitor from Runway Four eccentric and likeable.
—“Speaking of the Domain Building,” Grudge said. “Can we go there? I know it’s nearby. I’ve studied the map. I don’t want to climb it just yet. I’ll do that with Sally. But I’d love to get a shot from ground level.”
—“Why not?” Burns said, being totally amenable. “It’s only about ten minutes from here.”
—“Thanks.”
The two men continued on through the city streets.
—“So,” Grudge asked. “You didn’t feel like following your father into the family business?”
—“Nah. Cutting hair for a living wasn’t my bag. From a young age I was attracted to journalism. And in fairness to my parents they were always supportive. Town Islanders and Freelanders in general set great store by education and my folks were no exception.”
—“Your country is great,” Grudge said. “People pull themselves up by their bootstraps. Don’t get me wrong. I’m not saying there’s anything wrong with being a barber. I’m sure your father was a hardworking honourable man. What I’m trying to say, as a citizen of Runway Four, it just doesn’t work like that for us. The Party holds

all sway and we're assigned our roles from birth as cogs in the wheel of state. That's why I'm so full of praise for Sally's writing. It's enabled us to get the hell out of there—if only for a spell."
—"You did well there, Grudge. What a girl. Beautiful! How did you guys meet? Moreover, how in the name of God were you let form a relationship and travel here? If the country's as authoritarian as you say, it's incredible."
—"Like I said, Sally's writing's the reason. It opened many doors. I met her in a library as it happens. She was lucky. After her article came out, Chairman Young took a shine to her."
—"It's an amazing tale, the Grudge and Sally saga," Burns said. "And I'm sure it ain't over yet."
They came upon a building called the Showplace of the Nation—a music venue of world acclaim. Again, Grudge paused to take a photograph. He took several shots in quick succession. One or two passersby cursed him for blocking their path. Grudge ignored them, while Burns tried to assuage their annoyance with smiles.
Pictures taken, they continued their walk.
—"Jesus, you sure as hell like taking photographs." Burns said.
After a while, they reached the base of the Domain Building. Architecturally, it was a marvel. They stared up at its majestic form. Grudge pointed the SLR upwards. He had only taken one shot when a powerful feeling of foreboding came over him. He was gripped with an urge to race back to *Money* and embrace Sally, and get the hell away from the Domain Building. A premonition so faint he could not see it, struck him, and the same hunch he'd had earlier when looking out *Money's* window hit him again: it was on this building he would make his name. In an instant he became afraid.
—"Actually," he said, making an excuse. "Can we go back now, I'm jet-lagged?"
—"You're finished already? That's a surprise!"
From across the street, Puck Hellson's eyes watched them walk away.

***

Back at *Money*, Kathryn and Sally were bonding like beer buddies on a hunting trip. Kathryn, her computer open, was flying through screens showing Sally some of the stories she'd worked on in her career to date. Quite a few of them were scoops that had reached national prominence. Sally was impressed. Kathryn Harrington was nothing if not professional. Her whole setup: the good looks, the renown, the cool workplace, the cool city, were all things to which Sally was attracted. She felt fate had conspired to bring her here today, and vowed to equal Kathryn in her line of work and not waste this opportunity in Freeland. Like Grudge, she thought about defecting and would speak to him on the matter soon. She worried about her parents in such an eventuality, fearing their fate would be grim.

Another part of her buried deep detested Kathryn and all she stood for, and cared not a jot for the fate of her parents. Sally shuddered to feel so callous and knew not where the feeling came from.

Pausing from the computer, Kathryn threw her by asking.

—"Do you love Grudge? You guys seem such a well-suited couple."

Sally found the question a mite prying. Nevertheless she answered openly.

—"Yes, I love him. And I've never felt like this about a man before. He's special and deep and sensitive, and he's been through so much in his life. The story of his parents and what happened to them is harrowing. He never had it easy in our society and yet he's still standing. I'm so proud my writing enabled us to come here."

—"They are beautiful sentiments," Kathryn said. "I wish you both a long life together."

Again, something in Sally told her that this was all folly and to turn against Grudge. These conflicting feelings completely unnerved her.

Burns and Grudge returned to the office then and all four sat round making final plans for the trip to Mountain Lion Correctional Facility.

Clement Topcliffe looked in on his charges to see that everything was alright. After several minutes he walked out beaming, pleased everyone was getting on so well.

***

That evening Sally and Grudge dined out downtown in a place called Satay Dreams. They were in terrific form as the poppadoms arrived, still gobsmacked about how opulent their apartment was. The only sour note was the presence of a G-Man from the Runway Four embassy several tables from theirs, keeping a beady eye on them as they ate.

Despite the presence of this diplomatic ghoul, they enjoyed their meal luxuriating in the richness of Freeland where everything from the furniture to the food was just so much better than R4, that benighted strip of earth.
During dessert Grudge said.
—"We've got to stay here, Sally, you know that?"
For a moment, Sally was confused. Did he mean the restaurant? Why should they stay here any longer than their meal took? Quickly, though, she copped on. He meant Freeland, and never going back to Runaway Four.
—"But, Grudge," she said. "If we did, imagine what they'll do to my parents. I'd love to stay here, of course. I'm only a day in the country and I can taste the delicious freedom. But they'll torture or possibly kill Jett and Jane!"
Grudge peeked at the embassy man. The goon-cum-ghoul was looking their way and trying—and failing—to make it look like he wasn't. Grudge was reasonably sure the fellow couldn't hear their conversation. Something, however, niggled: what if the authorities back home had planted a listening device on either he or Sally. Maybe it was the Town Island air, but he could no longer live in such fear and paranoia. He cast them aside.
—"It's a desperate situation alright," he said. "And what a decision to have to make! But we're going to have to decide, and in the coming days. If we put our minds to it we should be able to think of a way to get your parents off the hook."
—"Don't fool yourself, Grudge. That's wishful thinking, and you know it is!"
He could see she was close to tears, so he said no more as the waiter cleared the empty plates and put coffees in front of them. He knew the National People's Congress was coming up in R4 and that the Generals and Chairman Young would want Sally there to make a speech. It was almost certain her parents would be killed if she defected.
—"Look, don't get upset," he said. "We'll get through this, whatever it takes. Let's go do the interview tomorrow, enjoy our apartment and our time in this great city, and we'll keep the momentous stuff till later."
She smiled as he touched her hand in reassurance. And again a callousness that had seized her earlier in Kathryn Harrington's

presence took hold of her and she secretly laughed at the thought of her parents being executed. She was shocked by her own thoughts and did her best to bury them deep in her subconscious.
They finished their coffees, settled the bill and went back via Middle Park to the apartment. They made intense love with the windows open onto the balcony and the sounds of the city—by no means asleep despite the late hour—filling the room. When they were finished Sally scampered over to the windows and closed them shutting out the outside world. They drifted off to the land of Nod like hibernating rattlesnakes. They needed all the rest they could get. Tomorrow was going to be a big and busy day.

***

Somewhere past the sun, in the far reaches of the multiverse, in a place where the arguments of Pope Richard hold no sway, and in fact are seen as simply the pointless chatter of the human race, the throne and around it the assembled higher and lower winged beasts, and all the fallen ones, is abuzz with a feeling many centuries since last felt. That feeling is a hodgepodge of excitement, hope, hatred, lust, fear, anger and pride. There's also a good deal of gluttony, greed, sloth and envy thrown into the mix. The King of Hell is in the throes of this emotional maelstrom. The battle has been joined, and all his plans, he believes, are about to come to fruition. Galmount is in place. Grudge's hopes are up. He's in Freeland with the woman he loves, and believes that he's about to break free.
The winged beasts sing their praises to the Prince of the Night. The multiverse resounds with this evil sound, while the Prince of Peace is nowhere to be found. Where are the songs of the good? The sleeping shepherd cannot be roused. His slumber has a drunken feel to it. Meantime, Puck Hellson is primed and ready to pounce. Where, oh where, are the higher angels? Where is God at this momentous juncture in space and time, and in those places outside of both? Down on Earth humans ponder it all. They have their secular saints and their religious ones; their two opposing systems of making sense of the world. Even so, no one is any the wiser ever. Perhaps the two systems are not as opposed as people think? The oceans, the mountains, the rivers, deep space, the stars, it is all consciousness? We are inside something that of itself thinks? The power of thought contained in a rock? Is it unlikely in the extreme, or quite possible?

It was Galmount's inherent goodness that got the King of Hell interested in him in the first place. The man was flawed but he nonetheless thought thoughts that of themselves could further empower the force of goodness in the world. It had to be stopped lest some kind of revolution took place.
The war was being won. More than any previous century, the scales were tipped in evil's favour. The violence in the world, the race hate, the child killing, the child rape, the suffering of the animals (how *they* needed a saviour!), was all a testament to one salient fact: the Devil had found work for many hands—idle and busy—to do.

***

The next morning Grudge and Sally walked into *Money* magazine. The big day had arrived. They were heading upstate to interview the serial killer Archie Shaw.
—"Don't worry about what you'll write," Grudge told Sally as they rode the elevator. "You'll be inspired. You just have to be adequate, and your adequate is like most people's excellent."
—"Thanks," she said. "You're my rock. If I was a church, you'd be my pope."
The elevator doors opened. There to greet them was a smiling Shawn Burns. He was keyed up and ready to go. He's a real wide boy, Grudge thought, the kind of guy who could sell sand to the Arabs.
—"You guys look happy, even loved-up dare I say," Burns said. "Let's go straight to Clement. Kathryn's there already. He wants to say one last thing before we go."
They headed, enthusiastically, to the boss's office.
—"Right, good morning people," Topcliffe boomed when everyone was assembled. "First off I want to wish you luck. This is a challenging but important assignment. Also, I want to say that we've had contact here at *Money* this morning from the authorities in Runway Four."
Grudge and Sally pricked up their ears. Was it Chairman Young they wondered (telepathy tingling between them), and more importantly, if it was him, what the hell did he want?
Topcliffe continued:
—"The authorities have very kindly offered to print our Archie Shaw article in their media when it's written, on the condition that it's run through their censorship board first."

—“They’ll cut it to shreds,” Kathryn said. “I wouldn’t get too excited about being published in Runway Four. I mean no offence to Grudge and Sally but your country is such an oppressive place. I really can have nothing but disrespect for it, and its rulers.”
—“No offence taken,” Sally said.
—“Ditto,” Grudge added.
Kathryn was right. The R4 censorship board would gut the article. The promise to publish it was merely a propaganda ploy to show the Freelanders what an open society Runway Four was. Nobody in power in R4 seemed to get the fact that running the piece through a censorship board kind of killed any hopes they had of affecting openness. Despite the fact that Grudge and Sally were thousands of miles away, Young still exercised control. Last night’s spook at dinner was a case in point; one of a number of shadowy bureaucrats who had tailed them since they’d arrived in Town Island. All these tactics, however, just increased their desire to defect.
—“Well, that’s fine, then,” Topcliffe said. “I’ll have to give their offer more thought. Meanwhile, get going guys. Shawn will fetch the car from the car park and pick you up on the street. Just wait for him in front of the building.”
They barrelled outside and after a short while Burns pulled up. Everyone piled into the car. Burns negotiated the Town Island traffic with practiced ease. Pretty soon they were out of the city and cruising to Mountain Lion on Interstate 77.
Grudge and Sally took in the countryside that flashed before their eyes with more keenness than Burns or Kathryn, who had seen it all before.
Conversation was minimal. All the planning had been done back at the office. After about ninety minutes they arrived at the prison. There will be signs along the way, somebody (a girl) had once told Grudge, and he saw that was the case today after they passed through the checkpoint at the bottom of the drive that led to the main block of the facility. *Hang House* the sign said with a black arrow pointing to a garage-like building to the right of the drive.
That’s where I was headed back in R4, he thought, had I not been saved. Why was I rescued? The question presented itself with a considerable degree of urgency.
They reached the main door. Climbing out of the car and surveying the building Sally became emotional and had a vision that one day

she would write a big novel—one of those works of fiction that manages to be both pulp and high art—and that this visit to this supermax today was very much written in the stars.
The party of four went inside. The warden was there to greet them—Burns was reminded of Doctor Chilton from that old movie—and once they'd gone through airport-style security "Chilton" led them to the wing where Archie Shaw languished.
This was Archie's moment in the sun, though it was to take place in a windowless interview room a short distance from his cell. Journalists from Town Island, and some up-and-coming foreign broad, were coming to talk to him. Kathryn Harrington had left word that it would be more than her arriving. He'd even brushed his teeth for the occasion. On the orders of the warden he was brought, in chains, to meet the delegation.
Archie sat on one side of a table and faced the four visitors. Two muscular prison guards stood round the walls, their presence reassuring in such a bleak room.
The strange guard who had been puzzling Archie of late had been transferred in recent days; his message passed on, his work done. Archie wasn't worried in the least about what he would say in this interview. He knew that the right words would come. He stared at his interrogators, the young guy—the broad had called him Grudge, what a stupid name!—looked cocky and intelligent. Archie would have given his favourite leg or even one of his testicles to have the opportunity to inflict a slow painful death on that attractive body. All Archie's victims had been women and it was a source of great regret to him that he had never killed a man. He often fantasized now from the confines of his cell that the first thing he would do if he ever got out was find a male victim. But he knew he would never see civilian life again, never walk in the sunny uplands of freedom. He had become a caged beast.
Kathryn began by introducing everyone. Archie nodded at each person in turn giving them a blast of what he thought was rich charisma but was in fact deep creepiness. Sally found him off-putting in the extreme. Grudge and Burns stared at him blankly sizing him up for the sicko he was.
—"Thank you for asking me here today, Mr Shaw," Kathryn said. "And for accepting my colleagues' presence, too. We hope you'll

cooperate and answer our questions truthfully. We want this to be a satisfactory visit for you and for ourselves."
Archie gazed at her. He looked pleased immensely. Boy, was he going to enjoy this.
—"I'll tell you what I can, ma'am," he said. "But I guess when it comes to my crimes, it's all been said already in court."
—"Well, we'd like to get your perspective on it," Burns said. "From the vantage point of today, after you've served some prison time and the crimes themselves, the seven murders, are fading ever more into history."
—"What the fuck?" Archie said, his voice rising. The guards at the wall flexed. Archie noticed and brought his tone down. He continued.
—"There ain't no need to speak in that insulting manner, mister. Fading ever more into history? My crimes shine on forever. People don't be thinking bout nothing else. I electrified this land. My seven murders ain't fading. No way!"
Archie's little speech was indicative of what a monumental egotist he was. Here in his dingy prison home he was convinced he had not been forgotten and left to rot, which in fact was what had happened. The case of Archie Shaw was just a flicker in history as people in the outside world moved on with their lives and on to the next sensation. The only ones who still gave him a thought, and even then not that often, were the relatives of his victims; and all they thought about were ways to kill him, slowly and painfully.
Kathryn gave Sally the nod to ask a question. Sally obliged.
—"Tell me, Mr Shaw?" she said. "Can you give us some indication of what it was that motivated your crimes? As simply as you can please, what made you go out and kill seven women?"
This question seemed to annoy Archie. In his view it was impertinent, like asking Picasso what motivated him to paint Guernica. The art—in Archie's case the slaying of seven spotless women—spoke for itself. There was no need for the artist to explain. When you're explaining you're losing, as the saying went.
—"My art, my murders speak for themselves," he bawled.
Sally and the others were taken aback. The guards in the room stepped forward. One of them told Archie to pipe down and be more respectful towards his questioners or the interview would be ended and he would be taken back to his cell. This warning calmed him

slightly. He did not want to go back to his cell. He was enjoying the attention. It was his ego that had caused him to bawl and he would do what he could to keep it in check.
But he could not keep his temper in check no matter how hard he tried. He attempted to stand up even though he was chained to the floor and the table. The guards pushed him down by the shoulders. He fixed his eyes on Sally.
—"Alright, alright," he said. "Get off me. I'm calm. I just want to say one thing and then this interview is over and you can take me back to my cell."
—"What is it, Archie?" Kathryn said. "Tell us."
—"It's the murders in Runway Four, I heard about them sure," he said. "And I know this girl here, Sally Popplewell, has been writing up on them and trying to solve them."
—"What else do you know, Archie?" Sally asked. "Do you have fresh information? I could write a new article"
—"Tsk," Archie said. "You and your articles. It's all a ruse. She's behind them all." He was nodding furiously at Sally. "The killings, all the shocking deaths. Talk about being in cahoots with Lucifer! And you, Grudge, you're a dead man!"
Once more, despite his snares, Archie attempted to stand up. He tried, pathetically, to lunge at Sally. One of the guards clubbed him with just the right tautness on the nape of his neck. Archie shut up and was dragged back to his cage-cum-cell, got beaten and was tied to the bed. There was always a high price at Mountain Lion if one got out of hand.
Warden "Chilton" came to retrieve them from the interview room. Through rooms and doors he took them to the airy front of house. Despite themselves the others felt cold towards Sally. Grudge wondered if death was nigh; his own especially.

***

Rattled by the experience of the fraught interview they bundled back into the car and made for the city. Silence ensued for the first few minutes till Burns broke it.
—"What a fucking nutjob," he said. "Full of himself, too. A classic narcissist."

—“At least we can be sure of one thing,” Kathryn said. “He’ll never see the light of day again. He was just rambling at the end. He knows nothing about the Runway Four murders. How could he?”
—“He’s got it in for you, Sally,” Burns said. “What’s this about you and Old Nick in cahoots?”
—“I haven’t the faintest idea,” Sally said.
They all felt it, a sense somehow that Sally knew more than she was letting on about what Archie Shaw had said. Though, none of them entertained the notion for long. It was too preposterous to think Sally was in any way behind the murders. Surely, Shaw was just a ranting madman?
Ideas, intuitions, impressions bit at Grudge’s mind.
—“I’m not so sure he knows nothing,” Grudge said. “I’ve a hunch, and I think I’m right. He’s a messenger.”
An awkward silence filled the car. The comment was left hanging, and indeed brushed aside by Burns who said.
—“I think that’s enough grim prison stuff for now. I’ve no doubt Kathryn will hammer out a terrific piece, right up to her usual standard. Archie was useful in that regard.”
—“I think I will, Shawn,” Kathryn said. “And with Sally’s help it’ll be something special.”
—“We’ll be back in the city in about an hour,” Burns said. “I can drop you guys out in midtown if you wanna do some sightseeing. Kathryn and I will head back to the office. You can follow us in later and help with the article. You might as well do some touristy stuff while you’re in Town Island. You said you wanted to take in the Domain Building with Sally, Grudge. There are tours every half hour up to the eighty-fifth floor.”
—“Great idea,” Sally said, and Grudge agreed.
He had noticed the Domain Building from many angles since arriving in Town Island. He’d been struck with the notion that the building would play some significant part in his life. He had even made it as far as its base in the company of Shawn Burns when a creepy premonition caused him to flee. Now though he was most eager to scale its heights, and felt fate was at play in the matter.
—“Drop us near to it when we get to town,” Grudge said. “Sally and I are going to have some fun.”

The mood in the car lightened at Grudge's upbeat tone. The foursome spent the rest of the drive back to Town Island chatting pleasantly.
In the city Burns dropped Sally and Grudge at the corner of 33rd Street and Fifth in the heart of bustling midtown. They promised to be back at *Money* later that afternoon.
—"Enjoy the tour," Kathryn said, as the car door closed and the vehicle sped away.
—"This should be fun," Grudge said, tilting his head upwards to survey the architectural majesty of the Domain Building across the street from them a matter of a mere hundred feet or so away. A gaggle of tour guides was gathered—it was the same everyday—at the entrance to the building.
—"Let's go over and grab one of those guides," Sally said.
Meanwhile, on West 34th Street, Puck Hellson's nostrils grew all aquiver. He'd been propping up a bar since early afternoon. His orders from on high had told him to inhabit this vicinity on today of all days. This was it and he knew it. He knocked back his drink (*"whiskey, you're the Devil"*) threw some money down and headed into the street; a proxy agent for evil, the King of Hell steering him towards the tower of the Domain Building. Puck wasn't worried in the least about what to do when he got there. His instructions would arrive just when they were needed. As he advanced, pedestrians, as so often happened, gave him a wide berth.
Sally and Grudge had signed up for the basic twenty-five dollar tour from a young enthusiastic guide at the entrance.
—"My boss is watching," the guide had said, explaining his eagerness to sign them up. They were sold on the idea and now stood in the lobby of the Domain Building. The place had the unmistakable feel of Gotham City about it: large columns and lots of marble and gold. Grudge's excitement was high, as was Sally's to get to the top, yet Grudge's nostrils, too, were quivering. The fiend was coming. They moved through the lobby, showed their tickets to an usher and stepped into an elevator that would bring them first to the fortieth floor. There were lots of nationalities inside. An announcement gave some brief information on the building in several languages. From what Grudge's ears could gather, Italian, Polish and Japanese were all in the mix, as well as his beloved English.

As they sailed skyward, Puck Hellson was entering the lobby having signed up for a tour hastily on the street. He knew what he was doing. He was primed, ready and about to spring. It wouldn't take long. By carrying out the Devil's orders, salvation would be his. The guide who had sold Hellson his ticket was choking to death on a pretzel in the street before a shocked crowd. A grace note on Puck's part, who hadn't liked the way the chap had spoken to him.
Hellson showed his ticket and caught the next elevator—side by side to Sally and Grudge's—to forty. He was behind them by only a matter of four or five minutes. For some reason he noticed his cadre of ghouls could not be summoned to accompany him on this hunt.
Grudge, Sally and an assortment of tourists stepped out onto the fortieth floor and were ushered by a guide along a corridor to another elevator which would take them to the viewing deck on eighty-five. Grudge had his camera ready, eager to shoot the views. Sally smiled at him, so pleased to be in his company and with the way things were unfolding for she knew Puck was coming. And she belonged to Hellson now.
Two minutes behind at this stage, he was hot on their heels. In the parallel elevator he ignored the pesky tourists and focused all his energy on carrying out the commands of Satan.
Grudge was awestruck when he stepped onto the viewing deck and saw the greatest city in the world laid out before him. Sally simply glanced at the metropolis and then looked back over her shoulder towards the elevators as though expecting to see someone she was waiting for emerge at any moment. The throng of tourists peopling the deck drank in the views with the enthusiasm of hardy climbers atop an arduous peak. Everyone walked around in wonder, cameras clicked and oodles of film was shot. Grudge had a flashback—he didn't know where it came from—of George Harrison's time here in 1963. Grudge hardly knew who George Harrison was, yet he saw his skinny frame frolicking round the platform brandishing an old-fashioned camera and a mysterious smile. Without further ado, Grudge started taking photographs, too. Town Island from this height was a revelation. He saw the harbour, and the famous statue, and Naught Ground, where the towers were destroyed on 8/10 in the most spectacular act of terrorism ever carried out on Earth. Something wasn't right, though, and Grudge could sense it. Cold fear along with the cold air at this altitude hit the nape of his neck.

Puck Hellson appeared on the viewing deck, his eyes ablaze with sick purpose. He saw his target, the tall guy taking pictures with the good-looking bitch next to him. They'd last spoken on the tram in Bludgeon. It was Grudge Galmount. There was a glow of goodness from him—an aura—that revolted Hellson to his core.
Puck walked towards Grudge. People stepped out of his way disturbed by the sight of him. Through all the centuries, he'd never lost his ability to terrorize. He pulled a knife from his coat. He was ten feet from Galmount. Sally saw what was happening and stood transfixed. An overwhelming urge to fuck Puck Hellson gripped her; to have sex with this messenger from Hell seemed to her the most desirable thing in the universe. Hellson by now was as crazed as Michael Abram, when, on that fateful night in Henley-on-Thames, he'd hurled a statue of Michael the Archangel through the Beatle's window. Sally, though, was no Olivia Harrison to smash a lampstand over Hellson's head. Instead, she looked adoringly at the fiend as he advanced.
In a flash—the sunlight on the steel of the knife—a security guard rounding the platform saw what was going on.
—"Look out, sir!" he warned, as Puck lunged but failed to plunge the knife into Grudge's heart. Grudge skipped back deftly like a boxer. He started chanting mantras at his attacker. To his relief, the mantras immobilized Puck. This supposedly powerful demon began to wilt on the spot. The staggering views of Town Island were ignored as the tourists turned to watch the tussle. Sally remained transfixed. Grudge kept moving, floating like that famous butterfly. He pulled a heavy torch off the belt of the security guard and started bludgeoning Hellson with it on the head. The demon slumped to the ground injured.
The security guard —startled that Grudge had stolen his torch— drew his gun and along with a colleague who'd joined him made to arrest Hellson. Rather than suffer such ignominy, and filled with shame for having failed to kill Galmount, Puck got to his feet, prised open a gap in the protective railing, and jumped off the Domain Building.
It remains unclear whether or not he died when he hit the sidewalk eighty-five stories down. When they went looking, the authorities found no body, save for Sally's who, in an act of grievous devotion, followed Hellson over the side.

The crowd gasped as the guards squawked into their walkie-talkies, and Grudge dusted himself down. I'm going have to defect, he thought.
A spook from the R4 embassy looked on disappointed. He knew by the look in Grudge's eyes he must report to his superiors the news that Grudge Galmount would not be coming back to Runway Four. The cops arrived and took statements. Later on, Grudge had lots to talk about at *Money* HQ. They got plenty of copy from his words. Hellson was gone, and so was Sally. He would have to start anew. God was by.

The End

Printed in Great Britain
by Amazon

69647614R00104